Frame Change

(A Nina Bannister Mystery)

by

T'Gracie and Joe Reese

For information, email **Cozy Cat Press**, cozycatpress@aol.com or visit our website at: www.cozycatpress.com

COZY CAT
P R E S S

ISBN: 978-1-939816-48-1

Printed in the United States of America

Cover design by Karri Klawiter
http://artbykarri.com/cover-art/

1 2 3 4 5 6 7 8 9 10

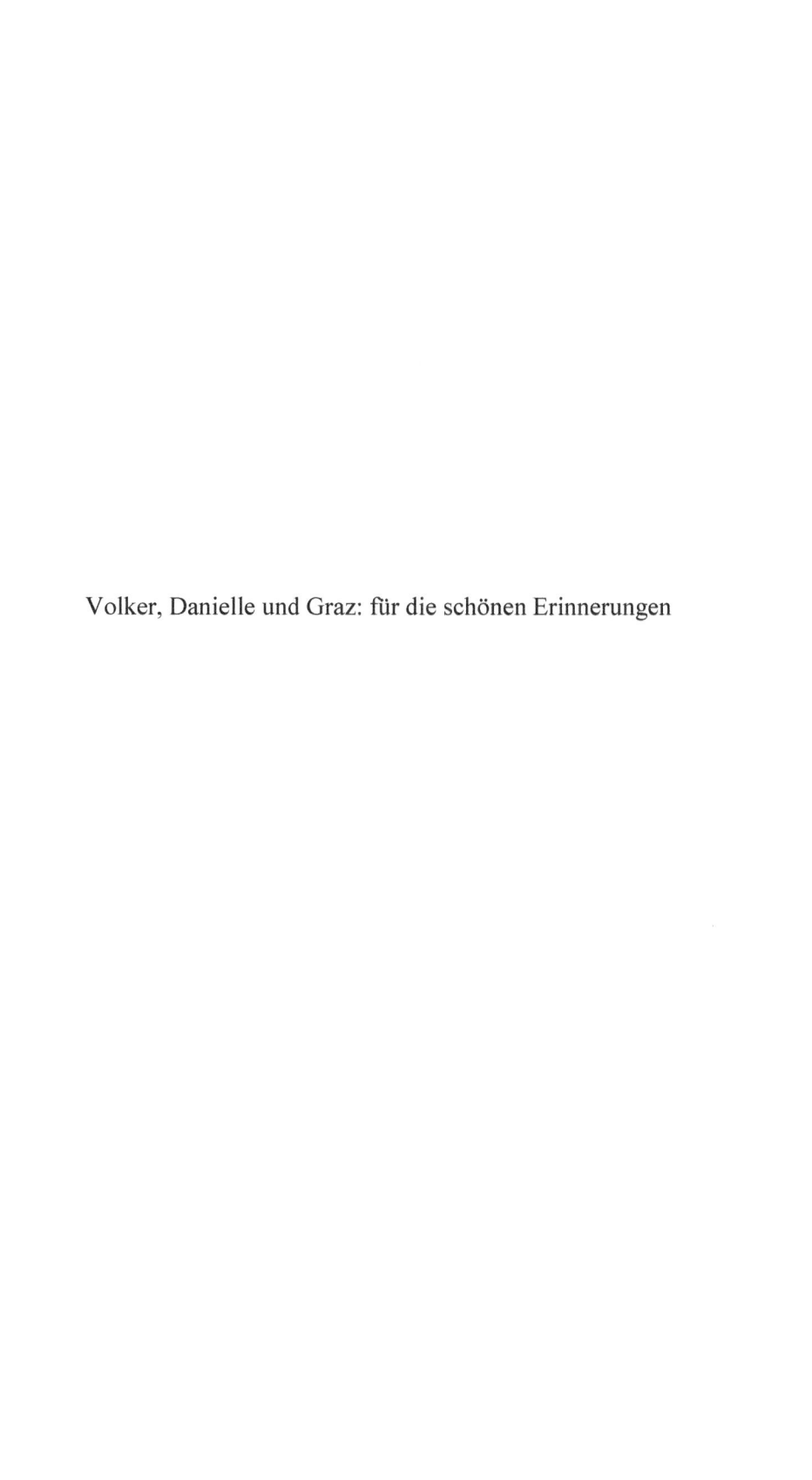

Volker, Danielle und Graz: für die schönen Erinnerungen

PROLOGUE

Margot Gavin could remember the day perfectly.

She could, in fact, remember everything about the interview. Down to the last word, the last gesture.

How strange!

It had now been almost a year. At precisely nine thirty on the morning of Tuesday, October 14, she had entered her office prepared to deliver a standardized speech informing a young applicant for the position of docent at The Chicago Art Museum that she would not be accepted for the position.

She had opened her desk drawer, taken out of it a package of Galois cigarettes, and regarded the applicant, whose name was Carol Walker.

"They will not let us smoke anywhere in the museum, and so we have to go outside to a small area between the buildings. I hope you don't mind, Ms. Walker."

"I don't mind."

"You should mind. It's barbaric; but then rules are rules."

She had not met this young woman, but the Director of Educational Resources, Rebecca Simpson, had delivered an unenthusiastic, even scathing, report of the previous day's interview.

"I just don't—I just don't see that she's qualified at all. She does have a degree in Art History from…I don't know where; but she's primarily a literature person. She spent last year teaching English at some junior college. She just doesn't seem to have the—well, the credentials for an institute of our standing."

And here she was. Small, unimposing woman, rather slight, dark hair worn in bangs.

But something about her eyes…

And so she'd taken a package of matches from the same drawer—for she intended to smoke anyway, of course, rule or not—lit her cigarette, and blown smoke upwards, gazing out the window behind her, through which sailboats could be seen, seemingly motionless, idle, as sailboats always seemed to be.

"You don't smoke?" she could remember asking.

"No."

"Not ever?"

"No."

"Drugs of any kind? Sorry, but I must ask these things."

"No. Never."

"Not even marijuana?"

"No."

"My God, what are we teaching our children these days? Ever been arrested?"

"No."

"I had been, at your age—what are you, twenty five?"

"Twenty eight."

"Twenty eight! Well that changes the figure, doesn't it? I had been, at age twenty eight, arrested five times, two of them even in this country."

She could remember thinking then about the speech she was supposed to be giving:

'While we certainly appreciate your enthusiasm, you must appreciate that, with such a large number of applicants…"

And…

"There are a number of other museums in Chicago, smaller, but more equipped to serve as training grounds for young people wishing to become involved in museum administration. I could suggest…"

And she could remember wondering why she wasn't giving the speech.

"And you are from?"

"Georgia."

"I see. I was once in Atlanta, for a conference."

"Our farm is east of Atlanta. North of Athens. In the mountains."

"You're a farm girl."

It was at that point she could remember thinking that this girl, this Carol Walker, had a very nice smile.

"Timber raising. Sheep raising. Never off the farm until I was nearly twenty or so—then somehow I got to go to Europe."

"And you loved it."

"Yes. I'm a language nut. And an art nut. I lived in classrooms in various cities; and museums. I almost slept in the museums."

"I'm sure you did. Yes. I'm sure you did."

There had been a pause, and Margot could remember herself drawing hard on her Galois and saying for some reason:

"I once blew up a warehouse. Quite by myself, actually. There was no one in it, of course."

"That's good."

"I don't know. There are things to be said on both sides of the issue. In your interview yesterday with Rebecca Simpson you made a horrible pun."

"Yes. I'm sorry about that."

"She asked you how much money you'd expect to earn. And you said you only wanted to make a docent living."

"Yes."

"Why ever did you make such a horrible pun? And in an interview! Why, child, would you do that?"

"Stupidity."

"Stupidity!"

"Yes. Must have been."

"It's a very old pun, you know. I must have heard it first at...where, Oxford? No. Sao Paolo. My God, what was I doing in Sao Paolo?"

"Don't know."

"No, you wouldn't, of course. But a crucial interview, competing against so many other very qualified candidates. Were you so incredibly naïve as to think the thing original, or so incredibly stupid as to find it funny?"

"Both."

"You would only make nine hundred a month, you know."

"All right."

"Do you have a personal life?"

"No."

"Good, so you can be flexible."

"I'm nothing if not flexible."

"What do you understand concerning the duties of a docent here."

"Nothing."

"And yet you applied for the job."

"I thought I would learn what a docent did, after I became a docent."

"I see. You tried teaching for a time?"

"Yes."

"I know because I read your teaching evaluations. The ones from—what god forsaken junior college was it?"

"There were several."

"Yes, that's true, now that I'm remembering. Dr. Simpson told me about them, and…well, let's see what it says here—ah, you didn't send in the mid-semester attendance reports, and the Dean of Liberal Arts emailed you and told you that the omission was 'inexcusable.'"

"Yes, she did."

"Is that why they fired you?"

"They didn't actually fire me; they just said I shouldn't come back."

"Did you read your student evaluations?"

"I never saw them."

"Of course, you didn't; why should they show them to you? Several of your students said you were 'the best teacher I ever had in my life.' Those exact words. What do you think of that?"

"I suppose it shows the sad state of public education in this country."

"What's your favorite painting?"

"One on the third floor. It shows a town in Prussia."

"Sourmire. French painter. He was a guest of the Duke of Brandenburg."

"It's a small town, you can tell. There's a castle up on the hill in the middle of town. But the painting is about the main street. Only a few people are out. Some horses tied to hitching rails. It's summer, and very early in the morning. The light is—I can't really describe the light, but you can't forget it. And it's cold. It's summer, but it's cold."

"How do you know it's morning and not evening?"

"I don't know; but you *do*."

"Yes, you do, don't you? Yes, you do. Well. Rebecca Simpson hates you and suggests that we not hire you."

"I'm sorry she hates me."

"Don't be. She's a chicken. Do you have any questions?"

"One or two."

"Go ahead, please. Ask."

"I was wondering what I was supposed to do here."

"Oh, I don't deal with that kind of thing. Anything else?"

"No, I don't think so."

"Then, that's it. I have to go outside and smoke. Oh, by the way: try to develop some bad habits, won't you?"

"I'll try."

"That's all we can ask. Good day."

And Carol Walker had left.

CHAPTER ONE: THE AMATEUR PAINTER

Fall meant school for the children of Bay St. Lucy, and it meant a slowdown in the tourist trade for the shopkeepers and bed and breakfast owners, who heaved a collective sigh of relief, even as they stared toward the financially-challenging months when peace of mind was at hand, and money was not.

A difficult choice.

Early September—to be precise, the weekend of Friday, September 9 through Sunday, September 11—meant something different to Nina Bannister.

It meant a reunion with her best friend Margot Gavin, who'd shut down her plantation hotel The Candles for a period of some days, said adieu to her husband for an equal number of days (Goldmann had business in Chicago to deal with), and made the eighty-something mile trip south in her Volkswagen, pulling into the village in mid-morning and taking possession of one of the rooms in Elementals: Treasures from the Land and Sea, the bed and breakfast which she still owned.

And which Nina now ran.

It was splendid. Margot arrived early enough so that the two women could still reasonably trek over to Bagatellis' and buy bagels, and still sit in the cool garden and drink coffee.

It was the same old Margot, kaleidoscopically garbed, smoking again, craig-faced and wild haired, and utterly outrageous.

Marriage had proven tolerable only because she and her husband, early on, had so tired of it that they'd decided to consider themselves divorced and merely carrying on an illicit affair with a total stranger, or, better still, a married stranger.

This entire line of reasoning made no sense to Nina, of course, but not much else that Margot had ever said did either, so whatever.

The two of them still laughed like schoolgirls.

And then there was, of course, the opportunity for Nina, sitting beneath a huge hanging fern and sipping her second cup of dark roast, to recount all of the fantastic goings-on aboard Aquatica, the floating oil platform which Nina and Hector Ramirez had somehow saved from blowing up.

That took a bit of telling.

And it made her, Nina realized, mousy retired teacher that she was, just as outrageous in Margot's eyes as Margot was in hers.

So it was all blissful until about ten thirty or so, when Margot took a closer look at the paintings which now encircled the garden.

Nina had been afraid of that.

"Those paintings—what are they?"

The best answer, of course, would have been:

"What paintings?"

But they were there, all twelve of them, all just as Nina and her friends had hung them there two days ago, as colorful by-products of the class they'd all just finished taking.

"What paintings?"

Might as well try, anyway.

"Those paintings! Those paintings you've hung around the garden! The ones where Ramoula Peters' works should be! And Elsie Garvin's! What *are* those paintings, for God's sakes?"

"Well..."

"And Tom Mitkin! There's nothing up there by Tom!"

"Actually, Margot..."

"Nina, what is happening to my shop? Our shop? What are you doing? Who painted those things?"

"I did. At least one of them."

Silence. A huge macaw should have shrieked at this moment, this pregnant pause, in order to add drama to the situation.

But Elementals possessed no such huge bird.

Pity, Nina found herself thinking.

"You did?"

"Yes. I and…"

Another pause.

Where oh where was that bird when one needed it?

"…I and some friends."

"Some friends?"

"Yes."

"What friends?"

"The class."

"The class. I'm sorry but I find myself repeating everything. I'll try to stop that. So—what class?"

"My painting class."

"How can there be such a thing as a 'painting class'?"

"I don't know. But there is. Was. It's over now."

"Thank God."

"Oh, I don't know. It was a lot of fun, really."

"Nina—look, look up at the wall. Those twelve paintings are all the same. All exactly the same."

"I know. It's easier that way, painting I mean."

"I'm sure it is."

"Anyway, Emily Peterson came in about a month ago with an ad for what she called a "Wine and Watercolor" class. For fifty dollars apiece, people—women, actually—who were beginning painters could come and meet at O'Doule's Pub. There would be wine. She'd have the easels set up, supply the paint, and…"

"I think I know what's coming, and I'm going to be sick."

"Supply a painting that we would all copy."

"So you all painted the same painting."

"Yes, the seascape with the old lighthouse, the choppy waves, the storm in the distance, the…"

"I can see what's in the painting."

"I didn't think I would be any good at it. But it was late June, and the Aquatica thing had just ended, and I had a lot on my mind. I couldn't really sleep. I kept seeing that shark eat Brewster Dale, well, you know, after he'd threatened to kill all of us. So I thought, 'why not try it'?"

"Oh, Nina, there are so many reasons. You should have called me, dear."

"They're not so bad, are they?"

"As opposed to what?"

"But they aren't really all the same. See, that one there above the clay pot? Patsy Stevens did that one. Can you see that the roofline on the old shack is—I don't know—kind of whompejawed?"

Margot lit a cigarette, drew hard upon it, and then held it menacingly out to her side, as though preparing to use the burning end as a kind of detonator.

"Of course," Nina said quietly, "that might have had something to do with the wine."

Margot said nothing.

"We all thought it would be a good idea if we could hang the paintings somewhere. So I volunteered our space. It's not for long, you understand. And by the way, weren't there some great painters who just painted the same things over and over again?"

Margot had stood up, though, and was wandering around the glass-topped table aimlessly, like a water buffalo that had been stunned by a blow to the head by a pickax.

Nina continued:

"The impression people, I mean?"

With a great show of concentration, Margot managed to answer:

"The Impressionists?"

"Yes! Yes, that's them! Didn't one of them just paint water things all the time?"

"Water lillies. Monet. Monet's Water lillies."

"Right! So, they're all hung somewhere, I've read, in a great big circle. Like we have here."

"It's the Louvre, Nina. The Jeu de Palm. Part of the Louvre."

"I knew it was something like that. But isn't that what we've got here? Like the Louvre?"

Margot sat down again, stared for a time at her cigarette, then stamped it slowly out, as though trying to inflict pain upon it.

"Part of the Louvre," she whispered, her breath hissing like a snake though the dissipating smoke cloud. "Elementals. Now part of the Louvre."

"And look! Look how my second wave, the one that's almost reached the shore, is just a little frothier than, oh, Stephanie's, which hangs there over the clock. I was worried because I didn't have enough of that slate gray paint that water sometimes looks like—slate gray, I mean—so I thought about trying to borrow some, but nobody else seemed to have any either, and we were about out of wine, and so I thought I'd just substitute a little of the pure white. We all were given a lot of pure white at the first of the session. I thought it might make the wave look like 'not water,' but actually it kind of frothed up on the canvas, and I think it looks pretty good. If you compare it to…"

"We have to take them down."

Nina looked at her.

"Well, we were planning to take them down in a couple of days, of course. But we thought if we could give Emily the advertising…"

"We have to take them down now."

"You don't think just…"

"No."

"But if I..."

"NO!"

"Oh, all right. I have to say, though…She could not say, though, being interrupted in mid-protest by the jingling of the front bell and the jingling of Alanna Delafosse, who, having heard of Margot's visit, had brought pound cake.

"Nina! Margot!"

She swept through the front room as if it did not exist, and entered the garden area like the cataclysmic event that she was.

Margot, on the other hand, still seemed somewhat numb from having experienced twelve almost identical (except for a few whompejawed lines and too-white waves) paintings, and could only respond by lurching forward and uttering:

"Uhhh!" while Alanna enshrouded her and exuded for a few massive and dangerous breaths:

"It is *so wonderful* to see you again! I'd forgotten whether you eat pound cake, my dear—but I so hope you do!"

"Uhhh!"

"You must tell me everything! How is life on a plantation? And your marriage, are you loving every blissful moment of it? How long can you stay with us? You must have dinner with me—and Nina of course—at the Auberge; I simply insist on it. We're getting the most delicious oysters! What time did you arrive this morning? Was it a difficult drive down? Did you come via the interstate? The interstate is so fast, and there are so many trucks, huge trucks that run over everything in their path. But on the smaller roads there are the speed traps. It's never easy to..."

And then Alanna, her eyes darting upward to watch for angels that might have been attracted by her enthusiasm, saw the paintings.

There was silence in the room while she studied them, her head swiveling.

"Oh my God," she finally whispered.

Nina spoke, but nothing came out.

She felt like the proprietor of a horrible prison camp, upon opening its doors to the victorious army.

"They're all the same painting!" gasped Alanna.

"Well, actually they're from my class. We..."

"We have to take them down."

"Margot and I were just talking about that. I thought..."

"We have to take them down! Margot, I'm so sorry that you had to see this. In your shop."

Margot nodded, weakly:

"If I could have been warned..."

Alanna embraced her again, and the two women seemed to weep on each other's breasts for a time.

"None of us knew. None of us knew."

The embrace lasted an interminable amount of time.

Then finally, the three of them—Nina, Margot, and Alanna—took the two small ladders that the shop possessed, and, much like Roman soldiers standing before the cross, took down what they saw before them.

The process of taking down the identical seascapes, wrapping them carefully, and preparing them for the safe return to the Monets and Pisarros who'd painted them by numbers—and then rehanging the actual paintings that had preceded them on the walls of Elementals—took almost an hour.

That made it lunchtime.

Sergio's by the Sea.

Where they found themselves seated beside a large plate glass window that would have overlooked the Gulf of Mexico if Sergio's had actually been located by the sea, but, since this was not the case, actually overlooked the parking lot of a supermarket that happened to be next door.

No matter.

The shrimp cocktail was supreme as usual, and the remoulade sauce went far toward healing Nina's hurt feelings.

"Nina darling," said Alanna, sipping some of the cold iced tea that accompanied the shrimp, "I did not intend to imply that your painting, and those of your fellow students, were insipid or uninspired."

"But that's what you think, isn't it?"

Alanna nodded, so that her purple turban came dangerously close to the flame of a candle that burned uselessly in the center of the table.

"Of course, I think that the paintings are insipid and uninspired. What I meant to say was, it was callous of me to *imply* that. I should simply have said nothing at all. After all, what are true friends for, if not to ignore the peccadillos of other friends."

"Here, here," said Margot, taking a twist of lime from her gin and tonic—all right it was early, but it had been a traumatic morning—and laying it carefully on a small dish that the waiter had provided for just such a purpose. "My thoughts exactly."

"You both," asked Nina, "think I have peccadillos?"

"Not many peccadillos," said Alanna, consolingly. "And frequently what in others might have seemed peccadiloish has proven in your case to be good solid instinctual reasoning. Hence the fact that you have basically saved Bay St. Lucy and the rest of the coast twice in the past year or so."

"Here, here," said Margot, who apparently had decided to pay a majority of her attention to her gin and a smaller part to the creative responses expected in scintillating conversation.

Nina continued doggedly though.

"You don't think in this case my painting is truly..."

"No," said Alanna.

And that stopped the conversation for a time.

It remained motionless until Margot, having half-finished the drink by now, said quietly:

"I was, on the other hand, Nina, thinking about something you said when we were talking about the paintings."

"Something intelligent?"

"No, something stupid."

"Damn."

"But perhaps useful."

Another pause.

A pair of porpoises played and sparkled and leapt in the frothing ocean two miles to the east of where they would like to have been seated, and a tan Volvo pulled out of the parking lot fifty yards to the west of where they actually were seated.

"You were talking about the Impressionist paintings in the Jeu de Palme."

"Yes, I thought that since we had all of our seascapes around on the walls..."

"Hush."

"Sorry."

"But, listen, both of you. Alanna, do you have openings for cultural events to be held at the Auberge this summer?"

"Yes, darling. We have a number of concerts and theatrical events, but…"

"What about painting?"

Alanna shook her head:

"Nothing."

"Then I have an idea."

"Tell it, by all means."

"All right. It has to do with a young docent I hired just before leaving The Chicago Art Museum last year."

"A docent?" asked Nina.

"Yes, all museums, or nearly all of them, hire docents. These people are a bit like graduate students. Their main job is to conduct tours showing the paintings to museum patrons, and explaining various facts about the works and the painters. At any rate, this particular docent was named Carol Walker. She was completely unimpressive during her initial interview, and, in fact, I was advised against hiring her. Something about her though…"

Margot shook her head.

"Something about her piqued my interest. It was almost completely intangible, but it was there, nevertheless. An ardent love of painting, and everything about it. Well, at any rate, I hired her. Within a few weeks, she had developed a method of lecturing about paintings that was—well, completely revolutionary. She connected a series of computers which she set up in the middle of a particular gallery with lights that she had somehow secreted around the room—and she was able to create a kind of holograph. A new visual world that engulfed the patrons as they stood there. I only saw a few of her presentations before I left to come to Bay St. Lucy. But I was completely overwhelmed by what I saw. At any rate, Ms. Walker apparently remained hated by some of the museum's higher ups—unimaginative administrative types—but her following increased. I got word a month or so ago from various people that the museum had received a very large grant to help them explore the possibilities of multi-media presentations within the museum."

"It sounds fascinating," said Alanna. "But how…"

"Why don't we invite Carol Walker to come here and give one of her presentations, say, in July? We can surely afford the multi-media apparatus. And the woman owes me her job. Surely she would come."

And thus the idea was hatched.

Carol Walker would come to Bay St. Lucy.

And the old Robinson mansion, erstwhile hangout of gangsters and thieves, would now become the home of Monet's Water lillies.

CHAPTER TWO: BOXES

At approximately the same moment on a Friday afternoon that a plot was being hatched to invite Carol Walker to Bay St. Lucy, the young woman herself was preparing for a meeting with Rebecca Simpson, a museum administrator who'd never liked her.

The office she was to report to was near the entrance to the Modern Wing.

Carol entered a door that led off the main corridor and was engulfed in a series of smaller corridors, by a stream of men in white jackets pushing wheelbarrows in front of them. The men all had on blue caps. There was no writing on their uniforms. But she did note that the men walking toward Rebecca Simpson's office were pushing empty wheelbarrows, and the men coming away from her office each had a large brown cardboard box, identical, approximately two cubic feet in dimensions.

"Carol! Come in! Sit down!"

It was the first time she'd been in Rebecca Simpson's office.

It was, at least today, not so much an office at all, but a meeting place of corridors, a kind of wheelbarrow traffic circle around which boxes circled endlessly, coming from somewhere Carol could not discern, and clattering noisily down a staircase she did not know existed.

"OVER THERE! "

"NO! GET THAT ONE! LEAVE THOSE TWO!"

Somehow in the midst of this chaos, was a desk, gray topped, with what seemed innumerable tiny half moon curves imprinted in it, as though the same hand had studiously pressed a thumbnail a thousand times, at random locations, into its ugly, ever-so-slightly malleable surface.

"NO! LEAVE THAT ONE!"

"YES! LEAVE IT...IT DOESN'T GO WITH THE OTHERS!"

The men, she could see, were unable to negotiate the steep stairway with the ponderously loaded wheelbarrows, and were forced to carry the barrows by hand, one man grunting with each end.

"Please, sit down, Carol."

"Here?"

"Yes. Right there—it's all right."

"What—what are they doing?"

"Who?"

"These men."

"With the wheelbarrows?"

"Yes. What are they doing?"

"I don't know."

That was the last that was said during the interview about the wheelbarrows, although the circulation of barrow-boxes continued with what seemed to be innumerable men involved in the parade

"Carol, don't you check your email?"

"No, I—it's been—a busy weekend."

"Have you gotten any of the messages I've sent to the docents?"

"I just found them. A few minutes ago."

"Well—Carol, I hardly know where to begin—so much has happened. You really do need to check your email"

"I know. I will in the future."

Rebecca Simpson was dressed in brown and looked, Carol realized, like one of the boxes. She had a square face—a bit more flushed than the boxes but otherwise identical—a square torso, square nose, square eyes, and an enigmatic interior.

"Well, I must tell you then, that Educational Services has received an anonymous grant."

"I see."

"It's quite large."

"That's good."

"Yes, we're very excited. You did not receive any of the emails concerning this?"

"No."

"I sent the first ones out on Friday morning, around nine o'clock. Did you not receive that email?"

"Probably. I'm sure I got it, but—I really haven't been checking emails this weekend the way I should."

"Then I sent another group of emails around three o'clock that afternoon. Did you receive that email?"

"I'm sure I did."

"There was a request for a reply."

"I just really didn't check any of my emails this weekend."

"Then…"

Each of the words was identical: a two foot cubic pasteboard word, crossing the gray desk in a wheelbarrow, and heading toward stairs leading downward, downward…

"Then I sent another email on Saturday evening. Did you not receive that email?"

"No, ma'am. I mean—I'm sure I did, but I really haven't been checking."

"And finally, I sent another set of rather lengthy emails yesterday evening. There were two emails, plus several attachments. Did you receive those emails, and those attachments?"

"I'm sure that, when I check, I'll find them."

"PUT DOWN THAT WHEELBARROW! NO! NOT THAT ONE! THE OTHER ONE!"

"So you received none of them?"

"No. That is, I probably got them. I'm sure they came through. I just haven't gotten to read them."

"I see."

"BE CAREFUL WITH THAT ONE! THERE ARE SPRINGS IN IT!"

"Well. I guess I must assume that you don't know what was in any of the emails."

"That's true."

Rebecca Simpson sighed heavily, the clear scotch tape holding her flaps together, straining as she did so.

"Then first, Carol, I have to thank you; and thank you with great sincerity."

Finally, Carol thought.

Why?

Although she already knew why, it was appropriate to ask.

"This grant has to do with multi-media presentations."

With my *multi media presentations*, she thought, but said nothing.

"A great part of the grant earmarks funding for multi-media, in-museum, instruction. I'm sure you're aware—as I pointed out in my emails, and in the attachments—that there is a great potential in using computer technology to bring out aspects of color, form—to create, actually, a new paradigm. Have you read anything by Ronald Marskin?"

"No."

"But…"

Then a shake of the head.

"I had suggested you read some materials by Marskin. Did you not receive *that* email either?"

"I guess not."

"My God. My God. Why do I send these things?"

Nothing to be said to that.

The wheelbarrows continued to clatter. Whatever the boxes contained, there had to have been an endless supply of it.

"Marskin's book deals with the use of computer technology in Visual Arts Instruction. I think it would have helped you, especially given what seems your area of interest. But there isn't much to be done now."

"No, ma'am."

"At any rate, Carol, I just wanted to thank you for the presentations you've given here in the past months. Whatever have been their deficiencies, they certainly have not lacked in enthusiasm. You have a true love for what you're doing and I'm sure that's going to hold you in good stead in the future, as you gain in the professionalism needed to go with it."

Carol realized for the first time:

She's firing me.

My God, she's firing me.

"Are you firing me?" barely able to recognize her own voice.

Silence for time. Then:

"This has, of course, not been an easy decision. I've reviewed many of your presentations—almost all of them, actually—and, Carol, there are just too many problems. I barely know where to begin."

Neither did Carol, who, dumbstruck, could only stammer: "I'm fired?"

"I think it's best that we go—in different directions."

"But—I mean—what kind of problems?"

Rebecca Simpson shook her head, looked up at the ceiling as though appealing to God for patience, and then took from her desk a yellow notebook filled with black scrawl-marks that looked like so many tarantulas frozen in motion over a field of ripe grain.

"I…"

More shakes of the head.

"Morris and Company established in 1873. Eighteen seventy three, Carol? That's just not the kind of mistake you can make here. At a smaller museum, for a less sophisticated audience…Carol, I've gotten protests! Some people have used the word "appalled."

"Which people?"

"Well, of course, I can't go into that."

"I keep getting requests, bookings."

"Yes, and we keep hoping these…these truly unforgivable gaffes will lessen. But they don't; they just keep getting worse."

"WATCH THE STAIRS! IT'S WET ON THE SECOND STAIR!"

"And, Carol—you've missed two meetings. I announce these docent meetings very clearly via email. But—it's as though you don't even check your email."

"I guess I just…I thought things were going well. The people seemed to like what I did."

"They like the theatrics of it. But we're not an entertainment business, Carol. We're not a troupe of trained monkeys. This is scholarship. Serious scholarship. I don't think we were able to make you realize the gravity of that."

"I'm sorry. I—I just can't believe that you're firing me."

"These things are never easy. And I can promise you, this is a decision arrived at by all of us in the division, after very difficult thought. All I can tell you is that, after that thought, and a great deal of agonizing, we feel that, at least at this point in time, the museum and you should go in different directions."

Like what? Carol wondered. *East?*

"I did want to give you this, though."

She handed Carol a plastic-covered card.

"This is a special "Friends of the Museum" card. If you present it at the entrance, you will be allowed in free at any time during the coming year. We do want you to come back to the collections. Often. You have made some very good friends here, Carol. Please—do not be a stranger."

"I won't," she said, taking the card.

"Now, if there's nothing else…"

"No. No, thank you for telling me."

"That's quite all right. Can you find your way out?"

"Sure."

And she did.

In the basement of the Art Institute of Chicago is a miniaturist exhibit of furniture. It is a series of shadowboxes, each a cubic foot or two in size, and constructed with exquisite care to reproduce rooms from various cultures and time periods. There is a sitting room from a plantation house in Virginia, circa 1765; a kitchen from a Tudor mansion during the reign of Henry VI; the drawing room of a Biedermeier dwelling in Berlin, 1868. The rooms are lighted with great care, and various scenes—people mowing hay or sitting on a lawn—can be seen through the window.

Carol had always loved this part of the museum. It quieted her when she needed quieting, inspired and energized her when things in her mind were too quiet to begin with.

She had pulled a chair before the farthest of the boxes, one labeled "Carpathian Landowner's Villa, circa 1923, and had lost herself in it.

"They've put the chair," said Carol, to herself, "in the wrong place."

No one wanted her.

"How funny. The chair is in the wrong place. It destroys the order of the room. The stupid museum. They've put the chair in the wrong place. And they've fired me. What will I do now? Where will I go?"

Her cell phone rang.

She took it out of her purse and flipped it open.

"Hello?"

"Carol?"

"Yes?"

"This is Margot Gavin."

"Oh, Margot!"

"Carol, we have a lot of money here in Bay St. Lucy, which is a town on the gulf shore in Mississippi. We'd like for you to come down and give one of your incredible presentations. Just name your price. And let us know what kind of equipment you need. I know you're busy, but—do you think you could squeeze us in?"

It took her fully two minutes to stop crying, so that she could say 'yes.'

CHAPTER THREE: TRANSITIONS

It took the better part of a week for Nina to get over Margot's and Alanna's response to her entry into the world of art.

At every trip to Bagatelli's, the word 'insipid' came into her mind.

At every step she took along the shore line, she heard the phrase 'take it down now!'

Every sight of the frothing waves on the incoming tide reminded her of her own masterful use of white in the seascape that she and twelve others had painted with such care.

It wasn't that *bad,* she continually told herself.

Or maybe it was.

Margot had been, after all, for many years, the managing director of The Chicago Art Museum.

She probably knew *something* about these matters, or so one would think.

Gradually these thoughts dissipated into the mild sea air, and were replaced by visions of the great spectacle which was to happen in only a few days at the Auberge des Arts. For the apparently quite talented Carol Walker had replied to Margot's telephone invitation to say that, yes, there was an opening in her schedule; she could come quite soon to Bay St. Lucy, and, yes, she would be delighted to give a presentation.

On Monet's Water lillies, as it happened.

As for the equipment necessary, it was quite easy to obtain, from any good store that specialized in computers and electronic devices.

Of which there was one in Bay St. Lucy and an even larger one in nearby Hattiesburg.

And so the date was set: September 16.

Three days away.

There was nothing to do, then, except look forward to it.

Well, almost nothing.

There was worrying to be done.

For something was definitely wrong with Penelope Royale.

Nina had heard rumblings for some days.

"Somehow she just doesn't seem the same."

"I know—it's—something's bothering her."

But she'd given little credence to such mutterings.

True, Penelope and Tom Broussard, married a little less than a year now, were the unlikeliest of couples. He'd been a rebellious student in Bay St. Lucy's high school, managing to get himself expelled and then sent to jail before taking a turn for the worse and becoming a writer. For her part, she'd also been expelled from the high school (on numerous occasions, actually), but, as opposed to Tom, who usually did no more than get into fights or insult various classmates or teachers, she'd actually managed to do severe and costly damage to the physical plant.

Now, she'd become the town's Tugboat Annie.

If Tom was Marlon Brando she was Marie Dressler.

Their marriage, though, had seemed to work out, for the simple reason that neither of them acted married.

Neither of them changed lifestyle in even the smallest degree.

Penelope continued to live at the far end of the wharf, in a corrugated iron shed beside her square, flat bottomed boat, The Sea Urchin.

Tom continued to live in a square, flat-bottomed shack in the most disreputable part of town.

She continued to live for only two things: fishing and obscenity.

He continued to live for only pornographic writing.

So it was hard for Nina to believe either could be dissatisfied with the arrangement.

But such was clearly the case, no doubt.

She realized it early on Wednesday morning as she approached the shed and boat, walking gingerly along a quay moistened by a small predawn shower and still slightly slippery.

"Hey, Penn!"

This was her standard greeting; it almost always called for Penelope to emerge from the shed, clad in dungarees, hip boots, and a plaid shirt, beaming, and saying something like:

"Hey you------------! Ready to----------------------some------------------------- and get some---------------------- fishing done?"

The dirty words varied, of course, but they were always fiercely imaginative and even quite poetic in a Dantean sense, if Dante had only been a bit more daring in his wanderings through Hades, and a bit less concerned about being excommunicated.

It was just Penn saying, 'Hi, let's go fishing!'

Because they did go fishing every week.

It had become a part of each woman's routine.

It gave Penelope a chance to keep up with the comings and goings of her favorite ex-teacher (the only teacher, actually, who had not attempted to have her removed, not only from the high school, but from the city, and even the state).

And it gave Nina a chance to be sure that Penn was still living comfortably in the far west end of the wharf, and thus would not be a danger to any of the town's infrastructure.

It also supplied Nina with four or five nice, foot-long whitefish (They sometimes caught other things, of course, but whitefish was their prey of choice), which Nina would put into her freezer and thaw for various evening meals.

So it worked out nicely for everyone concerned.

Except, of course, the whitefish, but that was matter for a different time and place.

It was thus highly surprising this particular morning when, as a reply to Nina's cheerful greeting, Penelope could only stare somberly at her across several buckets of bait and other aquatic refuse and say, quietly:

"Good morning, Nina."

Uh oh.

Something definitely not right.

"You ready to go fishing, Penn?"

"Sure. Bait's all ready. I've got your lines rigged. Come on and we'll get started."

Nina nodded and continued to approach the boat, but she was already genuinely concerned.

"How's Tom?"

"Oh, he's fine."

"And your business?"

"Going well. Had three parties last week and two more scheduled for the next few days. It's not summer business, you know, but it's holding steady."

"Glad to hear it. So. Where are we going today?"

"Oh, I don't know. Maybe over in the Bay. Maybe out toward the oil rig. There seems to be some action out that way. Several of the other captains have taken sea bass. Just whatever you want to do, wherever you want to go."

"Sure."

Well, that settled it. Penn was sick.

No obscenities at all.

What could be wrong with her?

Her color was fine.

She moved around in a sprightly enough fashion, juggling thirty or forty pound barrels of this and that as though they were weightless.

But she was not swearing.

Nor did she swear during the entire ceremony of starting the boat, easing it through the various slips and other docks—usually one or two of the other fishing boat pilots would have left a line adrift or moored unevenly, breaking an unspoken captain's code and eliciting from Penn some such outburst as:

"Flynn, you ---------------------! If you ever ------------------
----------------- that again I'll------------------------- and you won't have enough----------------------------- to ----------------
--------------------------your----------------------for a ----------
--------------------!"

Or something similar.

But this morning, the boat just chugged its way out to sea.

What was going on?

The wind freshened; there was a slight chop in the surf. Nina basked in the morning sun as she sat in the prow and turned occasionally to watch Penn steer.

She probed.

"How's Tom's newest novel?"

"It's coming along all right."

"He hasn't gotten arrested any more, has he?"

"Just once, last month. But the other guy in the fight didn't press charges."

"That's good."

"Yeah. I guess."

What was wrong with her?

Maybe nothing.

Maybe she was just feeling blue, or moody.

Sometimes that happens to everyone.

But no—this was something completely different.

And the reason Nina knew it was completely different was as follows:

After fishing for little more than an hour, they came within half a mile from the offshore oil rig that could be easily seen from Bay St. Lucy.

This was not Aquatica, the huge drilling station that Nina had, incredibly, saved from utter destruction some bare months before, and which was still going about its mammoth pumping business more than ten miles out.

No, this was a much smaller installation; but still, it had its own business to do, and it employed drillers and riggers, and it fed them, and it threw overboard as garbage both the food they did not eat and the remains of the food that they did.

Fish came to eat these things.

One of those fish struck Nina's line just as she was musing about what could possibly be wrong with Penn, and whether she should possibly ask something like: 'Penelope, are you all right? Have you been getting enough beer to drink? Somehow you just don't seem to be…"

WHAM!

Huge strike!

The rod bent double in Nina's hands; the reel buzzed, and the prow of the boat was pulled in a tight circle by the submerged aircraft carrier that was now pulling them:

She heard the voice from astern:

"You've got a -----------------------! Don't------------------ --------! Just -------------------- the -----------------------, and then --."

It was then Nina knew that real trouble was at hand, and that something was terribly wrong with her friend.

For things had become exactly reversed.

It was as though Penelope Royale had been turned inside out, her entrails outside of her and her skin hidden within.

Penelope—the real Penelope, the normal Penelope— could never engage in casual conversation, which she had been doing for the past hour with Nina, without swearing.

But she had not sworn.

Not one bad word had she uttered.

On the other hand, she could not talk about fishing when a fish was actually on the line in any other than stolid, serious, prose.

"Hold the rod tip higher. Give him a little more line."

Now all of that had been reversed.

Penn was swearing while giving actual fishing advice.

This was tantamount to an otherwise normal person drinking heavily in the morning.

It presaged evil.

What was wrong with Penn?

Whatever it was, its symptoms were to worsen.

For after five minutes of battle with the fish—it seemed like half an hour, and Nina's forearms had begun to ache— the struggle began to go her way, and the tiny spot in the churning green ocean where line entered water was now no more than twenty feet from the side of the boat.

"Watch----------------! The -------------------------- is going to-----------------"

Jump.

And the fish did jump, leaping and writhing and spraying and flashing in the sun, its t-shape now a full two feet out of the water.

Hammerhead shark.

HAMMERHEAD SHARK!

Nina's first impulse was simply to throw the rod away and tell Penn to take them both home.

Then she thought about *Jaws*.

"You're gonna need a bigger boat."

The shark whapped flat back into the water then, but the fight in him was doubled, and the boat began to skull even faster in the direction of the Christmas Tree-lighted rig.

Was he intending to take them under it?

And then it happened.

The thing Nina was probably never to forget.

The thing that showed her, clearly, just how ill Penn really was.

For 'ill' was the only way to describe it.

Penn rose from her pilot's seat in the stern of the boat, made her way to a storage compartment, which she opened, and pulled out a forty-five automatic.

This was, Nina remembered, the same weapon that had been used during a tense confrontation at the Aquatica.

It had saved their lives then.

Was it to do so again?

No, it wasn't.

Because Penelope, who in any other circumstances, in any other normal life, would have sighted the gun carefully, waited until the next leap, and—BAM—blown the two-foot shark completely apart so that nothing remained save a circular mass of chum and red writhing intestines, purpling up the water—

—simply watched that next leap.

And did nothing.

Nothing at all.

Until, with her face frozen on the horizon, her eyes seemingly peering out beyond the shark, and even beyond the oil rig, she carefully lifted the lid of the storage compartment, and gingerly placed the weapon back where it had come from.

Then she produced a hunter's knife from the broad leather belt she was wearing. She leaned over the side, and, with a deft movement, severed the fishing line.

"To hell with him," she said, quietly.

What was wrong with Penelope Royale?

For Carol Walker, the day following her firing began in depressing darkness. By the time she left for Pilsen, a scudding layer of gray clouds washed over the city, turning umbrellas inside out and soaking the sidewalks, which glistened in the glare of headlights. Rain—especially unseasonably cold September rain—made everything harder. Crossing Michigan Avenue, bumping into people who had their heads bent into scarves and their eyes fixed on the pavement...now crossing the sidewalk, remembering it was four forty-five and people would be sprinting desperately from the seventy-eight bus up Wabash toward Union Station, up toward Ogilvie—avoiding bicyclists, who seemingly did not care who crossed their paths...watching fearfully, furtively, all of the people in the world, who were running, peddling, hurrying, mumbling...just panicked by the fact that it was Friday afternoon and THEY MIGHT NOT BE ABLE TO GET TO THE SUBURBS ON TIME!

Of course, in these same stations—Union, Ogilvie— equal numbers of people just as harried, were pushing each other off the platforms, out of the trains, through the revolving doors, down the escalators...just as panicked that it was four forty-five and THEY MIGHT NOT BE ABLE TO GET INTO THE GREAT CITY OF CHICAGO ON TIME!

She made her way up the stairs to the Pink Line Wabash stop. There, seated on benches, huddled beneath warmers, clustered shelterless and peering down at the tracks below them, or the city stretching westward—people were miserable. No one smiled. A few read newspapers, but most seemed close to despair, blankness, complete lack of touch or contact. Here and there, up and down the platform, a group of teenagers ran into each other and giggled, or pushed each other precariously near the chasm over the electric tracks. Everyone else in the station hated them intensely.

Finally, the train came; she squeezed her way onto it, wondering vaguely if someone would try to pick the pocket of her trench coat, wondering vaguely if she would care.

Twenty dollars were folded carefully in the shirt pocket of her blouse.

She was to meet a man named Michael in Pilsen.

She'd gotten an enigmatic, typed note late the previous afternoon, in an envelope containing a twenty dollar bill.

HEARD ABOUT YOUR FIRING. BAD LUCK. HAVE A NEW EMPLOYMENT OPPORTUNITY TO PUT FORTH TO YOU. MEET ME AT 216 BLUE ISLAND ROAD IN PILSEN. USE THE MONEY TO BUY FOOD. KEY IS UNDER THE MAT WHEN YOU ENTER FROM THE STREET. (THERE WILL BE BEER IN THE REFRIGERATOR.) MICHAEL

What a strange thing for her to be doing!

She thought she could remember this 'Michael' person.

He'd been at one of her presentations, and had introduced himself.

The last name was German, she thought, *but she could not remember it.*

What she did remember was that he was slight of build—not too much taller than she herself—and that he had a nice smile.

Had she been attracted to him?

Surely not.

After all, she'd seen him no more than two minutes.

Certainly she had not been attracted to him!

Would he ask her to go to bed with him?

Or would he have too much old world gallantry, Germanic reserve—simple courtesy?

Going to bed with Michael...and in Pilsen, for God's sake.

Who went to bed with anybody in Pilsen?

She would not do it, of course. It showed too little respect for herself, for her values, for her upbringing.

Besides, he was not the German of her reveries. *That* German was tall. That fantasy German had the unruly lock of hair that all young German men seemed to have, as well as the habit of constantly throwing it back upon his head, constantly rearing his neck and shoulders violently upward so as to get rid of the stupid cowlick, get it far back from his face, making her ask herself as she saw the activity taking place over and over again, thousands of times each morning, millions of times by the end of each day...

"Why don't you just cut the damned thing off?"

But this Michael did not have such an unruly lock of hair; he had a neatly trimmed goatee.

There was, in short, practically nothing at all sexy about Michael.

She did not find him particularly attractive.

And she would not go to bed with him.

She descended the stairs from the Pink Line station and began walking toward Pilsen. She was going through the hospital district now, and felt the same curiosity as she always did when visiting Pilsen (which she did with some regularity on festival days or holidays). She liked Pilsen. The trip into it always amused her, though, and disturbed her: the complete trip was divided, as Gaul had been, into four parts: in the northern neighborhoods, where she lived, people walked aimlessly, having been told that doing so would keep them healthy; in the Loop, everyone walked desperately, attempting to get into or out of the Loop as fast as possible; in the hospital district (through which she was now walking), no one walked at all, except for some rats, either dead or dying in the gutters.

In Pilsen, on the other hand (and she was now approaching Blue Island Street, a main artery)...in Pilsen, everyone was happy to be where one was. Exactly where one was. People moved, but circularly, not linearly. They did not want to go anywhere else, and, if they had come from somewhere else, it had been long ago to allow them to shake off the remnants of any type of displacement.

They were content to be behind the counters of innumerable Taquerios, making Boraches, or Gorditas, or Empiezas—and smiling through the windows at the people on the street, who, cognizant of the area's rules against linear motion, sat upon benches and gazed into the restaurants, ogling food.

Or they were content to sit upon stone porches leading up to row houses, with a ten foot plot of garden in front of them, and seven deliriously happy children tumbling over themselves, screaming in ecstasy.

Or they sat in dark taverns, watching soccer games that never ended, and were accompanied by low rumblings of commentary from wall-bound televisions, from which, at precisely ten minute intervals, desperate screams of "GOL! GOL! GOL!" flooded into the barrooms, leaving the spectators, who were sipping one Carte Blanca after another, completely unmoved.

She entered a small place she'd discovered some months before. She bowed and smiled at the woman behind the counter, and the woman smiled back. They said some words in Spanish, then they bowed again and continued to smile. The woman was muscular and ravenblack-haired, but none of that mattered. All of it—her body, breasts, legs, white camisole top, red flower perched provocatively behind left ear, earrings dangling circular and golden below flower—all of the various aspects of her existence were obscured like daytime stars by the sun-like brilliance of her smile. It simply wiped everything else out. There might have been a great, even, sea of dull blue-white around it, but it was so dazzling as to make even that evanescence perceptible to the human eye.

"Ahh, dos Churachos…"

She responded to Carol's hesitant order as one might respond to news of a birth.

"DOS CHURACHOS!"

"Y tres gorditos com pollo…"

"TRES GORDITOS CON POLLO!"

After a time, the order was placed, amid much celebration and congratulation (MUY BIEN: TRES TOSTADOS! PERFECTMENTE!)—and Carol had the feeling that even the loafers, passers-by, children, and non-leashed dogs (Thank God—finally dogs without leashes)—were nodding in approval, as though she were not buying dinner but taking communion.

"GRACIAS! MUCHAS MUCHAS GRACIAS!"

Six dollars and seventy-three cents for a brown sackful of aluminum wrapped—things. And seven small plastic cups filled with evil-looking multi-colored sauces. Red sauce; green sauce; brown sauce; milky white sauce...

Several people nodded at her as she left the taqueria, and, through the plate glass window, she could see the woman behind the counter jumping up and down, waving both arms in the air, and screaming, "ADIOS!"

She turned the corner, walked by two Catholic churches, a Lotto shop, a music store, four more taquerias—and came to the apartment where she was to spend the night, not going to bed with Michael.

It was a nondescript row house, green paint peeling a bit, but otherwise all right. On the steps of the row house next to it, a small boy sat perfectly still, watching her. He could have been a brown statue with a black, tousled wig. A cold north wind rustled through the wig, moving dark strands of hair here and there...but the statue itself did not move, and, as Carol ascended the stairs leading up from the street, she wondered how a young human could remain so completely motionless.

She opened the door and walked, a bit uncertainly, into the dark vestibule beyond.

Immediately before her was a doormat.

She bent, lifted the mat corner, and found a small silver key.

Then she ascended stairs that creaked slightly with her weight.

The apartment was on the third floor landing.

A bit more out of breath than she should have been (she attributed that to the sixty or so pounds of Mexican food she was carrying), she inserted the key in the door of Apartment 367B and unlocked it, then used her knee to push open the door.

The apartment, vacant, stared back at her.

It was the opposite apartment of what she expected from Michael, knowing as she did of his association with some of the wealthiest people in Chicago. She would have expected him to have the use of an elegant penthouse apartment somewhere on the lakefront. Michael's apartment would be carpeted, picture-windowed, electric-kitchened, stunningly sunlit, blue lake water and motionless sailboat-viewed, and utterly, eternally, silent.

This apartment was ragged and, in every respect, questionable.

The wooden floors creaked; the large, single, dininglivingkitchen room, (the three divisions separated by walls barely begun and never finished) lacked furniture, except for two chairs placed oddly and haphazardly, as though having come to rest after some natural disaster—and the entire far half of the area glowed with innumerable rays of fine dust floating in the air.

She put her purse on the couch beside the nearest wall, shed several layers of clothes, dumped the load of aluminum-wrapped unknowns in the kitchen, and inspected the bedroom.

It was an actual room—not too large, but possessed of a door. The bed was neatly made, and if it did not have blankets or bedspreads, it did at least have two pillows and a tightly made sheet that was either black or very dark blue, depending on how many clouds were regulating the light coming through the small window above the bedstead at any one time.

Dinner. Dinner.

She returned to the kitchen.

She opened several cupboards and drawers, found knives, forks, plates.

She set a small table that stood by the magnificent kitchen window, and then she opened the refrigerator.

There was nothing in the refrigerator except a bottle of mayonnaise, a package of Cotto salami, and fifty bottles of beer.

Carefully she laid out dinner.

Chorizos on a platter; empiezas on this plate; gorditos, arranged by meat selection, on a separate plate; the sauces set out side by side…

…should she pour a glass of beer for Michael?

He might like that.

She found a clean glass (She was forced to admit that all of the kitchen was cleaner than she might have expected from a single man, and this was clearly the apartment of a single man), and poured the beer.

She looked through the window; a small market seemed to have been set up, blocking the street below, and there were sounds of laughter. Two motorcycles chugged and potted directly before the adjoining building; unbelievably skinny boys threw themselves upon the motorcycles as though they were jungle gyms; the motionless boy who'd been seated earlier on the steps remained motionless…and several women, all of whom looked like the woman in the taqueria, made florid gestures telling everyone what to do, which everyone ignored, smiling.

Dinner set, Carol returned to the couch, took a book from her purse, and glanced at her watch.

Five forty.

Michael had said he would arrive at six thirty.

Being a German, he would undoubtedly be punctual.

She began to read, her mind half on the book dealing with the life of Canaletto and his fascination with a particular building in Venice—and half on the evening ahead.

She looked forward to dinner. Michael was enigmatic to her. She wanted to know more about his background.

She liked talking during dinner.

And, she could not deny, she looked forward to the chance to talk about herself.

She had not really done so for some time.

True, she often chatted with the other docents…

…but it would be nice if this 'Michael,' whom she barely remembered, would be someone who could actually converse.

Someone who might listen, if she talked about herself.

For now, though, Canaletto and his canals. Then Michael; then dinner; then a long talk, winding this way and that, taking unexpected leaps as good essays and good conversations do—while sitting by the kitchen window, hearing rain that had now begun spattering on the glass panes, and watching as the small festival grew on the street below them.

So thinking, for more than half an hour, as the room darkened, she lost herself in the brightening Venice of Canaletto.

At precisely six thirty, there was a knock on the door.

She rose, crossed the door, and opened it.

Michael took two steps into the room, pushing her backward slightly. Then he cupped his hands beneath her buttocks, and, with astonishing ease, picked her straight up. He carried her across the room, laid her carefully in the bed, and undressed, as she undressed.

Within seconds, he was touching her, and she him.

"Has it been," she whispered, "long for you?"

She could feel the warmth of his lips as they breathed into her ear:

"It's always been," he whispered, "about the same length as it is now."

She sighed, saying, just before she put her tongue into his mouth:

"This is a problem; we have the same sense of humor."

"Don't worry," he answered. "I won't be using it for a while."

And then he was on top of her.

At eight o'clock the next morning, they were sitting beside the window, drinking coffee.

The day was brighter. Pools of water below on the sidewalks reflected rooflines, and from several buildings, roosters crowed.

There were few people on the street; the small market had cleared from the night before.

Carol wore a man's shirt that Michael had found in the closet, and nothing else. Michael was in his boxers; she was amused by the scarcity of hair on his chest.

He looked, she thought, like a boy.

"We can't do this anymore," he said.

"You are," she answered, "such an endearing sort of man. Say it again; I love to hear it."

"We can't do this anymore."

"Why not?"

"It's a bad idea."

She sipped from the cup in front of her and nodded:

"That's what I kept telling myself during the fifteen or sixteen times we made love: 'This is a bad idea; this is a bad idea.'"

"No, it's true. I have something better for you, though."

She looked at him: the morning sunlight made his goatee golden, and his eyes, which had seemed green the night before, were now blue.

"Your eyes," she said, "keep changing color."

"That's to my advantage."

They were silent for a time; the perennial, inevitable, mélange of guitar and accordion that defined Pilsen could be heard floating above all the roofs, out all the windows, up through the battered and brick-crumbling chimneys.

Michael reached back, took a pot of coffee from the stove, and filled his cup; he held the pot toward her. She shook her head. He shrugged, put the pot back, and said:

"I want to offer you a job. I'm offering it to you because I find you truly impressive. You know art; you are creative; and I think I could depend on you."

"You know all this from watching one multi-media presentation?"

"I've watched you a great deal more than that. And I've made inquiries."

"You've been spying on me?"

"Yes."

"Well, I suppose I should be flattered."

"What you should be is wealthy. You should be spending time in Paris and New York. You make no money as a mere docent, nor did you as a community college teacher. But I think that I can change all that."

"How?"

"I'm a kind of broker. I help wealthy people acquire paintings. Specifically, I help one person acquire paintings."

She looked at him, and, for perhaps the first time, he stared straight back at her. It was, she noticed, a contest of eye-wrestling, just as they might have had a contest of arm wrestling.

And, just as would have been the case with arm wrestling, neither won.

Finally each looked away. She said:

"Are the paintings stolen?"

"Of course they are. But all paintings have been stolen at one time or another."

There was, she thought, little to be said to that.

Finally, she smiled and asked:

"You want me to be your mule?"

He shook his head.

It was such a pity, she thought, that he did not have the long, unmanageable, lock of straw blond hair that her fantasy German had. The hair he did have was straw blond, as it must have been; but it lay quietly in place, a continual disappointment to her.

"Mules carry drugs," he said.

"Who carries paintings?"

"Rich people."

"All right. Tell me more."

He leaned forward:

"Listen. This is not brain surgery…"

He said the word 'brain' with a 'w;' it was his only language flaw. Otherwise, he could have come from Iowa. Except that he was not big enough.

"There are a great many paintings floating around The United States now. They are part of a large cache of masterpieces that were stolen by the Nazis toward the end of World War II."

"Stolen from whom?"

"Stolen from a group of wealthy Russian/Jewish families who lived in the Caucasians. Somehow they have become— available. I work for a man named Beckmeier. He has a number of residences, but his main seat is in southern Austria. He has a castle there."

"A castle?"

"Yes. Schloss Eggenburg. It's only a few miles from the Slovenian border, in very rugged country. At any rate, Beckmeier is assembling there what he feels will be the largest private collection in the world."

"But the authorities…"

"In that part of southern Austria, Beckmeier is the authorities. He just has to get them there."

"That's where you come in?"

"Yes. And you. If you will work for me."

"For how much?"

"Twenty thousand dollars for each painting you deliver."

"My God."

"Yes. And there should be one painting to deliver each two weeks. I'll give you the painting somewhere in Chicago, and a plane ticket along with it. You fly to Frankfurt, then change planes and go on to Graz."

"Graz?"

"A city of a quarter of a million, some ninety miles south of Vienna. It's the closest hub to Beckmeier's estate."

"I loved Vienna. I never got to Graz."

"Now is your chance. You will land at the Graz airport and be met by a limousine. Other instructions will follow. You'll be back here in three days from the time you take off."

"All right. That all makes sense, I suppose. But tell me, Michael: what pleasure do people get in hording stolen paintings?"

"I have no idea. I'm not an expert in the human soul. I am an expert in moving paintings. "

"What paintings are we talking about?"

"Rembrandt: Portrait of a Rabbi; El Greco: Mary Magdalen Before Christ on the Cross; Bruegel: Harvest; Van Gogh: Portrait du Docteur Gachet—the list goes on.

"But I have to keep asking: why me?"

"Because when I ask you to fly to Paris and rent an apartment in the Seventh, I don't want some stupid American asking me if I'm talking about baseball innings. And if I ask you to fly to Hannover and, for two months, disappear, I want to know that you will fly to Hannover and disappear."

She got up from the table, walked into the apartment for no particular reason, went from one nondescript and randomly placed piece of furniture to another for a time, and then returned.

"What's the downside?"

Michael paused for a time, then said:

"The Jewish families want these paintings back. If they find out you're carrying them…"

"What? What will happen to me?"

"You will simply disappear. No one will ever hear from you again."

She took a deep breath:

"That's a pretty significant downside. And what about the police?"

He shook his head:

"That is not a worry. The police will not bother you. Look at yourself: who in Interpol is going to say, 'There's an art thief.'"

Then he leaned forward:

"Now I need to leave. It's almost nine o'clock. I have an appointment. Will you think about my offer?"

"I don't know, Michael…"

"Just think about it."

"I don't think I could do this kind of thing. It's just that, I have an elderly father back in Georgia. He's very ill, and our farm…"

"You need money."

"Yes. But Papa is such a traditionalist. He's always been so proud of me…"

"I'm not surprised by that."

"Before I left for the great city of Chicago, he just kind of waved his hand out the window and said, "Carol, Carol…beyond the peaks. Beyond the peaks…""

"So now you get the chance to go beyond the peaks."

"I'm not sure this is what he'd have had in mind."

"You have to decide. And you need to decide soon."

He finished dressing and walked toward the door, then looked back over his shoulder:

"By the way, you should wait half an hour or so and then leave. The guy who lives here will probably be home around ten."

"Who lives here?"

He smiled, cupped his hand around her neck, pulled her face gently to him, kissed her, and said:

"I haven't the slightest idea."

CHAPTER FOUR: AND THE FLOWERS BEGAN TO DANCE!

The salon in Bay St. Lucy's Auberge des Arts was finally ready.

It had taken Margot Gavin, working in conjunction with Alanna Delafosse and Nina Bannister, two full days to prepare it properly.

And now young Carol Walker, standing inconspicuously by, in a corner of the room, looking, in her big black-rimmed glasses, like little more than a naïve school girl, was going to supply…

…what?

"You will not believe her presentations, Nina," Margot had said repeatedly.

That, and not much more.

Just that, because with her knowledge of computer technology and audio visual capability, she had astonished the passers-through the Chicago Art Museum, establishing, even after just a few months of residency there, a new standard in the ability to make art works come alive.

"A lot of people," Margot had continued, "know about holographs, and the way to create visual worlds, to put people inside planes and tunnels and walls that don't really exist. But these people are mostly engineers and scientists. Carol is an art lover. How she learned this stuff, I don't know. But she did."

Which was, Nina realized, glancing at her watch, about to begin.

She caught a glimpse of Margot, who was scurrying here and there, and who had just enough time to return a smile.

And she looked at Carol again.

Silent Carol Walker, standing straight in her corner, the only grown woman whom Nina could remember seeing who looked mousier than she herself looked, and who had even shorter brown hair—and, for that matter—a shorter body.

There—she did glance up, and around the room.

It was not a circular room, so it could not approximate the Jeu de Palme in Paris where the real Gardens sat silently, working their magic.

But, otherwise, it was a room of similar size.

Several clocks scattered around the Auberge began chiming, sonorously.

Eight PM.

Carol Walker moved to the small podium that had been set up against the far wall of the room.

People in the front row—somehow Alanna had been able, at very short notice, to attract a select group of art lovers, many of them French, from as far away as New Orleans— smiled at her, nodding occasionally. There were undercurrents of whispers. Nina could hear a few phrases of English, but mostly French, the long, guttural *uuuuuuhhhhh* that seemed to separate every three or four words, as though only in this language was space built in for thought. The women, most in their forties or fifties, were stylishly outfitted, but the men were dressed as European men always were when they came to the United States: they wore shorts and sandals, as though they were on safari in a third world nation.

And so, it was time.

Carol touched the first switch on a computer stand that had been set up beside the podium. Lights began to dim in the room.

Second switch: sound. Debussy from a first well hidden speaker, then a second, then a third. Quiet, elegant, clean and dreamlike Debussy, now filling the spaces between the paintings, breathing through the room.

The third switch created the hologram: there was a single gasp as silver light engulfed the island of people seated in its midst, and the fences, walls, paths leading to the Gardens of Giverney all opened and moved around them. Then Monet himself, his beard, his eyes, smiling, almost moving about through his rooms, his brushes...

....finally, all of the images in the room engulfing them, all of the holograph, all of the powers of the monitors and computer programs and encoded mathematical impersonal scientific technical amalgams stored like nuclear beauty pent up before them...all of these things exploded in color...

...and the flowers began to dance!

"Ah, mon Dieu!"

"Mon dieu, mon dieu!"

The gardens, the gardens, moved in sequence, orbiting around them. Everywhere there was light. Splendid light. Light as Monet must have seen it, clearly had rendered it. But he had rendered it condensed, captured with frames; now it gloried out as it must have existed in his own head, filling the room that now represented his brain, overwashing the walls and wires and doorways that disappeared before its heat and intensity and magnificence...the light of Monet's mind, brush—the light of Monet's magnificent Gardens.

The gasp continued as the flowers appeared, darkened, emerged, budded, sang around them.

Then Carol began to recite:

Laforgue:

"Au-desssus des etangs, au-dessus des vallees,
Des montagnes des bois, des nuages, des mers,
Par dela le soleil, par dela les ethers,
Par dela les confines des spheres etoilees..."

(Above the brooks, the valleys,
The mountains of trees, the clouds, the seas...
Beyond the sun, beyond the firmament,
Beyond the confines of starry spheres...)

The words were *known*, Nina realized immediately, rather than memorized, because Laforgue could not be memorized but simply had to appear, as the light did. Nina could never understand how people memorized poetry. Memorizing a poem violated it, hardened it, took from it its passion and birth.

No, it was clear that Carol Walker loved this poem and thus knew it, in precisely the same way she loved and knew the pictures radiating around her.

"La Nature et un temple ou de vivants piliers
Laissant parfois sortir de confuses paroles;
L'homme y passé a travers de forets de symbols
Qui l'observent vec des regard familiers."

(Nature is a temple where living pillars
Let, from time to time, confused words escape,
Men pass from time to time through the forest of symbols,
Observing them with familiar indifference.)

Nina could only watch, only listen, fascinated.

The person at the podium was not herself while reading these lines…this was not her voice, her consciousness. She had become someone else, as, probably, all great artists do from time to time. But that did not matter. Important was only that the lines be read perfectly, with the same somnolence and meter that the works themselves…that the light itself and the mirroring images, the blues and aquiline grays…demanded. The light changed; it obscured, focused, contracted, limiting itself in frame to one painting, *The Waterlilly Pond*, with the marvelous bridge overspanning it; the crowd turned slightly to see that the picture itself hung directly behind them—but then they forgot about the thing within the frame as the water and flowers and arc exploded outward around them and a new light flooded through the room drawing from their collective sense of wonder even more gasps, more repetitions of:

"Mon dieu—mon dieu…"

The Waterlilly Pond was not behind them in a box; it surrounded them. They all, under the spells of Lamartine, de Muset, Cambriole, Debussy—and of course Monet—became part of a new world that the computer had allowed them to fuse into.

And then it ended.

The last thing needing saying was said.

Carol turned off the computer.

The actual world, white and noisy and bare-floored and useless, returned.

For a moment there was silence…

…and then the crowd engulfed her. English, French…it all flowed over her:

"It was so beautiful!"

"How did you do it?"

"C'etait merveilleuse! Vraiment merveilleuse!"

"What—what was it, how did you make the light be so— so…all over!"

"Your French is so wonderful Are you born in Paris? Where did you learn this?"

"When will it be again? Does it happen for all paintings?"

"When will you do this again?"

And on and on.

Nina could only stand, fascinated, at the back of the crowd, while this young woman answered question after question, all with perfect aplomb.

Until finally there was Margot standing nearby, bending, whispering harshly:

"Nina, we've got to get her out of here; she'll collapse with exhaustion."

"She seems," answered Nina, "to be doing all right."

Margot shook her head:

"Yes, but that has to be exhausting. Let's spirit her away on some excuse of other. We'll depend on Alanna to take over hostess duties, and we'll go…I don't know, maybe to a restaurant or something. Maybe to Elementals."

"No, let's go to my place."

"You're certain?"

"Sure I am. Carol's a painter. She'll love sitting out on my deck and looking out at the ocean by night."

Margot nodded:

"You may be right."

And so the matter was decided.

And within half an hour, the three of them—Margot, Nina, and Carol—were, in fact, sitting ensconced above the incoming tide, a half moon glowing above them, cold Chardonnay simmering in three glasses in front of them, and Carol speaking of the water in the same amazed tones that the crowd had been speaking of her presentation only a short time before.

"How long have you had the place, Nina?"

"Several years now. Ever since my husband passed."

"My God, how I envy you! I have a little efficiency apartment near the Montrose stop on the Brown Line. It's all right, but, when I look out my one barred window, I see streetcars. You see this. I can't imagine why you're not constantly painting portraits of it."

"Well, in fact I…"

"Ummm," interrupted Margot.

There was an uncomfortable silence for a time, then the crashing of a particularly large wave, then Nina:

"I'm probably better as an English teacher than a painter."

This led Margot, who obviously wished to speak of Nina's painting skills as little as possible, to say:

"But we want to hear more about you, Carol. Some friends called me two weeks ago to tell me about the multi media grant. How much is it, exactly?"

Carol sipped her wine and said quietly:

"It's a quarter of a million dollars."

"My God. And how are you planning on using it?"

"I don't think that decision has been made yet."

"Well, I'd assume some of it will go to pay you a much higher salary than you're getting as a docent."

"My salary is going to change, that's true."

"Are you getting a new title? You won't be a docent anymore, I assume."

"You're right again. No more docent."

"Nina, when Rebecca Simpson first interviewed Carol for the job, she asked her how much she'd expect to earn, and Carol answered…"

"I'm fired, Margot."

The world stopped for a second.

The sea froze.

A flock of gulls that had been thinking of flying overhead and defecating on the deck, petrified and remained thirty-five feet above, awaiting instructions on what to do next.

Margot's mouth was open; Nina's mouth was open.

Furl crept onto the deck, looked up at Carol, who had not changed expression, and asked:

"What?"

(This was asked in cat, and so it came out something like 'rrrrggggghhh?' But everyone pretty much understood it.)

Margot, having heard her cue, repeated:

"What?"

"I'm fired."

Now, for the first time, Nina could see tears shimmering behind the black horned-rim glasses.

"That's impossible!"

A shake of the head.

Now the glasses off, being wiped by the napkin on which the wine glass had sat.

The gulls, released from their spells, continued on across and up into the inky night sky.

"That—that simply couldn't happen!"

"It did."

"Who…"

"Rebecca."

"That chicken! That, that…"

"Margot," said Nina, quietly, "remember you're not Penelope."

"I can when I want to be!"

"No. It doesn't become you. You curse like I paint."

Margot glared at her:

"*Never* say such a thing to me again!"

Nina shrugged.

They sat for a time.

Nina poured more wine.

Carol drank hers and attempted to smile:

"Thank you. Thank both of you. It's the first time I can remember smiling for several days."

"Why," asked Margot, "did you not tell me before, child?"

"I guess I just didn't feel like talking about it on the phone. And I wasn't sure you'd want me to come down here, if you knew I'd been fired."

"How ridiculous! Of course we'd have wanted you to come! But the question is now, what to do about your firing?"

"I'm not sure there's anything to do about it."

"There has to be! I know I've been gone for more than a year, but I still have some influence. There are still certain measures I can take."

"Like writing a letter?"

Margot shook her head:

"I was thinking more in terms of murdering Rebecca Simpson."

"You could do that?"

"Oh heavens, yes! Or Nina could. We've had several murders here in Bay St. Lucy in the past year. And Nina always seems to be able to solve them."

"I don't commit them though," said Nina, thoughtfully.

"Yes, but you could if you put your mind to it! And then it would be much easier to solve them."

"I think," said Nina, "that we're getting drunk now. It certainly sounds like we're getting drunk."

"We've each," said Margot, "had a glass and a half of wine."

"But it's strong wine."

"Carol—Carol, this is simply incomprehensible. What reasons did the woman give?"

"Factual errors in my presentations. Poor scholarship."

"Oh, pooh! You bring to life an entire world of paintings, and she's worried about whether something happened in 1871 or 1872?"

"That seems to be the case."

"And what about the director?"

"Powerless, apparently. Rebecca has been working behind the scenes for months. Apparently several members of the Board are on her side."

Silence for a time.

Finally Furl asked:

"Rrrgggghhh? Reeghhh? Arg?"

It was the question that had to be asked, of course. Nina herself would have waited to ask it, but she knew Furl to be both impetuous and undiplomatic, and so she was not surprised that he had blurted it out.

The summer air translated it as diplomatically as possible, but it still came wafting over the table harsh and crimson in the Mississippi breeze:

"So what are you going to do now?"

The question that always seems to be coming up in life, usually dead on the heels of what had only moments earlier appeared absolutely certain about what we were going to do now.

And Carol Walker looked it straight in the eye, shook her head, and gave a perfectly clear answer, which was:

"I don't know."

Furl, seemingly satisfied, padded off the deck and into the living room.

Carol continued, trying to hold back tears, and succeeding partially.

The sobs were a different matter, and so the next few sentences came out sounding in English the way the earlier questions by Furl had come out in cat.

"I have—a little money."

Margot shook her head:

"I know you've always lived in a thrifty way, Carol. You don't do the things a good many young people do. Eat or drink. Things like that."

"No."

"But given what they paid you, you could not have saved much."

A shake of the head.

Then:

"I don't think I'm going to get hired as a docent again. Not after what they'll say about me."

"Teaching?"

"Maybe. But not until the fall, and then only as an adjunct. There's a little money in that, but…"

She pursed her lips:

"The worst thing is the situation at home, on the farm."

"You are," Nina interjected, "from…"

"Georgia. East of Atlanta. North of Athens."

"I remember Margot telling me that."

"Yes. The farm has been in our family for a long time. The longest time. But my mother died prematurely some years ago, and my father is now in ill health. Whether we can keep the land or not…"

From somewhere in the center of town, the wail of a siren could be heard.

"Well, anyway, I've got to do something. The only possibility is to go back to Chicago and look for something secretarial. I don't have too much experience at that sort of thing, but surely if they see my background they might…"

"Stay here," said someone seated at the table.

It was Nina.

Margot and Carol looked at her.

Then Margot nodded:

"Of course. Of course, Carol. Stay here in Bay St. Lucy."

"But—but…"

"Child, it makes perfect sense. You can help Nina out at Elementals. I can't pay you a great deal, but I'll bet it will equal what you had been making. You can go back to earning a docent living."

"But…but…where would I stay?"

Nina leaned forward:

"Stay here."

Carol looked at her, in something like wonder:

"But you don't have room!"

"I have a couch that makes into a bed."

"You wouldn't mind?"

"Of course, I won't mind."

"What about your cat?"

"Furl will hate you for a while, but he isn't the one who makes the big decisions."

More wine followed.

Then a second bottle.
And thus it was determined:
Carol Walker was to be a citizen of Bay St. Lucy.

CHAPTER FIVE: GETTING TO KNOW YOU

The following weeks were idyllic ones for Nina. Carol Walker slipped into her life like a well-oiled bespectacled little piston, which chugged away quietly and efficiently as it worked within the machine that was daily life in Bay St. Lucy.

She took possession of the couch and made a bed of it, having at least six inches of upholstery to spare after stretching out her slightly more than five-foot frame.

She somehow made friends with Furl, an astonishing feat, but one which could not be doubted after seeing the animal stretched out and purring on her lap as she sat mornings with Nina on the deck above the beach, chatting about this and that, softly scratching cat dorsal hair with her small white fingers.

She made friends also with Signor and Signora Bagatelli, who, during her first few morning visits to their bakery, behaved in a manner so polite and courteous as to evince deep mistrust; but who, after slightly more than a week's time and five trips' worth of poppy seed bagels, began to ignore her completely as they shouted insults at each other and threw up their hands in the despairing gestures that were their morning routine.

She repeated some of the things Margot had already told Nina, but in more detail, and in language that painted portraits as she talked.

"I loved our farm. Still do, I suppose. My father raised sheep there. I can remember walking out in the pastures, very early in the mornings. There was always a blue mist rising up out of the valleys, and you could hear mourning doves cooing in the pine thickets."

"Brothers and sisters?"

"No. Just me. A Daddy's girl. I was a tomboy, always outside, always climbing trees. Sometimes in winters, the snow was pretty deep, and I would go cross country skiing. Not many real friends. Just a kind of loner."

"College?"

"Three years at the university. Then I had a chance to study in Europe. My father cried when I left, but they knew it was the chance of a lifetime."

"Where did you go?"

A big smile then, and slightly more animated petting of Furl, who seemed to be envisioning the life that was being recounted along with Nina.

"Arrrgghhh," he said, meaning "Go on."

"Vienna."

"Aha."

"From the most remote mountains of Georgia to the great city of Vienna. I remember arriving by train at the central train station. I went to the university and was shown my room. Then I ventured out into The Old City. It was about ten in the morning, I remember. My God, how fresh everything smelled, and how bright it all was! The shops and markets and street vendors and painting stalls and huge umbrellas springing up over little tables in the sidewalk cafés. I was just sucked into the city. One narrow little street after the other. I walked all day. But then, for that matter, I walked all semester and then all year. I took courses in German as well as painting. I picked up German quickly. Then French."

"I loved," said Nina, "your reading of the French poem."

"Yes. I have a gift for languages, or so I'm told."

"You have a great many gifts."

And she did, Nina told herself continually during those weeks.

One of the gifts she had was opening little cracks, through which Nina began to think that she herself might escape out into the vast world, of which she'd seen so little.

One morning, in particular—it must have been no more than ten days after Carol's arrival—the two of them were in the kitchen, washing up the breakfast dishes.

"But Nina, the thing that surprises me: you love literature so much...."

"Well, I've spent a great deal of my life teaching it. Literature, and history..."

"But why have you never actually gone to Europe?"

"I don't know. I suppose Frank and I had everything we wanted here in Bay St. Lucy."

"But—not even the thought of a summer trip?"

"No. The law is a very demanding profession. Frank was able to take no time off during those first years. He even worked Sundays. Then the firm began to prosper. He took on one partner, then another. But that didn't mean more free time. It meant less. The cases don't go away just because it's summer."

"Then why don't you go now?"

She could remember smiling, wringing out the wash cloth, and shaking her head.

"I'm too old now."

"Nonsense! You sound like you're an invalid!"

"Probably I soon will be."

"Well, if you put it like that, we all will be some day. That's the reason to live now."

"I would be completely lost in a city like Vienna."

"No, you wouldn't. You'd have a guide."

"What guide?"

"Me!"

And from there, it had gone forward, the great plan of Carol Walker and Nina Bannister that, sometime, when the money was a little better, they would sail to Europe.

They talked of it, planned it.

Visualized it.

Carol gave Nina a book about the great Habsburg Empire.

And Nina, just as she had immersed herself in the intricacies of women's basketball only a little more than a year before, began to travel back in time.

To 1278 when King Rudolf and the horrible Ottokar met in battle on the Field of Marchfeld, and Rudolf, victorious, became the first Holy Roman Emperor.

Then forward to 1477 when the young and fabulously handsome Maximillian journeyed to Burgundy to wed Marie, with whom he was to be head over heels in love, until her death a short year later in a fatal fall while the two were riding horseback.

She read:

"There is a story that some years later, when he had become Emperor, he begged the Abbot Trithemius of Wurzburg, a clever man known for his skill at working magic spells, to conjure up Marie's spirit from the realm of the dead. The Abbot agreed to do so, on condition that Maximillian would on no account speak to her. But when the image of Marie appeared out of the shadows of the room, wearing, it was said, the same blue dress she wore on the day of her fatal fall, Maximilian could not restrain himself; he cried out a single endearing word and she vanished from his sight."

What stories! she found herself thinking.

And so she continued to read.

She read about Charles the Fifth, and about his interview with a stubborn and unreasonable monk named Martin Luther; she read about the defenestration at Prague, and how it led to the horrible Thirty Years War; about 1683 and The Great Siege of Vienna, when the armies of Suleiman the Magnificent were said to be spread around the city for miles, and the people panicked, and the walls were breached, and only bare mattresses stood between the Turkish forces and the destruction of all Europe—

—and Count John Sobieski of Poland arrived with his soldiers in the nick of time, September 13, and, after a fierce battle, saved the city.

Then knelt at the feet of Emperor Leopold and said: "I am glad to have rendered you this small service."

And day and night she read.

She read while having coffee, while puttering at Elementals, while waiting to doze off to sleep at night.

About the grand eighteenth century and Empress Maria Theresa and the prodigy child who sat on her lap and then astonished the people in the grand music salon of the

Hoffsburgs who had no idea they were witnessing the phenomenon that was Mozart.

She read about Archduke Johann, and how beloved he was.

And, of course, she read about Sarajevo.

And how that signaled the end of it all.

So, more and more, she could talk with some degree of expertise about their trip.

These talks occupied more and more of their time, as they walked along the shore at tide's end, as they wandered through the innumerable shops and stores that were the heart of Bay St. Lucy—as they met various of Nina's acquaintances for lunch or brunch or early dinner or late breakfast or whatever—and as they puttered about in Elementals, hanging a painting here and moving a huge clay pot there.

So that the reverie of actually going to England with Carol did take shape more and more firmly in Nina's mind.

As did another reverie.

A melancholy one, to be sure.

But a reverie nonetheless.

This little girl with the mousy bangs and the horned-rimmed glasses, and the quiet, easy demeanor…

…if Nina had ever had a daughter…

…that was one of the gentle sadness's of her and Frank's otherwise fine life together.

They had planned during the first years, of what life with children would be like.

It had not happened, of course.

And now, here was this younger copy of herself, sharing her thoughts, moving in and out of her mind as though a part of it.

A gentle reverie.

Then it would pass.

But she allowed herself to play within it while it persisted.

And there was, of course, another aspect of Nina's new existence: the world of painting. For, with only a little encouragement from Carol—she had resumed her lessons, only this time augmenting them with advice from her new roommate. Color, perspective—these were things that Emily Peterson had, of course, talked about, but not at great length... But, at any rate, there were now four easels standing around the deck, and on them: Seascape #1, Little Red Lighthouse #3 (she had thrown away the first two, since they each contained a dog that, given the probable scale of the lighthouse, would have been approximately seven feet high), Old Fishing Boat #2 (Bad coloring on number one), and Field of Flowing Wheat #1 (her personal favorite).

This idyllic existence ended on a Tuesday afternoon.

It was a day that Nina was to remember for a long time to come.

She had spent the morning at Elementals. Carol had stayed home to finish the dishes and do a load of laundry.

Nina returned to find her sitting not out on the deck in the glorious Mississippi sunshine but in the living room, on the couch, Furl in her lap.

She had clearly been crying.

"What's the matter, Carol?"

A shake of the head.

"I've just gotten word; a call on my cell phone."

"Word of what?"

"It's—home. Father is very ill."

"I'm so sorry."

"We've been expecting this for some time. But there are other problems. We may lose the farm."

"My God."

"I've got to come up with some money."

"Carol, if there's anything I can do—I or Margot…also, Jackson Bennett is a superb attorney. I'd be happy to introduce you to him."

"No. It's going to take a lot of money. A lot more than I could possibly borrow, or wish to borrow."

"Do you have…"

"I have one possibility. I was offered a job some time ago by…well, it doesn't matter."

"What kind of a job is it?"

"Not a particularly pleasant one, but one that I'll probably have to take on now."

"Where is it?"

"I'll need to go back to Chicago. Then there will be some travel involved."

"When will you be back?"

"Probably soon, if everything goes the way I expect it to."

Then the smile that Nina had come to appreciate so much:

"Keep the paint fresh. And don't forget to keep working on your paintings."

And that had been that.

Michael's full name was Michael Gellert. He'd been born some thirty-five years earlier in a village not far from Osnabruck, in Germany. He'd been an average student in the Gymnasium, then an average student at the Technische Hochschule in Munster, then a far below average painter. He had not, in actuality, succeeded at anything in life until he became an international art smuggler. And at this occupation he was quite good.

It was ten forty-five at night, and wind had turned cold across Lake Michigan. The fact that it was not yet October meant nothing. He had approached the Museum of Natural History from the south, coming over from Lawrence Street, the Mercado, now deserted, and the freeway overpass, watching the vast building itself grow ever larger, but ever darker. It was the darkest night he'd ever seen. There were no stars, of course; but there seemed to be no clouds either, nothing moving, out in what must have been the lake, or above it in what should have been an early autumn sky. Everything, though…the wide, silent sidewalk, the great slab of angled granite that must have been steps, the museum itself…everything had been ink-drenched, and the world was completely black, save for the greenblueyellow Ferris wheel on Navy Pier, far in front of him, and the lights of the skyline itself, frozen white and motionless, looking down on him as he slowly approached downtown.

"Keep walking."

This, he knew, was his employer, Beckmeier, but he had no idea how the man had approached him. He'd seen no one, did see no one until the figure was simply there, striding along with him.

For a time they walked silently. Immediately to their left, the museum continued to loom. It was too big; they could never get around it—and the lake, to their right, was only the rumor, the myth, of a lake. There was no water to be seen, no boats, no wavelets lapping against what must have been a concrete quay; they were simply there, utterly alone and soundless, walking down the vast edges, drear and naked shingles of the world.

"I have learned," the figure said, finally, "the location of a particular painting. I've also made arrangements to acquire it. I need you, or one of your people, to transport it for me."

The wind had begun to howl. It bit into both of them like a razor,

"Where is the painting now?"

He turned his head and was aware of a slight upward movement in the collection of clothing moving beside him. It could have been a shrug.

"In California. It will arrive here tomorrow."

The museum, finally, was behind them now. But they were still completely alone. He could discern, turning his head back over his shoulder, the pillars of the museum's entrance. Was someone there, moving from behind one to another? No. His imagination.

He was getting jumpy as he approached middle age.

He would have to guard against that.

A figure approached them, wildly, improbably, on a skateboard. It seemed a cross between a scarecrow and the masthead of a ship, leaning away from the wind that tore into them, and being rushed along before it, passing soundlessly between them and the lake.

"What painting are we talking about?"

"A Dürer."

For a moment, he could not speak. He did not know whether to blame this unseasonable cold on pure shock; but he simply waited; let his steps carry him along, the great sidewalk looming on either side of him, until his mind throat and mouth coordinated themselves into words.

"My God."

This, he admonished himself, was the best he could come up with.

"Yes," came the reply.

"You have a Dürer?"

"Yes."

"The Chicago Art Museum doesn't even have a Dürer."

"They have two sketches; I will have a painting."

"What painting?"

"Hase."

"We're talking about one of Dürer's Hasen? His rabbits?"

"Yes."

He paused for time, as the same process of speech coordination in the midst of impossible conversation repeated itself.

"How much is it worth?"

"It's priceless. But I will pay you one hundred thousand dollars to transport it to me, from Chicago to Graz."

"All right."

The two were silent for a time.

So...do you want to move this painting for me?"

"I'm not sure. I may have to think about the matter."

"There's no time. The painting needs to get to Austria. And damned quick."

His warning antennae picked up something in the air.

Something was wrong.

"Why this sudden urgency?"

"You know the former owners want these paintings back."

"Yes."

"Have you come, given the nature of the business you have chosen..."

"Import/export."

"Ha. Yes. Well, if you wish to call it that. At any rate, have you come to hear of 'The Red Claw'?"

"No. And what do red claws have anything to do with recovering stolen art?"

"Because of the man who is reputed to be their leader. No one has seen him. No one even knows what he looks like. But he's reputed to be a particularly nasty fellow. He does not treat couriers well, when he finds them transporting the paintings of his people. These couriers simply disappear."

"Still, the name…"

"Lorca Reklaw."

"Ah. I see."

"Yes. The Red Claw. Reklaw was apparently the name of one of the largest of the families. Do research on the thing, if you wish. With your contacts…"

"Yes, yes. You can depend on it. If I do this, I shall come to know with whom I am dealing."

He breathed deeply, then said:

"This will take a special operative. Someone completely unknown."

That part of the matter is entirely up to you."

"All right. Let me think about it. Give me until tomorrow morning. I make some contacts; talk with some of my people."

"Fine. If you decide that you want the job, be in front of Union Station tomorrow morning, eight o'clock. Someone will be there to give you the details. Also, of course, to give your half of your fee. As has always been our arrangement."

"All right."

"Very well then."

And the figure was gone.

The end-of-the world loneliness of the back side of Field Museum gradually gave way, as he made his way through the park. By the time he reached the Art Institute, the city was somewhat itself again, with people either going too fast or nowhere at all. The cabs were lined up in their usual place, directly opposite the Russian Tea Room, pointing north on Michigan, awaiting the end of the concert at Symphony Hall. He caused some consternation among the drivers by selecting the third taxi, and not the first (there was a good deal of pointing and recriminating in, he guessed, Pakistani or an offshoot of it)...but finally he solved the problem by giving ten dollars to both drivers.

Then he got in the third cab.

"I want you to take me to Damen and Montrose. There's a possibility we may be followed. Take a circuitous route. Don't go the most direct way. Keep looking behind you. Stop every now and then, as though you're studying a map, or trying to figure out where you're going. If you think we're being followed, stop at the nearest bar or tavern, and let me out. Can you do that?"

The driver's expression was now quite earnest.

"Can do."

And the cab pulled away.

The city slid past them, cold, jagged and garish in the wind. He could see the driver as he glanced into the rear view mirror, turned left here, right farther up, avoiding, as he had hoped, Lakeview Road, meandering down side streets that he did not know. He could not withstand the temptation to look around from time to time, but he saw only headlights, glaring in what now seemed to be a mix of rain and snow. Save for the runners, the park was deserted. Cars had been parked along the quiet streets bordering it, but there was practically no traffic at all that he could see.

The trip took them thirty minutes. Finally, though he recognized the statue marking Lincoln Square. they turned onto Montrose, made their way down it, and parked almost beneath the CTA line at the Ravenswood intersection.

He gave the driver a twenty dollar bill, then got out of the cab and made his way up the street toward the apartment where he'd been staying for the past week.

The great U-shaped building folded its black brick wings around him as he made his way through what had been a garden in mid-summer, but what was now only a repository of wilted straw. He opened the front door, glanced at the letters in the mailbox and decided to ignore them. The second door leading into the hallway, which should have been locked, was not; it stood six inches open into the dimly-lighted stairwell, and he wondered a moment if he should worry. But two things stopped him: first, the memory that the door, swollen with moisture, was almost always like this, and he'd come to expect it—and second, the complete lack of anything else to do except go up the stairs and into his apartment.

He began climbing the stairs, all the while thinking about the problem.

A Dürer.

A DÜRER!

The Red Claw.

He needed someone special for this job. Someone who would not stand out.

So thinking, he put his key in the lock and opened the door.

The apartment stared back at him.

He entered, took off his light jacket, then sat on the couch, staring out the window.

The wind was rattling now in the panes of glass. The window had not been installed properly, or had somehow warped away from its facing. It did not matter which; except that there was a jet of frigid air funneling through a gap at the top of the lattice glass, chilling the room.

Outside, though, no one passed on the side street; the windows of the building itself were black, and nothing seemed to move inside what he could see of the curtains. It was the quietest building he'd ever encountered. He'd always appreciated that, prized it; but now he would have welcomed screaming babies in the adjoining apartment, or the sonorous pounding of bass guitars floating from whoever lived downstairs, and had always been the case where he had lived before, regardless of city, regardless of nation.

There was none of that here, though.

Only silence.

Until his cell phone rang.

He flipped it open.

"Hello, Michael?"

"Yes?"

"This is Carol Walker."

And with that, he knew his problem was solved.

CHAPTER SIX: AN EASY JOB

The following day, at four PM, a cab dropped Carol Walker at O'Hare International Airport.

She made her way toward Concourse 2, looking for United Airlines.

The check-in lines were not bad.

She swiped her ticket, punched in the appropriate numbers, and moved toward Security.

She placed the backpack, which contained the painting she'd been given, wrapped in plain brown paper, on the conveyor belt, took off her shoes, took all objects from her pockets, stepped into the x-ray frame where she was patted down, searched, and searched again.

All this time, she watched as the backpack rolled on revolving metal bars into the hooded area where it was to be x-rayed.

Nothing was found in her bodily cavities. She took the plastic tray from its rollers, bent awkwardly to put on her shoes, somehow got the rest of herself together, and watched as the backpack as well as the painting it contained, slid into view.

She thought back.

Just this morning, quite early, Nina Bannister had taken her to the small regional airport at Bay St. Lucy.

Upon arrival in Chicago, she had called Michael

Several hours later, they had met beside the lake.

She could still remember the conversation:

"What do you want me to do?"

"I have a painting and a ticket for you to Graz, Austria. Your flight leaves today at five PM. You will be met at the airport and told what to do from there."

"And how am I to get this painting on the plane in the first place?"

"Carry it in your backpack, which you will stash in the overhead compartment."

"You want me to smuggle a priceless stolen painting in my backpack?"

He nodded.

"First rule: never leave the painting. Be sure that it never leaves you."

"All right, I understand. But—Michael—I've—I've not done anything like this before."

"I know."

"So why trust me with something this big?"

"Precisely because you have not done this before. No one knows you. You have absolutely no record of existing. Even the places you've taught would not remember you. The people who look for these things may be watching me...but they will not, cannot, watch any person such as you."

"Do you think they're watching you? Do you think they're watching you now?"

"It's my business," he answered, "to make certain they are not."

She could not find anything to say.

"I must be honest with you," he went on, quietly, "whoever is looking for this painting, is an agent of the Jewish people. Such agents will not bother with paperwork. If they do find you..."

"I know. They will kidnap me."

"Yes. You will disappear. But that isn't going to happen."

Before them were the lights of the park. They could see, in a circular glare of lights, people ice skating.

"So do you want to do this?"

"Yes."

"All right."

"What is the painting?"

"A Dürer."

"My God."

A Dürer.

And now, here she was, Carol Walker, international art smuggler.

She waited. People flowed around her like she was a rock in a stream. Several other attendants went on about the process of groping between people's legs and pressing hands flat against women's breasts. The people themselves, though, had entered a zone of non-suffering by dent of being somehow, for a time, non-human. They were not angry; they were not happy. They were neither joyous nor content nor displaying any emotion connected with life and vitality; between two points in their lives, they had become the "Airport-Dead:" not even personal abuse could return them to the ground, since they were, mentally, five miles in the air and moving faster than sound.

Thirty minutes later, she was boarding the plane to Frankfort.

As she attempted to put the backpack into the overhead compartment, the Dürer fell out, ripping the paper covering so that the painting itself was visible. The stewardess rushed over.

"You have a pretty picture there."

"Thank you."

"What's it called?"

"Rabbit."

"Could I see it a little closer?"

Carol showed her the Dürer.

"It's so cute! Somehow it doesn't look like most rabbits."

"It's by my brother, Dürer Walker. See the name in the corner?"

"I see! Your brother has real talent!"

"Thank you."

"You tell him to keep at it; he'll be painting real rabbits soon. Now, can I get you anything?"

"No, that'll be fine."

And, stowing the painting in the overhead compartment, Carol Walker settled back to fly to Europe.

Frankfurt Airport was no more of a problem than O'Hare had been. There were somewhat longer lines, but that did not bother her. She finally handed a bored woman her passport, and allowed two agents to look at her backpack.

Each of them regarded the painting with the same contempt with which they regarded her.

Then she changed planes and took off for Graz.

By late afternoon, she was in the city center, being dropped at the Main Square, or Hauptplatz, by a cab.

She got out of the vehicle, made her way through a crowd of people for a few steps, stopped, and breathed.

She had never been to Graz before.

It was a lovely place.

Red tiled roofs, a ring of mountains around the city...

And the hotel behind her came right from the nineteenth century.

She checked in and went up to her room.

Again, from another time. Great goose down comforters lay upon the beds, and wall-length windows let in the light of the sun, which was setting over city hall.

Situated directly under the window was an ebony desk, massive, incorruptible, and as subtly decorated with gold trim as an Austrian General's tomb might have been decorated with rank and insignia. The drawer slid open as though it had been permanently oiled, revealing a thick envelope and black ball point pens that had the weight and solemnity—not of utensils—but of artifacts.

She took the Dürer out of her backpack and propped it against the desk.

Then she opened the envelope.

Sure enough: a cashier's check for twenty thousand dollars.

She caught her breath.

It can't be this easy, she found herself thinking.

And, in thinking this, she was entirely correct.

END OF PART ONE

CHAPTER SEVEN: FRAME CHANGE

It was a big Friday night for New Orleans, an even bigger one for the French Quarter, and a bigger one still for Bourbon Street. LSU was playing Alabama the following day at three PM. That game was to be played in Baton Rouge, of course, but a distance of ninety or so miles meant nothing to ardent fans of: (A) big time SEC college football, (B) drinking, and (C) sex. (Well, all right, it wasn't *real* sex, since prostitution had been practically nonexistent in the Quarter for decades. But it was good *fake* sex, with pictures of naked or near naked women flashing in garish lights above all the bars, and naked or near naked women dancing on makeshift stages down inside the bars.)

Everyone pretended they were genuinely sinning, and they could all go back to Ruston or Opelousas or Tuscaloosa the following week feeling proud of their debauchery without actually having to pay for it in the afterlife, since they hadn't really done any of it in the current life.

And not only that, the Saints were in town to play the hated Dallas Cowboys on Sunday.

It was, in short, the kind of weekend the Quarter lived for.

By eleven PM, Bourbon Street was a sea of people, all shouting, all drinking, all being carried along like a brackish and slow-winding river which was running either toward or away from Canal Street, depending on celestial forces unknown to anyone being moved by them.

Michael Gellert blended into the scene.

He was a bit smaller than the football and sex fans who surrounded him on both sides, but he had learned over the years how to blend in with all environments, and he was doing so now.

As was the man walking beside him—Beckmeier, his employer. The man seemed out of place in New Orleans, but he was a man of strange habits, most of them unknown to the people who worked for him, as Michael Gellert did. He had, of course, appeared out of nowhere, just as he always seemed to appear out of nowhere, just as he had appeared some months ago near midnight on the far side of the dark and deserted Museum of Natural History in Chicago.

The man who was now saying, in that raspy voice that seemed always to be produced by vocal chords that had been burned by acid:

"Something has happened. You need to change your way of doing business."

Horns were everywhere around them: car horns, horns that resembled musical instruments, and devils' horns that seemed to sprout from the foreheads of florid and beefy men who were awaiting either hangovers or heart attacks, and not caring, at this point in the evening, which came first.

"What are you talking about?"

"The Red Claw."

"It exists?"

"Yes."

"How do you know?"

"I employ people other than yourself to move paintings."

"I'm aware of that."

"Last night I received, in the mail, a note. The note mentioned the name of one of these operatives, and said that I would not be hearing from her again. Nor would anyone else. It said that she'd been—well, 'taken.' The note went on to say, 'I have the painting that the operative was carrying. Thank you. Now I want the rest of them.' The note was signed, 'Lorca Reklaw.'"

"Where did he intercept the courier?"

"Montreal International Airport."

"And the courier's identity?"

"Is not something that should concern you."

"So what do you plan to do about this Reklaw?"

"I have several men in my employ. I pay them well to guard my estate in southern Austria, and the things that are in it. I like to think of it as a private museum, meant for the enjoyment of a few special people. No authorities have ever bothered me in connection with the pieces I possess and display. If they did, I would show them all appropriate papers, proving that I own the works."

"Of course."

"If this man Reklaw or any of his agents comes near my property—well, let us just say that I and my people would be ready, and would know what to do."

"I see."

"Nor do I intend to stop collecting. The paintings have been located and paid for. I want them brought to me, 'Red Claw' be damned."

"So what do you want me to do?"

"Be more careful. Avoid airports. Disguise the paintings."

"How the hell am I supposed to…"

"I don't care. That's what I pay you for—just do it!"

And, so saying, Beckmeier was gone.

By the twentieth day of October, fall had begun to arrive in Bay St. Lucy. The air was still somewhat warm, of course. But the sea breeze had freshened, the light had changed and become golden, and the sky, more brittle somehow, had deepened its shade of blue.

Nina and Carol were now settled into their routine.

Nina would work mornings at Elementals, while Carol stayed at the bungalow and cleaned up, or read, or submitted teaching applications for positions to begin at mid-semester.

Afternoons, the roles were switched, except that Nina took on the chore of buying dinner groceries.

And she painted.

It was remarkable, she found herself thinking, how therapeutic the hobby had become to her, especially when sweetened as it now was by her surrogate daughter, who praised her lavishly.

And it was about painting she was thinking at ten fifteen—about how skillful she might have become, and how much she might have added to her life had she started as a young girl and not an old woman—when the small bell tinkled on the front door of the shop and a slightly built, blond, young man stepped inside.

"Sorry—sorry to bother…"

There was an accent of some kind, perhaps central European, she wasn't sure.

But, at any rate, she stepped out from behind the huge potted fern she'd been watering and announced:

"No bother! Please, please, come in! Welcome to Elementals: Treasures from the Earth and Sea!"

The man smiled uncertainly, took two steps inside, and allowed his head to swivel around.

"What a lovely store!"

'Thank you!"

"You have wonderful paintings here!"

'We like them!"

"By local artists, I assume?"

"Most of them, yes. Some from New Orleans or Vicksburg or Jackson. We sell them on consignment. Please, feel free to look around,"

He did so, walking slowly, nodding in approval as he passed various pictures or pots or silverware displays.

"Yes, yes, all things of great quality."

"Well, Bay St. Lucy is an artists' village."

"So I see."

"You're new in town?"

"Just drove in. I spent last night in—where was it?—Starkville, I think."

"And you've driven down from?"

"Chicago."

"Aha. Here. Please. Sit down, and have a cup of coffee!"

"You're very gracious."

"No, it's no bother. We're nothing here if not homey."

He sat. She poured.

They smiled at each other across the small glass table.

"You're a long way from Chicago. What do you do there?"

"Investment banking."

"I see. Or rather I don't. I'm an ex-school teacher myself. 'Investment banking'—that's an alien world to me. I'm not even sure what investment bankers do."

"Neither are we!"

Obligatory mutual laughter.

"So you're making a driving vacation along the gulf coast?"

He sipped the coffee and shook his head:

"No. No, actually, I've come to Bay St. Lucy for a very specific reason, and I'm hoping—actually I was told elsewhere in town—that you might be able to help me."

"Me?"

"Yes. Are you Ms. Bannister? Ms. Nina Bannister?"

"Yes, I am."

"Do you know, then, Carol Walker?"

Nina was surprised and showed it.

"Yes! Yes, of course I do!"

The man across the table from her smiled:

"It is she that I've come to see."

"You are…"

"A very old friend. Well. Perhaps not so very old as all that. But a friend of some years' standing. Let me explain: Carol was teaching at a community college south of Chicago. College of DuPage. As it happened, we were both living in a small town near the campus. I was commuting each day into the city. And so, somehow, we found ourselves at a coffee shop one day—Starbucks, I guess—and started chatting. One thing led to another and we became—well, quite close. We remained that way up until last year when she began her duties as docent at the museum. We had talked about marriage, but…well, you know, those things don't always work out."

"Of course."

"I think Carol will always be a farm girl."

"From Georgia."

He smiled and nodded:

'Ah, yes, you have come to know her well, I see. At any rate, I think her ultimate plans require her to return home and be with what is left of her family, live on the land."

"Those were not your plans, Mr…"

"Oh, I'm sorry. Michael. You may simply call me Michael. The last name is—well, it's complicated."

"Very well, Michael."

"At any rate, our engagement broke off."

"I'm sorry to hear that."

"As I say, such things happen. The main point is that Carol has many friends in Chicago."

"I'm sure she does."

"We were all shocked to learn of her dismissal."

"She was, too."

"Of course, she was. She must have been. And the woman who fired her is such a—well, I can't say what she is. I must ask, though: how is Carol doing?"

"Very well. You probably heard in town, that she's staying with me."

"I did."

He finished his coffee and asked:

"May I?"

"By all means," said Nina, pouring another cup.

"This is excellent."

"We southerners enjoy our coffee."

"I can see."

"So, Carol's not expecting you?"

He shook his head:

"I must admit, no. And it's shameful of me not to have called her. But—I have gifts in the car from several of her friends, all of whom miss her, and miss her very much. We all feel that we were perhaps not 'there' for her when she needed us. She's a very quiet girl, as I'm sure you know."

"She can be, yes."

"And I think—we all think—that she may have felt more alone than she really was. So, a phone call…"

"Just wouldn't have been enough?"

"Exactly."

"And your mission is…"

"As you may have guessed. I'm here on behalf of the 'friends of Carol,' all of whom wish to talk her into returning to Chicago."

It was Nina's turn to shake her head:

"Well, I wish you luck. We've all come to be very close to Carol. Nobody in town wants to see her leave."

"I can understand that. But a small town such as this…"

"Sure. Ultimately, it's going to get boring for her."

"Or perhaps not. I don't know. At any rate, the last thing I wish to do is drive her into a corner. If she wishes to stay, so be it. But it's very important for me to see her, and simply tell her how many people wish her well. And, of course, to give her the cards, and the stuffed dogs—and a picture of the woman who fired her with obscene words written across it!"

More mutual laughter.

"If you don't mind my asking you…" began Nina.

"No, not at all!"

"I couldn't help noticing your accent."

"I'm Swiss. I grew up in Geneva, but my family moved here when I was eight years old. To New York. I went to business school at Columbia University."

"My."

"Yes, it's a very good school. And, I must say, I do miss New York. Someday I shall probably return there."

"But without Carol."

"Alas, it seems so."

"The farm girl."

"True, the farm girl. But I do not wish to trouble you further. Is Carol at present…"

"She's at my place. There's a map of Bay St. Lucy over there on the wall; I'll point it out to you. You can't miss it."

"You're very kind."

"Not at all. And I'm sure Carol will be thrilled to see you."

"I hope. I hope."

And so Nina showed Michael the directions to her shack.

And so she said good bye to him and watched him drive off in a rental car.

And so she had herself another cup of coffee.

He was a nice young man, and would have made a fitting husband for Carol Walker, she told herself.

Perhaps he yet would be.

The drive down, all the way from Chicago…
…yes, perhaps he yet would be.

Then she got up and began to putter around the shop, bathing in warm expectations that someday she and Margot might attend a wedding in Chicago.

She prided herself on an instinctual grasp of human nature.

And seldom had she felt such a closeness, such a positive sympathy for another person.

So she kept on puttering, having no idea that everything 'Michael' had told her had been a complete and utter lie.

Carol loved walking along the beach.

A pure child of the mountains, she'd never had the chance to experience the ocean before. There had been Europe, true, but her time there had been spent mostly in major cities such as Vienna, Rome, or Madrid.

But now she had time on her hands—a relatively new experience for her—and the sea beside her, the blue green ever surging, imminently alive and immortally evolving sea, which she found herself remarkably sympathetic to. She felt at home beside it. And in the same way she could not stop walking when she was in Paris—one quarter sucking her out from another and into its own personality, until the soles of her feet were blistered—in just that way, she could not turn around and go back home, go back to Nina's shack, go back to the few errands she'd been placed in charge of, go back to Bay St. Lucy, and to Elementals for her afternoon's work.

On this particular day, she knew she would be late.

Not that Nina would mind, of course. Not that the big smile would be any smaller, or the enthusiasm upon seeing her any less.

How lucky she'd been to find this place!

She relived the days since her firing as she trudged back along the hard-packed and foam-traced sand, the shack itself now looming before her some half mile distant.

The boxes, the boxes…

Rebecca Simpson.

The chicken.

Her presentation at The Auberge des Arts, extraordinary place that it was.

Then the need for money.

And her first trip to Graz.

Carol the mule.

How easy it had been!

There would be more trips now, she knew. Michael had made that clear. Perhaps one per month, perhaps one every two weeks. But she was to expect no more problems than she'd encountered on the first trip. And she would be receiving another impossibly large cashier's check with each venture.

Danger?

No. Michael had made that clear.

Who would want to hurt her?

And as for the paintings themselves, she had not stolen them. Nor had Michael, for that matter. They were simply out there in the universe, a strange cosmos of stolen art, drifting with the gravity of rich people's wealth from one secluded mansion to another. This phenomenon would not change, whether she had anything to do with it or not. What would change was her bank account.

And the day when she could go back to Georgia.

She reached the foot of the stairs leading up to the bungalow.

It was a bungalow, wasn't it?

No. With gray wood peeling, and screen door half torn, it was still a shack.

And thinking with amusement how much she loved it despite its dilapidation, she made her way up the creaking stairs, watching a pelican perched precariously on a pole sticking out of the shallow tide some fifty yards up the beach, and listing as a low cloud of gulls scudded over the incoming surf.

She opened the door.

The tidy living room welcomed her, as did Furl, who padded noiselessly across the hardwood floor and rubbed inquiringly against her ankle.

Are you still the same person you were yesterday evening?

I mark you as my property.

Coffee.

She needed coffee.

And so, single-minded, not even looking out on the deck or at the ocean beyond, the storms possibly coming up in the eastern sky, the oil rig close to shore—she attacked the coffee maker, opened the refrigerator, got milk, made the first cup quite strong, drizzled white liquid into it, set it on a cup, breathed deeply, took a first delicious sip, and turned to go out on the deck.

Where, at the table on the deck's center, Michael was sitting.

"Hello."

She stood as though paralyzed in the doorway.

What was he doing here?

The pelican on the pole in the ocean had as much right to be here, on Nina's deck, on her own deck, as did Michael.

Michael was Chicago.

Actually, Michael was indeterminate cities and indeterminate nationality and indeterminate vocation and indeterminate future or past—a shadow and nothing more.

But now the shadow was impinging on the clear blue watery light of her own private world.

"The door was open. I hope you did not mind."

She simply stared at him, chastising herself for her own inability to speak.

"Actually, Carol, you should probably be more careful. It's a dangerous world we live in, you know."

She found herself, an automated figure, moving on slow creaking gears and tank treads across the floor of the deck, until she was standing before him, looking down at him.

"What are you doing here?"

"I'm not unwelcome, I hope."

She knew nothing to say to that.

Of course, he was unwelcome.

What if Nina learned of his existence?

But that would never happen, of course.

Michael was too smart to let that happen.

"I have just met your friend, Nina."

Oh God.

What was going on here?

She watched, as the automaton she'd become seated itself and continued to stare open-mouthed across the table.

Nothing, she said.

And nothing was what came out of her cave-opened mouth.

So Michael was forced to continue:

"She's a charming lady. You're lucky to have found a home here. And I must tell you—this may work out for the best, for all of us. Now. May I have a cup of coffee?"

She nodded, still uncertain of what might come out if she tried to speak.

Then she went back into the kitchen to find another cup and pour it.

Then she returned it to Michael, faintly aware as she did so that she was still physically attracted to him.

Why in heaven's name was that?

No knowing about such matters, of course. But his smile, his strawblond hair, his casual white shirt open at the neck, and the dark green scarf he wore that set him off, made him a denizen of another continent—no, she was attracted to him, no doubt about it.

He took the coffee and gestured around the deck.

"These paintings? They're not yours, I hope."

She shook her head.

"No, they're Nina's. She and several other ladies of Bay St. Lucy are taking art lessons."

"They're dreadful."

"They're not so…"

"They're dreadful."

"All right. They're dreadful. But doing them gives her great pleasure."

"And me."

She looked at him.

"What are you talking about?"

"I think we might use them."

"Use them? How? And by the way, Michael, what the hell are you doing in Bay St. Lucy? Did you bring a painting? Do I have another trip to make?"

He shook his head:

"No, not now."

"Why not?"

"That's part of the reason I came down. We need to talk."

"About what?"

"About your trips to Graz."

"Have I done anything wrong?"

"No. But they shall have to stop for a time."

"Why?"

"It's getting dangerous."

She took a deep breath and sipped the coffee.

Of course.

It was too good to be true.

Just like the docent job at the museum was too good to be true.

Something always came up.

"How dangerous, Michael? What's going on?"

He looked beyond the deck, as though whatever danger was approaching might be topping the horizon at any moment, like an armada. Then he shook his head again and said, quietly:

"Let's walk on the beach."

She felt the approach of a half-smile, tried to suppress it, failed, and said through it:

"You think Nina's shack is bugged?"

"I don't know. But I'm absolutely certain that the ocean is not. Come on."

And so, within a moment's time they were back on the beach.

The tide, she found herself thinking, must have been coming in. Her footsteps from half an hour ago had been erased and were now under a film of ebbing and surging seawater.

"What is this thing that's 'come up'?"

"The Red Claw has come up."

She looked at him.

Was he joking?

The what?

And even as she wondered about these things, she fought back an urge to take his hand and act as though the two of them were lovers.

They had, in fact, made love, had they not? That bizarre night in Pilsen, with a dog howling beneath the window and the mournful sound of Mexican guitar music pulsing down the street—

—or had she merely dreamed that?

"The Red Claw," he continued.

"What are you talking about?"

"The paintings that I'm attempting to move, Carol. There's a group of Jewish—well, I suppose one could call them vigilantes, for want of a better word. They know that the paintings are out there. They also know that the paintings were originally stolen, by the Nazis, from several Jewish families who lived in the Caucasian Mountains. They're attempting to get these paintings back. They will not stop at anything to do so, and they don't choose to work with conventional police organizations. They use other methods."

"What other methods?"

"They kidnap couriers. The couriers are then never heard from again. I told you this before, I'm sure you remember."

"Yes, but, I thought, since I was not known..."

Michael shook his head:

"I thought you'd be safe. But now things seemed to have changed. This group is apparently headed by a man named Lorca Reklaw, the son or grandson or God knows what son of one of the original Jewish families."

"Reklaw. The Red Claw?"

"Yes. It's become his symbol."

"What would he do to me?"

"I don't know. I do know that, somehow, the ante may have been raised. And I came down here—originally—to give you a chance to back out."

"To stop transporting the paintings entirely?"

"Yes. I'm very fond of you, Carol."

"Good. Most people who go to bed with me don't like me at all."

"I apologize for that evening."

"Why? I thought it was pretty nice myself."

"It was unprofessional."

She shook her head:

"I never claimed to be a professional. I just struggle along."

"You know what I mean."

"Almost never."

"But now you must. Carol, if you want out…"

She did not even need to think about this.

"I can't get out. I need money. The last check was wonderful. But I'm going to need at least five more like that to give to my family. They need me; they depend on me. Now, if moving the paintings is no longer possible…"

"It is possible."

"But you said…"

'I said it has become more dangerous. I did not say it had become impossible. And the fact is that…"

"That what?"

"That you may have stumbled unbeknownst on a way to make things much safer."

"What are you talking about?"

"I'm talking about…no, just let me think it through for a time."

And so they walked, the buildings of Hatteras to the West coming dimly into view, through a late morning mist that had settled over the dunes.

Finally he said:

"Yes, it could work. Carol, you were a docent for a year?"

She nodded:

"Just over a year. Before…"

"Yes, yes, I know. I also know about your fabulous presentations. Indeed, that is how I became aware of you. But now, I must ask: as a docent did you learn to do restorative work?"

"Of course. That's one of a docent's main jobs."

"Can you do a frame change?"

"Sure. Again, that's one of the things museums do. There are great works that are four, five hundred years old. Frames need changing. Besides, the frame isn't a work of art; it's what's inside it."

"Indeed. All right. Then I'm going to ask you to do several frame changes, my dear Carol. We shall thwart this Red Claw. It only requires the skill of two people. The first is you."

"And the second?"

"The second is an artist who is about to become quite popular—about to be 'discovered,' really."

"Who?"

"Why your friend, roommate, and student: Nina Bannister."

CHAPTER EIGHT: ART FOR SALE

Thursday.

A delicious morning, cool, clear, the waves aquiline and translucent.

Carol Walker wanted to paint.

That was not her job, of course.

Her job was simply to wait.

It was ten o'clock; Nina was in town at Elementals.

There was little for Carol to do. Some cleaning. Another load of laundry for the two of them.

She was debating whether to read or...well, when one thought about it, there was nothing else to do.

So all right then, she would read. But read what? Nina had graciously made a nice little library of paperbacks available to her, but the titles were mostly mysteries, punctuated by high school literature fare, and neither seemed right for this particular moment. Janet Evanovich or Emily Dickenson. What a choice. All right then, she would...

There was a knock on the door.

She crossed the living room floor, opened the door, and found herself looking at a perfectly nondescript man. He was of average height, wore average wire-rimmed glasses, smiled an average smile, stood balancing himself carefully on average light brown shoes, and looked like he had no distinguishing marks at all except for his fingerprints, which, she decided immediately, had probably been burned off.

"Ms. Walker?"

All traces of accent had probably been burned off too.

"Yes?"

"I have a picture for you. It's a gift from a friend."

"All right."

He had propped the painting against the wall. It was carefully wrapped in brown paper, and was approximately two feet square.

He picked it up and handed it to her, saying quietly:

"Your friend wishes you well."

"Tell him, 'thank you'."

"I shall."

"Do you want to…"

"No, I can't come in. Other errands to run."

"All right then."

"Good luck."

He turned, descended the stairs, got into what surely must have been a rental car, and started the engine.

By the time the car had reached Breakers Boulevard, Carol was already on the deck.

It had been well prepared for the coming of the painting.

Four of Nina's pictures leaned against the rail of the deck. There were Old Red Lighthouse #2, Storm at Sea #3, Morning at Sea #5, and Little Red Barn #6 (Nina's favorite of the four, except that the cow was too large and thus out of proportion.)

The tools Carol would need, and which she had bought yesterday in one of Bay St. Lucy's surprisingly well-equipped art supply shops (well, Carol found herself realizing, not so surprising really when one realized that this was a town full of painters—amateurs, true professionals, and all shades in between). These tools she had stacked neatly in the living room beside her couch, having warned Nina beforehand that she intended to change some of the frames the painting class had provided.

First was the corrugated board. She wiped it clean with a towel she found in the bathroom, then carried it out to the deck and placed it carefully on the glass topped table, which she also carefully wiped clean.

Then a second trip: screw driver, linen tape, wire, and acrylic cleaner.

She placed them all carefully on the board, lifting her head slightly to watch the porpoises, whose daily passing Nina had warned her about. She greeted them mentally and imagined that they sang back to her, as Homer's sirens might have done.

Third trip.

Foam core backing. Mat board.

The instructions she'd received as a docent some months ago repeated themselves in her mind: "Prepare your acrylic. Peel one side of the protective liner off the side that will be touching the art work. Place that side face down on the art assembly (boards and picture), then peel off the other side. If you have ordered the acrylic with UV or Non–glare properties (she had), the side that should face up will be indicated on the packaging."

She looked.

It was.

So now…

So now…

She took a deep breath, returned yet again to the living room, lifted the brown paper package as though it were a new born child, and carried it out to the deck.

Carefully, carefully, carefully—she unwrapped it, the light paper falling in shards at her feet, hissing softly as it did so.

The paper shed itself, leaving the painting there before her in her hands.

"Oh my God," she whispered, trying as hard as she might to stop her hands from trembling.

"Oh, my God."

St. Sebastian, Tended by Irene and Her Maid.

She had expected one of several paintings Michael had mentioned.

And she had prepared herself for the coming of each individual work, much like a foster mother might prepare for the coming of an adopted—even if only for a short time—child.

So here was her child.

And there were the initials of the child's real father, the child's creator, subtly imbued in the dark, shadowy, lower right hand corner.

H.B.

Hendrick Tenbruggen.

She had admonished herself for knowing so little of the man, and for needing to do research.

Which she had, of course, done.

Tenbruggen. Ghent School, late Baroque, this painting finished last 1625.

She'd also done research on St. Sebastian, and the words stuck in her head:

"St. Sebastian. Died circa 288 AD. An early Christian saint and martyr. Killed (it is said) during the Roman emperor Diocletian's persecution of Christians. He is commonly depicted in art and literature tied to a post or tree and shot with arrows. This is the most common artistic depiction of Sebastian; however, according to legend, he was rescued and healed by Irene of Rome. Shortly afterwards, he criticized Diocletian in person and as a result was clubbed to death."

Words, words, words.

"For the depths," someone had written, "of what use is language?"

What use indeed.

Her hands continued to tremble.

The painting seemed to move in her grip, like a living thing.

Which it was, of course.

The figures, muscular and full bodies, circled the center of the canvas in the typical Baroque manner, but the face of Irene, staid and immensely calm, held the entire creation in quiet repose, as though nothing, not the emotions nor the pain nor the immensity nor the enormity, of the things depicted, were going anywhere without her say-so.

"Edle Einfalt," she found herself whispering, "Und stille Grosse."

Lessing's great description of the statue of Laokoon, a Trojan who tried to warn his countrymen about the Trojan Horse.

Noble simplicity and quiet grandeur.

And the arrows.

The arrows.

"Oh, you poor man," she found herself whispering, idiotically, since the poor man could not hear her.

Or...?

The arrows were small, seemingly no more than a foot or so in length.

But one, sticking in Sebastian's upper leg; and another, directly in his chest; and a third in his shoulder...

...no blood at all.

Sebastian's shadowed face, turned down toward the ground...

...and the stretching, almost writhing, body of the white-rag turbaned maid, as she attempted to untie him from the gnarled tree limb to which he'd been tied.

And all of it illuminated magically by light of a sun that had already set, and was glowing enough to radiate off distant crosses where other martyrs hung, watching night come, as they died.

"My God," she whispered again.

She was sobbing now.

And she was praying.

So were the figures in the painting.

Three hours later—she had worked quite efficiently, and the job had gone better than she could've hoped for; she walked into Elementals, carrying Old Red Lighthouse #6.

"Nina!"

"Hey, Carol, how's the morning been?"

"Great!"

"What have you got there?"

"Your lighthouse picture! I changed the frame on it. I think it looks really good now. You need to hang it!"

Nina walked toward her, shaking her head:

"Carol, I tried one time hanging my paintings and Margot..."

"I know all about Margot. But Margot isn't here. She won't see the painting."

"Alanna might."

"She won't either. And if she does, I'll talk to her."

"And say what?"

"That I know a few things about this business, too. Nina, this painting is really good. There's a kind of vibrancy about the colors…"

"Isn't the dog too big?"

"Don't worry about the dog."

"But, I…"

"Price it at $350."

Silence for a time.

"What?"

"Three hundred and fifty dollars."

"But no one will pay that much for one of my paintings!"

"Trust me."

"But…"

"Trust me."

And Nina did.

So the painting was hung, just above a display of clay pots from Lucille Davis (who also sold her pottery in Vicksburg and New Orleans).

And in this way, Tennbruggen's *St. Sebastian Tended by Irene and Her Maid,* disguised as Bannister's *Little Red Lighthouse #6 With the Slightly Too Big Dog,* was offered for sale, at the price of $350, in Bay St. Lucy, Mississippi.

Four days later, at eight fifteen on the evening of October 25, Nina and Carol had finished their dinner, cleaned the dishes, and were deeply involved in a game of gin rummy. It was one of those strange games where no one could seem to win. The pile grew more and more slender, and, though Nina needed only a five, a seven, or a king—and God only knew how little it would take for Carol to win—no such card was forthcoming.

Rain pounded on the roof of the shack—a cool front had blown into Bay St. Lucy at five PM and soft rain had started soon thereafter. Turning to harder rain, then turning to this.

And so there was no possibility of walking on the beach, or strolling out on the stone jetty, or ogling the fall fishermen on the long pier as they attempted to hook hammerhead sharks or whitefish. No, there were only two things possible to do on such an evening: reading (which would come later) or card playing (which might extend until later, indeed for all eternity if these particular cards never showed up).

Another draw.

Six of spades.

Damn.

Discard the three of diamonds.

Carol's draw

Four of clubs.

Would that do it for her?

No, apparently not.

Her discard.

The ten of diamonds.

Damn.

Rain rain rain.

Spatter on the sliding deck door.

Furl asleep beneath a cardboard box in the corner of the living room.

Carol drew, furrowed her brow, shook her head, wiped her glasses.

"Nina! Nina!"

A bull horn voice from the parking area below.

"Nina, for God's sakes!"

The voice seemed to grow more desperate.

Carol put down her cards and stared:

"What is that?"

Nina shook her head while rising and walking to the living room window.

"I have no idea."

She pulled the blinds back and looked outside, but for a time all she could see were shapeless gray forms through a film of rainwater.

"Nina! Are you up there?"

"Who is…"

She went to the door. She could hear Carol's voice from behind her.

"Are you sure you want to open that?"

She shook her head:

"No, but we have to do something to end this damned card game."

And so saying, did open the door.

Standing at the base of the stairs, dressed only in an impossible open-collared flowered shirt and stained white pants, was Tom Broussard.

Tom, hulking and unkempt at his best, now (at his worst) hulking and unkempt and soaked, was Bay St. Lucy's only genuinely successful pornographic novelist.

"Nina!"

His broad face upturned, his eyes gaping in horror, he reminded her of Stanley Kowalski, and if he'd chosen to shout 'Stella!' instead of 'Nina,' she would have thought herself in a play and would have attempted to remember her next line.

What was that line, anyway?

Everybody knew 'Stella!' Nobody knew the line that followed.

She knew she was supposed to depend on the kindness of strangers. But Tom was no stranger. So she had no idea what to do, except to step out on the stairwell platform so that she too was now getting wet.

"Nina, you've got to come!"

"Tom, are you drunk?"

"I don't think so."

"Have you been drinking?"

He nodded, floridly, dramatically, the nods almost amounting to bows, but his voice was flooded with rainwater and deep sobbing:

"Of course I've been drinking! But I don't think it's going to help!"

"Come up here! Get dry!"

He shook his head, water splattering from his tangled black mane as it would have from the tail of a black stallion that had just made its way out of a river crossing.

"Can't!"

"Why not?"

"We've got to get back to the boat!"

"Why? What's going on, Tom?"

"It's Penn!"

"Is she all right?"

"No, she's—oh God, I've never seen her like this!"

"Is she hurt?"

"I don't know, Nina, I don't know. You've got to come!"

"All right, Tom. But—do you want me to call 911?"

"No, this is a genuine emergency!"

"But what should we…"

"Just come! Just come!"

"All right! Let me get a slicker on!"

The rain was beginning to roar now, and the ocean was beginning to roar, and Tom was down there roaring, and Furl had disappeared into the bedroom.

Nina had half-finished the process of putting on the slicker when she heard Carol say, softly:

"Gin."

She looked over at the table.

Carol was laying down her cards.

"I only needed a…"

"Oh, the hell with you," she said, and went out into the rain.

It was toward an uncertain rendezvous with destiny that Nina found herself hurtling, the battered pickup truck Tom had somehow managed to find at an auction for scrap iron, splashing its way down Breakers Boulevard toward the mangy end of the harbor where Penelope kept her fishing boat, The Sea Urchin.

"Can't you tell me what's happened, Tom?"

"It's just—I can't believe it!"

'What?"

But he merely shook his head and gripped the steering wheel tighter.

Dark shapes flowed past them on the left and they themselves flowed out of Bay St. Lucy proper and into Bay St. Lucy improper, the cheapest moorings of the cheapest boats. And so went the progression: yachts with stately mastheads, expensive pleasure boats, less expensive pleasure boats, scows, garbage haulers, and finally Penn's Urchin.

They pulled to a stop, the rain rattling harder now than ever, and the quays glistening with oil and water.

She pushed open the truck door, which screeched in pain as metal tore against metal and the things that should have been oiled at some point in the vehicle's existence and never were, cried out in their vengeance.

She jumped from the truck's running board down into a six-inch deep puddle of rain or seawater—it hardly mattered which, the saline content of the substance having less relevance to Nina's existence at this particular time than temperature, which seemed something to be measured in Kelvin degrees rather than Fahrenheit.

"Come on! She's over here, in the shack!"

Nina would have thought about cursing because her sneakers had gotten soaked; but she was approaching Penelope Royale, around whom all attempts at obscenities always seemed amateurish, and thus hardly worthwhile.

They were running over the docks now, the square, flat-bottomed Urchin sitting tightly moored, rocking in the rain peppered waves, the equally square, flat-topped corrugated iron shed in which Penn and Tom incredibly and impossibly lived, now looming up before them.

They had gotten to perhaps twenty feet of the building's entrance when the front door burst open and Penelope lunged out. She was dressed in what seemed to be a torn and ragged sail from some schooner that had been washed ashore in a neap tide. *No,* thought Nina, *that was not precisely accurate.* Penelope was not 'dressed' at all in any conventional sense of the word. She was more accurately 'fitted out,' as though all of her limbs had become masts and crossbeams, and, having spent her entire life on the water, her entire being had finally evolved into more of a water craft than a human being.

And the vessel that she'd become was storm-tossed now indeed.

She filled the doorway.

She glared.

Then, her mizzen cannon doors opening, she let forth a volley of grapeshot and dirty words, all directed at Tom.

"You ---
--------!!! How could you --
-------------------------!!!! Don't ever try to ------------! If I------
-----ever ----------------------------!'"

As for Tom, he simply stood in the midst of the storm, big, vulnerable, and doomed, the Spanish Armada to Penelope's quicker and far more deadly English fleet.

He floundered.

He moved his arms but seemed incapable of speech.

From some half mile distant, one of the great tankers that frequently made its way whale-like along the coast let out a loud honking bray.

Penelope stared at it, and would have sunk it had not the distraction from Tom proved too irritating.

So instead, she let loose again upon him:

"You----------------------!!! You didn't have the------------
-------------- to----------------------------! And if you ------------
-------------------I would have--
-----!'"

Nina noticed for the first time that Penelope held a crowbar in her hand.

'She's, she found herself thinking, *'going to kill him. She's going to kill both of us.'*

She flashed back almost ten years ago when Penelope, who'd been her student at the time—as had Tom—(How had she survived those two?) had almost single-handedly, dismantled a drinking fountain.

But Penelope had been a girl at that time, a mere slip of a thing.

She was a full-blown woman now, and much stronger.

The muscles in her upper arms, or those left visible through tears in the sail she was wearing, twisted and corded themselves like thick ropes.

Tom, Nina could see, was watching those muscles too.

And the black, oily, seemingly weightless (at least to Penelope) crowbar.

My God, Nina found herself thinking. *What has he done?*

Then someone, insanely, took two steps toward the building (and thus also toward Penelope) and said:

"Penn! Penn, let us come in!"

Who had said this?

Whoever it was had now incurred the same stare that had been fixed on Tom.

It was Nina.

Damn, she told herself.

What was she thinking of?

(Of course, what was she thinking of, even being here in the first place?)

It was growing dark. It would have grown dark all on its own, even without the storm and the low scudding clouds to help it. It would have grown all cuddly and dark even without Penelope's foul and tempest like fog of thick obscenities to intensify it impenetrability.

But now, aided by all these things, it was dark indeed.

So why was Nina Bannister not home in bed?

"Penn, let us come in!"

Penelope stared at her.

"Nina, -- --!!"

Well, there was not much to be said to that.

So she simply stood there and listened to the wind blow.

The wind did that very well.

And after it had dispersed over the docks the last fifteen or twenty words of the torrent that had been unleashed, it slackened enough so that Nina could hear this second person (the lunatic) who seemed to be impersonating her, say:

"Just let us come inside!"

The crowbar arose now, and found itself being pulled back, as though Penn having become taken over by the spirit and form of Captain Ahab, it could have been launched at Moby-Tom Broussard.

"Nina, why did you let this------------------------------------- --!!"

"I don't know, Penn!"

"He's ruined me! He's--- ---------------. Nina, how could you--------------------------------- ------------------------------------?"

"I don't know, Penn!"

"But why did you even--
---------------------------------?"

"I don't know!"

"How-------------?"

"Don't know!"

"Why ----------------?"

"Don't know!"

"Then how---------?"

"Don't know!"

And with that answer, the crowbar fell clattering on rain-spattered concrete, and Penelope buried her face in her hands, her body wracked with seemingly inconsolable sobs.

Within a minute, Nina was hugging her.

And within two more minutes, the three of them were inside the building, in what passed for both living and bedroom, Penn sitting, sobbing, on the bed itself, Tom and Nina in massive sponge cloth objects that at first glance seemed creatures of the deeper reefs, but upon closer analysis must surely have been once manufactured as chairs.

"Now," Nina found herself saying, somewhat calmly, "will one of you two tell me what's happened?"

Both of them shook their heads.

"Penn, please. Whatever Tom has done…"

More head shaking, and low, quiet, murmuring:

"That………….! How could he……………….?"

"All right, then. Tom, you tell me."

"I'm sorry, Penn," he said, more to his wife than to Nina.

It did not seem to help.

She merely went on murmuring:

"How could you let this happen? How could you do such a thing? What did I ever do to you? Why did I deserve this?"

He could only shake his head.

"I don't know, honey."

"DON'T CALL ME THAT! YOU…..!!! DON'T EVER CALL ME THAT! NOW HOW DID THIS HAPPEN?"

"I don't know. I just don't know."

Silence for a time.

The beating of the rain.

The buzz of a dim electric light bulb hanging from a single, precarious wire in the center of the room.

Nina:

"All right. I'm going to ask you both one more time. Whatever this is, it can be dealt with. Whatever Tom has done, Penn, there will be a way around it. You both will find a way of dealing with this thing. Now, Tom, I'm going to ask you again. We have to put it into words. We have to get it out there. Tell me: what is it?"

He looked at her.

He took a deep breath.

Then he said:

"Nina—Penn's pregnant."

CHAPTER NINE: BREAKTHROUGH!

It has been noted earlier in this series, that certain towns and villages prepare for communal events such as weddings, births, and deaths by giving showers. Or, if they do not give showers (there being no such things as funeral showers), they at least bring food and say gracious things to and about each other.

This was not the case in Bay St. Lucy.

Bay St. Lucy, filled with shops and gifts and curios and fruit baskets and cute hats and non-abstract art and absolutely nothing of any practical use—did not give showers.

Bay St. Lucy *was* a shower.

It never stopped unwrapping and opening itself, and every turn around every corner in every one of its establishments elicited the breathless and wonder-filled statement/question:

"Ohhhhhh! Isn't that darling?!"

Penelope's pregnancy was the purest sort of just the kind of fuel the town ran on.

Word of it took some time to spread itself around Bay St. Lucy, of course, and by four o'clock the following afternoon there were still a few inhabitants-shut ins, gunshot victims and the sort—who had not heard of it.

But in the case of normal Bay St. Lucyans, it was pretty much standard fare and grist for the gossip mills that never ceased churning and generating life-giving information to THE PEOPLE!

A baby!

Penelope Royale and Tom Broussard were going to have a baby!

There were perhaps a few problems that had to be glossed over.

First, the source of the information, Nina Bannister, had been judicious in her reporting of it, leaving out Penelope's immediate attitude, which was not so much matricidal as homicidal.

This would pass, Nina knew.

Second, there were obviously going to be some things that this particular couple still needed, as opposed to more conventional couples.

A house.

Those kinds of things.

But that could all come later.

The thing that had to be dealt with now was:

The shower.

THE BABY SHOWER!

WHAT FUN!

So, of course, Nina found herself in the late afternoon, sitting in Elementals, and listening to the rain (which had not stopped, and which showed no sign of stopping).

She'd been hard at work for an hour, and sheets of paper lay beside her on the writing desk beside the cash register.

The sheets all bore the heading Elementals: Treasures from the Earth and Sea, written in Algerian script with small pictures of Neptune and The Earth in the upper right and left had corners respectively. They were filled with names, dates, gift ideas, and suggestions concerning shower themes.

It was late October.

The baby would arrive, probably, around late August of the following year.

No time to waste in planning.

Nina had wrestled for a time with the date choices. August 27 was a Friday night. But that was a little late in the month. If the baby came on the fifteenth, which was a possibility, then Penn and Tom would have to go for two weeks with no clothing to put on the child, no toys for the child to play with, no crib accessories for the baby to goo goo at.

No diapers.

Not a good risk to take.

So the decision was made: either the twentieth or the twenty-first, depending on whether the town preferred a Friday or a Saturday.

Of course, what if Penn were late?

Why then…

"Excuse me?"

What was that?

Someone was actually in the store.

What a terrible distraction!

Was there no respect for simple privacy anymore?

There was a SHOWER to be planned here!

Oh, for heaven's sake.

Oh, well…

"Yes, how may I help you?"

"I'd like to buy a painting, if it would be possible. I do hope it's for sale. I just found it, over on the far wall. It's quite lovely you know."

The person making these comments was a young slender woman dressed in zebra striped pants (the pants were black and the diagonal stripes white), with close-cut raven hair covering one eye (the left), and an English accent.

She might have been in her late twenties, early thirties.

But she was English.

What was she doing in Bay St. Lucy?

Didn't the English have their own beaches?

"Of course, of course—let's go and take a look. We just got some seascapes in yesterday, painted by Ramoula Peters. She does terrific work. And we sell a lot of paintings done by her. Or you might have been looking at the abstract that Paul Donovan brought in last week. Usually his stuff doesn't stay around very long—he's in great demand."

Nina rose and followed the woman across the room, making a note as she walked that two of the ferns needed watering.

"I'm sorry, but I failed to note the name of the painter."

"That's all right. I'll know who it is."

Also, there was a sterling silver set that someone had apparently looked over and not put back in the proper place.

Work work work all the time.

"Is this your first time in Bay St. Lucy?"

"Yes, yes, it is."

"Well, I hope you're enjoying yourself."

"I am, immensely! What a lovely little village you have! It reminds me of Cornwall."

"You're English?"

"Yes, from Sheffield originally."

"What do you do?"

"I'm actually in the import/ export business."

"Based in…"

The woman smiled:

"Quite a few places, actually. I tend to move around a great deal, or be moved, I suppose, if one were to put it accurately. Mostly larger cities, though—which is why I love occasionally to visit the smaller towns. Ah, here we are: this is the one."

"Which? I can't quite…"

"This one."

She pointed.

Nina looked, then looked again.

It was her painting.

Her painting!

"Yes, this is the one: I believe the note here beside it says, 'Old Red Lighthouse #6.' And the artist's name is 'N. Bannister'."

This could not be happening.

She was going to sell a painting!

She felt faint, unable to speak.

"This note says the price is $350. Is that accurate?"

"I—I…"

"That is quite a reasonable price, I must say. Can you tell me something about the artist?

"You're sure you want *this* painting?"

"Oh, yes, definitely! All of the works hanging in your shop are quite charming, really they are. But this one has…"

Nina waited.

What did this one have?

"It masquerades as a primitive, but I think it has a modularity that is paradigmatic of something more—how shall I say it? More vascularity than the primitives are able to conjure with. Don't you agree?"

"I...maybe."

"The interchange of color and structure envisages something Doyanesque. And although there's a truly scintillating aura of abstract clarity—no, no, 'clarity' is not the right word, maybe 'perfunctoriness'—there's this scintillating viscera, there's also something that eviscerates its own rubric even as it overshadows it."

"You don't think the dog is too big?"

"Oh, no, no, that seeming disparity is quite purposeful, and allows the force of the painting to, as it were, circle its own centers of gravity, becoming a kind of double star enhancing its own gravitational field, for want of a better phrase. Yes, it is, in short, quite wonderful. Do you know the artist?"

"Yes."

"Does he or she live here in Bay St. Lucy?"

"It's a 'she'."

"I'm not surprised. There's something definitely feminine about the entire conceptual framework. Men are more celestially tuned, women more 'of the earth.' And that quality emanates quite clearly from this."

"It's me, actually."

The woman stared at her.

This was, Nina found herself thinking, *the happiest moment of her life.*

She was celestially tuned.

She viscerated.

AND SHE WAS GOING TO MAKE THREE HUNDRED AND FIFTY DOLLARS!

TAKE *THAT* MARGOT!

And who really cared about the stupid old Chicago Art Museum anyway?

Did the paintings hanging there enhance their own gravitational field?

Did they possess perfunctoriness? Real, true honest perfunctoriness?

You're damned right they didn't!

"You painted this?"

Yes. You see, I took this class, and I…"

"Oh, my God. I'm so excited!"

"I'm not sure it's really…"

"It's *wonderful*! Please tell me: whom have you studied with?"

"Well, the class was taught by Emily Peterson…"

"Peterson. Peterson. Out of London?"

"Ruston, Louisiana, I think. Originally. Her husband owns a hardware store."

"Do you have other works?"

"Yes. They're out on my deck. There were five other paintings of this barn, but the colors weren't right."

"Will you be offering them to the public?"

Not if Margot Gavin has anything to do with it.

But to hell with Margot!

Down with Margot, up with Carol!

"Yes. Yes. I'll probably be replacing this one with, oh, I don't know: maybe "Old Red Fishing Boat #2.""

"And when will it be hung?"

"Probably…"

As soon as I can get home, get it, and bring it back here.

But why appear too eager?

If the paining was actually a double star creating its own gravity, and that kind of stuff—maybe I could price it higher?

"Probably a little later in the week."

"Wonderful! I may not be here by then…have to leave early tomorrow, busy schedule and all…but could you send me a picture of the work? I would definitely be interested in bidding on it."

Bidding on it.

BIDDING ON IT!

"I'll be happy to. If you'll just give me an address…"

"Of course, of course! Also my email address and my cell phone number. Now, you must tell me: where are your other works to be seen?"

My deck.

"They're not really available now."

"No museums at all?"

"No," Nina said, meekly.

"Then perhaps I shall be able to act as your purchasing agent. I do know a number of people with excellent taste. There's nothing more exciting than discovering new talent. You may expect more buyers to be dropping around. Now, I'm a bit rushed, so if I may pay for this with a credit card…"

"Of course, of course."

The paying process was taken care of.

Old Red Lighthouse #6 was carefully taken down and wrapped.

Goodbyes were said and congratulations were given (Nina being congratulated for transcending primitivism, the woman congratulated for finding out that Nina was transcending primitivism.)

The woman left, ringing the little tinkling bell above the door as she did so.

And Nina, left alone, raised both her arms straight in the air, shouting:

"YES!"

She was a painter, after all!

Within ten minutes, she'd locked Elementals for the rest of the day, unchained and started up her Vespa, and backed out of her parking place.

She did not really need the vehicle, of course.

She could have floated over the city.

She headed out onto Breakers Boulevard and navigated not toward home—although she looked forward to getting there—but to the most disreputable side of Bay St. Lucy.

She watched as the pets grew scruffier, the buildings more disreputable, the old cars in weed-grown lots more rusted and undriveable, and the air heavier with the scent of stale tobacco and unpaid bills.

Finally she came to the hovel of Tom Broussard.

Be here, Tom. Be here, Tom.

She knew he spent evenings with Penelope and afternoons here, drinking beer and writing his latest novel, whatever that happened to be.

She looked up, saw the empty porch, heard several dogs howling from an indeterminate distance away, and hoped that they were not unleashed.

But no, what was she thinking? Of course, they were unleashed.

What could she hope for, then?

That they were not rabid was about the best she could think of.

"Tom?"

Noise from within the house.

And then Tom Broussard himself, clad in a sweat-through undershirt, his chest arms cheeks legs feet and furniture all sprouting black hair that had never been combed, a can of beer in his hand, stumbled out onto the porch.

"Nina! Nice to see you! Come on up!"

She did so, wondering if the stairs leading up to Tom's porch were any ricketier than her own.

It was, she thought, holding onto the bannister in the silly hope that it might not fall to pieces before the stairs, a dead draw.

"Tom, how's Penn?"

He raised high the can of beer and let a smile whiten the otherwise totally black mass that was his head.

"She's great! All she needed was to talk to you."

"Well, I'm glad I could help."

"She's knitting booties."

"I can't believe that."

"Well, she is. And we've talked the whole thing through. In some ways we might not appear to be the most conventional parents..."

She made her way into the porch, stepping on piles of toxic clothing and kicking aside sixteen to twenty beer cans.

"I don't know what makes you say that."

"Well, we're a little different. No house. No dog."

"Tom, there are a dozen dogs just hanging out underneath your house here. I'm sure they're all very nice. Just grab one, put a collar on him, and feed him raw meat."

"You know what I mean, Nina. We're not exactly PTA material. Penn's out fishing all the time and I'm here in this shack writing dirty novels. It might be better if I had a real job."

"Oh? How much money did you make last year, Tom?"

"Two and a quarter million dollars. Something like that. But I think we're supposed to pay taxes so it may turn out to be less."

"So what job would you rather have?"

"Maybe I could teach."

"Don't be absurd."

"Naw, you're right. Anyway, though, a couple of nights ago, after you left, we went over all the problems. And there were a lot of bad things, of course. But we had one good thing going for us."

"Which was?"

"We just asked ourselves, 'Who's gonna mess with our kid?' And then it all seemed ok."

"See? Now that's what good parenting is all about."

"Yeah, maybe it is. So come in, sit down."

She did and she did, always glad to find a chair in Tom's main writing room, where she could sit and be absolutely motionless, so that something would not see her and attack her.

"Want a beer?"

"No, thanks. By the way, I pretty much have your baby shower planned. Mid-August at Elementals. Do you have any toys already?"

"We have fishing nets and harpoon gaffes that the kid might want to play with when he's older."

"You know he's going to be a boy?"

"Look at Penn; look at me. How could it be a girl?"

"Well, I guess that's one way of looking at it. Tom, I wanted to come see you because..."

She paused.

How could she say this?

She still did not exactly know; but she knew that, however it got said, Tom Broussard would have to be the first to hear it.

"Tom, do you remember how it felt, when you sold your first novel?"

He had smiled slightly before, but now the sun exploded in his face, causing a seismic grin so cosmic and nuclear in force that she felt its heat.

"Do I? Oh, Nina. A writer always remembers that."

"Tell me about it."

"I was living here. Had just gotten out of jail. I'd started writing when I was behind bars. The other guys gave me a hard time about that, of course. I got in a few fights a week."

"Must have been tough."

"The writing was tough. I didn't really know what I was doing."

"I mean the fights."

He shook his head:

"Actually the fights were the only fun I had. Without them, I might have gone crazy. But they kept me going. Anyway, by the time I'd been here a month, I had collected twenty or so rejection slips from New York and LA. They weren't really 'slips.' They were just cards saying they were overwhelmed with other submissions and couldn't look at my manuscript. They wished me every success, though, in what seemed a promising young career."

"But you kept on."

"Yeah, you have to do that. Finally—it was late one summer day, and the sun was going down. I was hung over, of course, and hadn't gotten up in time to check the mail when it arrived. I remember there was a phone bill, an electric bill, and a letter of some kind. I thought at first it was from some law firm telling me I was sued and had to go back to jail. I didn't want to open it. Finally I did, thinking that I might have to get out of the country, and, if I did, it would be better to do it that night."

"But it wasn't from a law firm."

"No. It was from a publisher based in New York. Croft and Sons. Small company, but...well, your first kiss might come from a small girl but you aren't complaining."

"No, I guess not."

"The first line read, 'Congratulations, Mr. Broussard.' I just hung fire there for a while, not believing it. It went on, 'We here at Croft and Sons have had a chance to review your manuscript, and we are highly impressed, both with your command of plot and your use of language.'"

"You remember it, word for word?"

"Oh, you never forget it. No real writer ever forgets the first acceptance."

"What was the novel?"

"It was a different kind of thing than what I'm turning out now. A lot more idea-oriented, intellectual stuff."

"The name?"

"*The Entrails Trail.*"

"Oh, yes. I remember that. I was very proud of you, being one of my old students. I remember thinking it was the dirtiest book I'd ever read. I still think that."

"Well, you've always encouraged me. And believed in me."

"Yes, I guess I have. Anyway, I got some news today, Tom. And I wanted you to be the first person I told the news to."

"What news?"

"Tom, I sold a painting."

"You what?"

"I sold a painting."

"Oh, my God."

"Yes. Isn't it unbelievable?"

He rose, crossed the room, and embraced her.

"Nina, I'm so proud of you! And Penn will be, too!"

"I'm just...I'm just still blown away. The woman who bought it—well, I can remember her words, exactly, just like you can remember your acceptance letter. She said, 'It masquerades as a primitive, but I think it has a modularity that is paradigmatic of vascularity.' Then she said, 'The interchange of color and structure envisages something

Dovanesque,' and she said it had a scintillating aura of abstract clarity and then she thought better and said it really had a quality of perfuntoriness and then she went on to say it had scintillating viscera."

"Do you know what any of those words mean?"

"No."

"What was the painting?"

"An old lighthouse."

"You painted a lighthouse that was paradigmatic of vascularity?"

"Well, it was a *red* lighthouse. Maybe that's what she meant. She didn't even mind the dog being too big."

"How much did she pay for the thing?"

"Three hundred and fifty dollars."

"Wow!"

"I know, isn't it wonderful?"

"Nina, you have to go out and celebrate!"

"But I don't know how to celebrate! I've never had anything to celebrate before!"

"You solved two murders, almost won a state basketball championship, and saved the gulf coast from complete destruction."

"I know but this is *art*! It *means* something!"

"Right! So I'm telling you, you have to celebrate!"

"How do I do that?"

"You get drunk, of course!"

"I can't get drunk."

"You have to get drunk; you're a painter."

"But I'll be sick the next day. I'll throw up!"

"Throwing up, Nina, is just another term for 'the interchange of color and structure.'"

"Well. You may be right."

"Of course, I'm right. Now where are we going?"

"You're going to get drunk with me?"

"Of course I am. This is a red letter day, a day you'll never forget."

"Okay. Shall we all go to Sergio's?"

"We'll *begin* at Sergio's. But what did you mean by 'all'? Penn, you know, can't drink. Not in her condition."

Nina shook her head.

Perhaps getting drunk wasn't that bad an idea, after all.

She already felt drunk, if it came to that.

But there was somebody else who would have to come with them.

Somebody else who would be oh so proud of her.

And who *might* actually understand the big intellectual words that had been used to describe the lighthouse that she, Nina Bannister, brought to life on canvas.

And, saying a brief good bye to Tom, a fellow artist—she went home to her own shack—to break the news to that person.

Darkness had begun to fall on Bay St. Lucy, and, as Nina Vespa'd through the lengthening shadows, she struggled to keep her mind on driving and away from the thousand trains of thought it seemed constantly to want to be boarding.

And speed. Keep the speed down.

Twelve miles an hour, twelve miles an hour…

…and there! Fifteen!

Fifteen miles an hour on Stonewall Jackson Drive. What are you *thinking* Nina?

She had a sudden vision of herself as the young Marlin Brando in a motorcycle cap.

But—was that so inaccurate?

He was an artist, she was an artist.

Different métiers, but…

Oh, and that was a good word, 'métier.' Perhaps she was allowed to use words like that now—French words, big three and four-syllable words like 'visceral' and 'perfunctoriness' and 'scintillating viscera.'

She was a painter!

And she owed it all to Carol Walker.

Perhaps she was talented, genuinely talented; but she would never have known it, never probably have even gone back to the painting class—would have always remembered the scathing comments of Alanna and Margot—Margo, who after all was only an administrator and not a genuine painter—had not Carol seen the paintings and also seen something, something, special about them.

And so she found herself deliciously curious as she approached her shack, stopped in the oyster-shell driveway, locked the Vespa, unhelmeted the helmet, stowed it carefully, and looked up at the porch.

What would Carol say upon hearing the news?

'Congratulations?'

'That's wonderful news!'

'I knew it all along!'

'What did I tell you?'

She climbed the stairs, unlocked the door, and pushed it open.

Carol and Furl were both curled in identical positions on the couch, each reading the same book.

Furl looked up; Carol looked up and adjusted her glasses.

"Hi," she said.

"I just sold a painting," Nina said.

The response to that was immediate:

"Let's go get drunk."

I'm already learning, Nina told herself, *about being a painter.*

Within five minutes, they were speeding (caution be damned! Fifteen miles an hour it is!) away from the sea and toward Sergio's By the Sea, there to meet Tom, who was to drive there in his truck.

Carol was sitting back on the passenger seat, her arms tightly wound around Nina's waist, as Nina's mind sorted through the wonderful drink menu at Sergio's:

"Digestif Spirits: Fernet Branca," and "Liquore Strega;" "How Edward Drinker Copes," which consisted of Speyside Scotch, Gran Classico, Blanco Vermouth, and Cranberry Bitters;" "Winter Cocktail: Rum, Fresh Ginger, All Spice, Lime, and Angostura;" "Feufollet, with Apple Brandy, Elder Flower, and Burnt Absinthe."

Margot, of course, would ignore these delicacies and simply say: 'Gin. A lot of gin.'

But what fun was that?

When they arrived, Tom was already standing beside the front door of the restaurant, dressed as he had been some few minutes ago.

And that caused a problem.

They were seated at a dark, corner table. They were given their menus. They'd begun to study them carefully (after, of course, the ritual of sitting down and profusely congratulating Nina, the Guest of Honor)—when the waiter arrived again, asking:

"I wonder—would Madam (this meant Nina, toward whom he was gesturing) and her guest (this meant not Carol who had the effect of disappearing into any room she entered and simply not existing until she decided to leave—but Tom, who was one of Sergio's few guests dressed in oil-stained (at least Nina hoped it was oil), off-white pants and a sweat through undershirt—please come with me for a second?"

They did.

He led them to a quiet alcove set just off from the cash register, and said:

"Madame should know, we here at Sergio's are not unaware of the difficulties faced by the homeless. In fact, if madam's guest would prefer to accompany me to an area we have designated in an alley behind the kitchen, we would be able to furnish him with a hot meal made from the left overs of the previous evening."

"Really?" Tom said, enthusiastically. "What kind of leftovers are we talking about?"

"Tom!" Nina said, almost shouting. "What are you talking about?"

"It's free food!"

'No! Now come with me! We're leaving!'

The waiter was ashen-faced.

"I'm truly sorry, Madame, if I've failed to…"

"You certainly *have* failed! Now good night!"

They discussed the situation in the parking lot. Tom said that he thought a lot of the restaurants Nina knew might have the same attitude, so maybe it would be better if the three of them went to a place he knew on the far side (his side) of town.

They agreed to this and he drove them to the place, which was behind an abandoned Dairy Queen. But even a quarter of a mile before they approached it, they could tell that it had been surrounded by a dozen police cars, their blue lights flashing, their sirens wailing, and their bullhorns braying out the words:

"Come out with your hands up!"

This did not portend well.

And so they thought further for a time, remembered that Penelope was sitting in her own metal-corrugated shack, alone, while preparing for motherhood, and that perhaps another night might be a preferable time for the drunken debauch they had—perhaps unwisely since Nina had never previously in her life drunk more than three glasses of wine at one time—planned.

By the time darkness had engulfed Bay St. Lucy, Nina and Carol were sitting on the deck, watching the ocean reflect a second ocean of stars, a candle burning on the table, and two glasses of Merlot sitting in front of them.

"What are you going to do with the money, Nina?"

"I don't know. Three hundred and fifty dollars."

"You could buy clothes with it."

"I don't need any clothes. I have jeans and several sweaters and t shirts. And sneakers. That's really all I need."

"A car?"

"You can't buy a car for three hundred and fifty dollars."

Carol sipped her wine, set the glass softly on the table, and leaned forward:

"Nina, it's not going to be just three hundred and fifty dollars."

"What? What do you mean?"

"I mean it's going to be more than that."

"How?"

"Because you're going to sell more paintings."

She could only stare across the table. A streetlight was reflecting blue in Carol's glasses.

"What makes you think that?"

"Because I know it's true."

"How is it true?"

"It just is."

"But..."

"We're going to select one painting a week. I'll work with you. We'll freshen and intensify the colors just a bit, maybe change the perspectives here or there. Then we'll take the painting down and hang it just where the last one was."

"You think this woman may come back?"

Carol shook her head.

"No, but there'll be others."

"Other people who want to buy my paintings?"

"Absolutely. *Little Red Lighthouse* #6 is just the beginning. Next we'll hang *Little Red Fishing Boat* #4."

"Number three."

"Whatever."

'And you think it will really sell?"

"I know it will."

"But...but, Carol, my paintings just don't seem that much better than the other people's paintings. I mean, the other people in the class."

Carol took a deep breath then, shook her head, and said quietly:

"You have to learn to look beneath the surface."

They listened for a time as the waves washed inward.

Carol continued:

"Not just paintings. A lot of other—well, 'matters.' Things just aren't always what they seem to be. You have to learn to look below the surface."

And so they sat, and talked.

They talked of the money, and how it would add up if put in a separate account.

They talked of selling ten paintings; and how that would produce three thousand five hundred dollars—and with that they renewed their earlier talk concerning THE GREAT TRIP!

THE TRIP TO AUSTRIA!

IT COULD BE DONE!

AND, BY GOD, IT WOULD BE DONE!

And, after a time, the tide had come in. It was almost washing around the support posts now.

The stars had moved and shifted their positions inexorably.

Nina had finished her third glass of wine.

They said good night. Carol lay down on the couch. Nina crawled into her bed.

She felt like a ten year old on the night before Christmas.

What was there coming up for her to see?

A new life?

What was coming up...for her to see?

She was, of course, to find out all too soon.

CHAPTER TEN: BAY ST. LUCY—DEN OF THIEVES!

During an unusually cool, dark, and shadowy month of November, the equally shadowy world of international art theft shifted its center from New York, Istanbul, Cairo, and Paris, to the deck behind Nina Bannister's shack.

At that shack arrived, on Tuesday morning November 3, Vincent van Gogh's *Poppy Flowers*. The work had been painted in 1887, three years before the artist's suicide. It depicted a small vase of red and yellow poppies. Van Gogh had, reportedly, painted it as a tribute to Adolph Monticelli, whose work he'd come across in Paris in 1888.

It was said to be worth fifty million dollars.

It was reframed on that Thursday morning by Carol Walker (who used a dark oak wooden frame) and covered by the painting *Little Red Fishing Boat #4*, which is still thought to be the first work by N. Bannister that was not a depiction of a light house.

The following afternoon (Friday), at precisely 2:15, it sold to an unnamed collector who happened to be passing through Bay St. Lucy and who had a faint French accent, for $350.

The money was within an hour then placed in the new checking account that had been created a week earlier by the artist, and which now had a total balance of $697 (three dollars having to be subtracted for service fees).

During the next week, a roughly similar process occurred.

On Tuesday morning, November 10, another Van Gogh arrived, this one the *View of the Sea at Schweiningen*. The same Carol Walker unwrapped it with her usual sense of exultation, looked at it for a time, and remembered: Schweiningen was a beach resort near The Hague. Van Gogh, working outside on the dunes, had struggled with a strong wind which sent grains of sand into his thickly applied paint. It was always said of the painting—

—she ran her finger over it—

—yes.

Yes!

There were still grains of sand that made the lustrous surface rough.

She was touching them now, sand granules that had perhaps been blown into, and then out of, the beard of Vincent van Gogh.

Another Nina Bannister painting (*Vase of Red Roses*) was duly stretched and placed over it.

Vase of Red Roses had no sand in its acrylic base, but did have, if Carol said so herself, the brightest and most intense red that the artist had yet been able to manage.

The following day: painting hung.

The following day after that: painting sold.

Checking account now slightly more than one thousand dollars.

And on and on.

The View of Auverse sur Oise, Paul Cezanne, not signed by the artist, who felt it unfinished.

Covered by *Old Yellow Mill Wheel*, completed (and signed, because it definitely *was* finished), November, 2013.

Sold the following day.

Nativity with St. Francis and St. Lawrence, by Caravaggio (magnificent use of the technique that had come to be known as 'chiaroscuro' referring to its innovative use of shadowing).

Replaced by *Two Porpoises Swimming in the Ocean, a Hundred Yards or So From Shore*, finished the last day of November.

Sold the following day.

Carol Walker's feelings during this process were ambivalent. She was ecstatic each week with the thought of actually getting to touch some of the world's greatest paintings, stolen though they were. She was also appreciative of the cashier's checks that accompanied each paining, checks that totaled considerably more than $350 apiece.

These checks she simply kept.

It was not time to go home yet; but that time was coming.

She thought often about the mountains, and the sound of wild dogs howling in the distance. The food she'd eaten as a girl and that she would undoubtedly eat again upon returning.

She thought of the relatives who'd passed on, and the ones who still lived there: people who had not seen London, or Paris, or Chicago. How would she tell these people everything that had happened to her?

But no more of that.

It was not time yet.

A few things had to be accomplished first.

And so, those things she thought about as she walked up and down the beach and helped prepare and hang the paintings.

But she also thought about Nina Bannister.

She loved the glow of pure joy in Nina's face when, each week with clockwork precision, she came home and announced:

"I sold another painting!"

And she loved the pure process of helping Nina paint, seeing her mix the colors, aiding her in basic techniques of design and perspective.

Her own mother had passed away so many years ago.

It was almost as if…

…doing the day to day chores together, chatting about nothing at all…

…it was almost as if…

But no more of that, because, in point of fact, it *was* (no 'almost' to it!) that she was lying to Nina Bannister.

Using her.

Nina Bannister was a retired teacher and principal from the village of Bay St. Lucy. She was not Vincent van Gogh, nor Paul Cezanne, nor Caravaggio, nor Rembrandt.

Of course, that was probably a good thing when one actually considered it.

Nina Bannister would almost certainly not commit suicide, even if the unthinkable were to happen and the discovery were to be made that the paintings being purchased in Elementals were disguised stolen masterpieces and not original 'Nina's'.

She would probably not even cut off an ear.

At most, she might cut off one of Furl's ears.

But probably not even that.

No, at most she would have a small laugh at her own expense, and realize that she was—Nina would have probably put it this way, English teacher that she was—'not Prince Hamlet, nor was meant to be.'

She would not be bitter.

But still it was wrong. It was wrong to deceive her like this.

Nina had taken in the recently fired and completely unemployable Carol Walker.

Bay St. Lucy had taken her in, for that matter.

And now she was tricking them all.

But, she then told herself, what choice did she have?

She was on a quest, a mission.

The people at home needed her, depended on her.

And how much harm could really be done? This process would go on for another two months, possibly three. Then she would announce that it was necessary for her to move home, to care for her aging father. A few tears would be shed.

Bay St. Lucy would cease to be a modern version of Casablanca, with no more Humphrey Bogarts or Ingrid Bergmanns or high class art smugglers or Van Goghs or Rembrandts.

True, Nina's sales would probably stop.

But with the money that had accumulated in the meantime...

She could give Nina the trip of a lifetime.

And this, she resolved, no matter what else happened...

...this she would certainly do!

Although she still felt guilty.

As for Nina, her life changed in a completely unexpected way.

Or, for anyone who'd ever lived in a small town such as Bay St. Lucy, perhaps not so unexpectedly after all.

Word got out.

Word always gets out in villages, and so, this being a village, it got out.

It got around town that Nina Bannister was selling paintings.

Very few people in town actually *sold* paintings, or at least not to the general public. Ramoula Peters did, and, occasionally, Emily Thompson did. But most of the paintings that left the shops and art stores of Bay St. Lucy had been painted by people in New Orleans or Vicksburg or such places and sent to the little sea coast town to be moved on consignment. If the actual painterly inhabitants of the town sold many paintings at all, the sales were to each other, or to relatives—sales made to buck one up and say, in a manner of speaking, "See! You *are* a good painter!"

Nina was selling her paintings to complete strangers. And she was making $1400 per month. With social security (another $1400 per month) and teacher retirement (another $1400 per month), she was practically getting rich.

So word got out.

After the sale of the first paintings, little of any consequence occurred, except the 'professional' painters of the town found their way more frequently into Elementals and stood for a long time beneath *Little Red Barn* or *Little Red Mill* or *Horse* or whatever—and just shook their heads.

Why are *these* paintings selling, and mine are not?

All of the people in Nina's painting class heard about the sales, and all of *them* came in (most having had some success in getting their works hung in The Stink Shoppe or various places, after being evicted by Margot and Alanna), and all of *them* wondered:

"Why are *these* paintings selling, and mine are not?"

But, finally, as the sales continued, it became obvious.

The intensity of colors was greater in Nina's works.

Her works *did* have true viscosity.

There was a shimmering, even ethereal, quality about her use of acrylics.

Even Alanna, having stopped in one day toward the end of November for a glass of tea, shook her head as she gazed across the room at *Fish in Wave*, and said:

"Nina, you have come so far since you began painting. The town is so proud of you!"

"I don't know. I'm not sure I'm doing that much different."

"Oh don't *say* that! The difference between these newer works and the ones I saw a month ago—well, it's simply night and day. You've found your voice, your mode of expression. There's a depth of feeling in your works that none of the others here in town can match. They are simply recording visual images, dear Nina; you are creating art!"

Well, okay then, thought Nina.

At least Alanna wasn't going to take her paintings down.

And at least Margot didn't know anything about what was going on.

And one day, Emily Peterson—the teacher of Nina's class—came in and said the thing that had to be said ultimately, that was to follow SALES as the night the day:

"All of us in the class, the ladies taking the class and I as teacher, are so proud of what you've accomplished!"

"Thank you, Emily. Of course, I couldn't have done any of it without your help."

"No. I may have made a few suggestions. But I can see now, looking at the painting of the fish there in the waves—what is it called?"

"Fish in Wave."

"Yes, that's a splendid title! I can see a kind of buoyancy in it that so few beginners could ever be able to master. But listen to me: we can hardly call you a beginner any more, can we?"

"Oh, I don't know..."

"The bottom line, Nina, is something that several of the members have asked me. Actually, they have asked me to ask you."

"Ask me what?"

"Well…would you take over teaching the class?"

"Would I…"

"Not the entire class, of course. But perhaps one or two classes a month? I'd pay you, of course. We have so much to learn from you!"

And so Nina moved her easel to the center of Emily Peterson's classroom.

And everyone watched as she painted.

And everyone nodded in approval.

And the money rolled in.

Which it did, for everyone concerned, including Michael.

As it happened, the second Tuesday in December (it was very cold in Chicago, and a fine snow was beginning to fall), he was making his way up the stairs to the apartment in Pilsen he'd come more frequently to use, for the purpose of doing two things: one, to accept a painting from an operative (Rembrandt's *Portrait of a Rabbi)*, and two, to have sex with this operative.

He reached the third floor landing, aware simultaneously of the soft murmur of guitar music from a bar down below on the street, and of the howling of the north wind off the lake outside.

The door, he knew, would not be locked.

It was not. He pushed it open.

The room stared back at him.

On its far side, extending into the dormer window space, was the well-made bed.

On the bed, lay a pair of zebra-striped pants.

He crossed the room and picked up a note that had been pinned to the bed cover.

He read:

"Thank you for the English lady. Sorry she will not be joining you for the evening. And thank you also for the painting. We want the rest of them."

The note had been signed:

"Lorca Reklaw."

Beneath the signature was the brightly colored (perhaps done with acrylics?) picture of a red claw.

END OF PART TWO

CHAPTER ELEVEN: A DICKENS FABLE

Two days later, Michael Gellert was in another part of Chicago, summoned there by a phone call from Beckmeier.

"Come. Come now. We must talk."

"Come where?"

Upon asking which, he'd been given an address.

This was strange. He did not know where Beckmeier actually lived, had never been invited into the life of the man.

Something was clearly happening.

He took public transportation—the Brown Line—to the Montrose stop, exited, looked around to see if he was being followed—knowing that anyone following him would probably be very good at the job, and not be noticeable—but looked around anyway, saw no one, and started walking toward the address he'd been given.

He felt as though he was in London.

The weather may have had something to do with that. It was postcard weather. Weather out of Dickens' London, in one of the 'good' chapters, where people were not starving and did not yet have tuberculosis. This was 'Evening of Christmas Turkey' London, the city at its gaslit best. A benevolent snow had begun to fall (the sky had been somber all day), each flake the precise size and texture of a pillow feather (no gloppiness), and able to descend of its own accord, pulled to the streets by gravity alone, wafting a bit this way and that, untouched by wind (of which, remarkably, there was none), and so beautifully backlit by streetlamps as to resemble a tiny part of the setting of an operatic Act Four, an instant before the first notes had been played.

All of the houses were the same. They were not "houses," in the sense that most Americans thought of "houses." They did not have carports. They were not made of red brick, nor painted white. They were identical, slate-granite gray buildings, set the same distance back from the quiet, broad sidewalks, precisely three stories high, with two windows in each floor, through the curtains of which could be seen shadowbox illustrations. If the setting was Dickens, the casting was Henry James.

Behind the curtains of every window, illuminated by a glowing yellow lamp, was some fragment...a flower, the corner of a painting, several glasses sitting on the dinner table—of exquisiteness.

The neighborhood was so quiet that he could hear, or thought he could hear, each individual snowflake falling on the sidewalk, and making the same sound a cornflake would make falling on a carpet.

Cars lined the streets as paintings lined the walls of museums—meant to be seen and not actually "used"— except the cars were snow-covered.

They did not move.

People did not attempt to drive them; not on these silent, shrouded streets.

They simply sat there, as symbols of wealth and ownership, bothering no one, and parked too close together to be extricated, even should the necessity have arisen.

He located the correct address and began climbing the stone steps leading to the doorway. Normally, he would have grasped the black metal handrail beside him, to keep from slipping.

But this was not the kind of snow one could slip on. It was a higher grade of snow—dry, quiet, and supportive— than was found elsewhere in the city.

He rang the bell.

There might have been a sound somewhere deep in the bowels of the great animal of a building looming before him; but it might also have been nothing more than the near-silent shifting of the earth's crust.

After a few seconds, a butler opened the door.

"Good evening, sir."

"I'm Gellert."

"Yes, sir."

"I think Herr Beckmeier is expecting me."

"Come in, sir. Let me take your coat."

He did so, then walked inside.

All around him were the soft colors of money and time.

Save for the butler, who, having carefully hung the overcoat was moving soundlessly away, he found himself alone.

He walked through the hallway, into the living room, along another corridor, into another living room (how many living rooms were there? How far back, and up, did this mansion extend?)—but his mind became fixed on things other than the physical dimensions of the house.

There...on the wall opposite what seemed a massive end table—hung Raphael's *Portrait of a Young Girl*.

No one, as far as he knew, even knew of the location of the painting, which was, he knew, generally referred to only as *The Portrait*.

It was like walking through a forest, unaware of the existence of silent eyes, motionless animals in hiding. Until something about the light, something about an adjustment in vision...something changed, and there were the shining-dime eyes of a rabbit in the brush.

No brush here, though.

Clear, straight, and unobstructed on the walls:

In the dining room:

Parable of the Vine, by Domenico Fretti

In the small library:

The Nativity, by Correggio's pupil, DiCredi.

And on the opposite wall:

A Correggio.

No copy, no offshoot, partially finished, somewhat damaged:

No, an actual Correggio.

The Adoration of Christ.

Who was this man, this employer of his, this Beckmeier?

He continued to wander through the mansion.

Finally, he found himself in a room even more intimate, and also darker, than any he'd seen before. A suit of armor stood at attention near the fireplace—all of the rooms had fireplaces—and a crystal chandelier hung heavily above, revolving slowly and inexplicably in a complete lack of breeze. He could see three paintings, one on each of the walls before and on either side of him: two deep green and red portraits he recognized at Chirico's, and a third which was unmistakably Caravaggio's *Nativity*.

His eyes adjusted themselves to the half-light, the quarter light, the almost complete absence of light…and in the glow of coals and the faint flicker of dying flames, he saw that dotted around the room, on various pieces of furniture, were thirteenth and fourteenth century metal chalices: Sansovino's terracotta *Madonna col Bambino*, and a small bust by Nanni di Banco.

"They're very fine pieces, are they not?"

For the first time, he recognized that his employer was in the room with him.

"Please—sit down. Something to drink? Brandy?"

"No, thank you," he said, allowing himself to be engulfed by a massive green leather chair. "I'm fine."

"You do not drink a great deal, do you, Mr. Gellert?"

"No."

"Admirable."

"I don't know."

"Yes, it is. Well. Thank you for coming."

"I had to come. I work for you."

He could see the man more clearly now: his half-shrug, his half smile.

"That will, regrettably, have to change."

"Why?"

"Circumstances."

"What circumstances?"

"Do I actually have to tell you?"

"I suppose not. It's Red Claw, isn't it?"

"It seems always to be Red Claw. He is somewhat of an irresistible force, something impossible to be reckoned with."

"What's happened now?"

The figure of Beckmeier was growing more clear now as Gellert's eyes adjusted themselves to the dim light in the room. He was dressed in a dark green silken robe; and with his silver hair, perfectly combed of course, his mustache, his goatee—he could have played Mephistopheles in *Faust*.

"He has apparently discovered my—my abode."

"You mean here?"

A smile.

Sulfur. Brimstone.

"No, of course not. This is merely a stopping place for me."

"A stopping place? With more than a dozen priceless paintings?"

"A place of transition. The paintings are brought here by operatives such as the ones you employ. They hang for a time and are admired by a few of my close…"

"Friends?"

"Acquaintances, my dear young Gellert. I have long since ceased to have friends. But as I say, they rest here for a time, these paintings, and then are transferred on to southern Austria."

Michael Gellert waited.

"There, in my Castle Eggenburg, I have over the years amassed a truly impressive collection."

"And now Lorca Reklaw has learned where this 'domicile' is."

"So I am told by my sources."

"What will happen?"

Beckmeier shrugged.

"What always happens when objects of true beauty exist. They will become, like suns, the center of violent universes."

"I assume then that you're not going to allow Lorca Reklaw simply to walk in and take back his paintings."

"They're my paintings. He's simply under the illusion that they are his. Or his people's. He's also under the illusion that he's invincible. That no one knows where he is. That he himself cannot be made to disappear."

"And he is wrong in believing this?"

"Very wrong. As he may learn quite soon."

"So a small war is going to happen."

"Perhaps not so very small as all that. But the hills of southern Austria are quite remote. It will be a war carried on, let us say, out of sight of the public. There are a few villages nearby. They employ constables, etc. But I also employ these people, and have for some time."

"You are the law of the land."

"I am simply a feudalistic leader."

"From the old days."

"From the better days, when the Hapsburgs ran Vienna, and the minor aristocracy ran the countryside. You know, if you visit the Franziskaner Kirche in Vienna, in the basement, where all of the Habsburgs are buried in lead coffins—you will see that the burial place of Franz Josef is covered in flowers. Fresh flowers. Brought in daily."

"I must remember to do that."

"Yes, do, dear boy. It will give you an inkling of why the people of the surrounding area appreciate—well, who I am, and how I live. But that is all mere background. Foreground is that our business has been, sadly, concluded. I shall be transporting these paintings to Austria—how I do so is not your concern. Then I shall, as I mentioned, move there myself. I've been home far too little. And I shall set about protecting the paintings I have, rather than procuring new ones. At least for the time being. As for you, whatever method you've been using for the past months—as effective as it has been—must now be terminated."

"I understand."

"Also, I must tell you—and this is not easy—"

"Go on."

"No one, who's been involved in this operation, can be considered safe. Not even you."

"You think Red Claw knows about…"

"He seems to know about everything. And everyone. Look to yourself, Gellert. And look to your people. I shall protect myself, and my paintings. I'm not at all certain I can protect you. And I'm damned sure I can't protect your operatives."

"You think Red Claw might…"

"I think Red Claw does not forgive. What he does to his enemies, I can only imagine. I've learned one thing. A strange thing, perhaps, an eccentricity of his—but something that seems to be a pattern."

"And this thing is?"

Beckmeier ran his palm carefully over his hair and then said, quietly:

"He does not like to kill people in this country. He feels apparently that The United States was a savior for his people."

"The Jews?"

"Yes. And so he does not like to—shall we say, 'soil' the soil here with the blood of people he takes to be anti-Semitic criminals. He 'transports' them. Usually with as little fuss and violence as possible. Then he—well, what he does then, no one seems to know."

"Nor wish to know."

"No. Nor wish to know. At any rate, then—look to your people. And now our interview, as our professional arrangement, is sadly concluded. "

They both rose and shook hands.

Beckmeier disappeared into the bowels of the great mansion, leaving Michael Gellert alone with the butler, who stood by the door holding an overcoat.

CHAPTER TWELVE: SMALL TOWN GOINGS ON

At that same time in Bay St Lucy, eight PM on the evening of December 3, Nina Bannister was teaching what had been Emily Peterson's Wine and Watercolors class.

The class took place in O'Doul's Restaurant and Bar, which was a relatively new Irish pub in Bay St. Lucy, and which, partially as a community service and partially to get known and attract a bit more business, had offered some of its downstairs space to be used one evening a week for the new devotees of painting.

"I'd make the red a little deeper."

"You don't think it would be too much??

"No, I think it makes the thingies on the mill wheel—what are those called?"

"Paddles?"

"That doesn't seem right. But the thingies are more dramatic when they're dark red, at least to me."

"Ok, Nina. You're the expert."

"Oh, not really."

"How many painting have you sold now?"

"I don't really know."

She had sold twenty. One just this afternoon.

Which she, of course, knew exactly.

She moved on to Patricia Smithson's easel.

"Patricia, I think for this one, the base of the mill…"

Etc. Etc.

They were all gathered on the downstairs floor of the bar, and next to one of the large picture windows.

Tables had been moved around so that they were in a semi-circle.

On each table sat propped an easel. Just in front of each easel, lying flat, was a paper plate, and within that plate were eight quarter-sized puddles containing acrylic paints.

Blue, red, green, white, black, and an indeterminate color which one of the students—Esther Ryerson—said was ochre, and another of the students—Margie Mason—said was mauve.

No one was quite sure.

At the front of the room, was a large easel. The canvas was bare and ready for Nina to start

Upon each easel was a canvas, blank at the beginning of each class. Affixed to the top of each of the students' canvases were miniature copies of Nina's original.

The students, for their first act of the evening, were to subdivide this canvas into four separate parts, as the copy had been divided.

They would then draw with pencil the various features— mill wheel, base, trees, storm in the background, cart parked in front—of the painting.

Nina grabbed her brush and instructed them to start with the background (it would take longer to dry; leaving space for the penciled-in features.) They would then add colors, to their liking.

Also, they could add other things—dogs, cats, children, cows, animals, lightning bolts—again, to their liking.

The painters could also order wine as they worked, and were urged to do so by the managers of O'Doul's, who enjoyed both the art of watercolor painting and the sound of the cash register.

"You don't think the base is too big?"

"No, Patricia, I don't. I mean, it's got to hold that entire mill thing."

"How about the background colors?"

"They look fine to me, except maybe the sky is too pale."

"Well, I was planning on putting a thunderhead in the background."

"Oh, I see. So you want some contrast."

"Exactly."

"That's fine then. Oh, can I get you another glass of wine?"

"If you would."

"Sure. What are you drinking?"

"Merlot."

"One Merlot, coming up."

She walked to the bar, feeling quite comfortable being both bar maid and painting instructor. She put in the order, and was joined by Emily Peterson herself.

"Nina, this is just going wonderfully."

"Well, I hope it is."

Everyone is learning so much!"

"I'm glad. I'm just painting what I see and trying to offer any tips I can."

"Well you're doing splendidly. So splendidly, actually, that someone is here to write about you!"

"Really?"

"Yes, here!"

A young woman stepped forward.

Nina had never seen her before, but she was perky and blonde, and she had both a strong handshake and a good smile:

"Ms. Bannister?"

"Yes?"

"I'm Elaine Grogan. I've just been hired as a Special Features Editor for the *Bay St. Lucy Gazette*!"

"Oh, how nice to have you in town. Do you like Bay St. Lucy so far?"

"Love it."

"I'm not sure there's a great deal to write about. We're a pretty quiet little village."

"Well, there's you to write about. Everyone seems to be talking about your talent, and the paintings you're selling."

"Oh, I don't think we should make too big a thing of it."

"Nonsense," interrupted Emily. "Anybody who has real talent ought to show it off!"

"Exactly!" echoed the young woman. "I have to tell you, I was in Elementals today when the lady bought that painting of the old oak tree. What was it called?"

"Old Oak Tree."

"Yes, that one. She was so knowledgeable sounding. I have to write about what she said when I do the article."

"She did seem enthused."

"I'll say she was enthused. I took notes on some of her comments that I overheard when she was raving about it to you. She said it had 'a laminating viscosity' and an 'ephemeral vibrancy.'"

"I think she was just being kind."

"Well, anyway, she sounded quite expert. So, anyway, I want to get as much background info on you as I can, find out how you fell in love with painting, how you developed your talent, and what your sources of inspiration are."

"I'll tell you whatever I can, but..."

"And, of course, there's one thing even more important than that! We have to get a group picture!"

"Here, here!" said two men sitting at the bar, who were not in the watercolor class, but who were drinking wine anyway.

Here, here!" said Emily.

"Here, here!" said all of the students, simultaneously.

So Elaine Grogan got out her pocket camera.

And everyone got together in a tight group.

And they raised their glasses.

And they shouted as one: "To Nina!"

And thus, the craft of painting was celebrated in O'Doul's Bar and Pub in Bay St. Lucy Mississippi.

The class lasted until ten o'clock.

By ten fifteen, Nina was home.

Just as she walked in her door, her cell phone rang.

"This is Nina."

"Nina, this is Patty."

Patty Brewster owned The Stink Shoppe, a boutique several blocks from Elementals.

"What's up, Patty?"

"Well, probably nothing. But..."

"Go ahead—what's wrong?"

"I was just working late tonight. Have you just been in Elementals?"

"No, I've been teaching the Wine and Watercolors class."

"Well, when I was pulling out of our store driveway, I saw a light on in one of the windows."

"Really?"

"And I thought, that's funny, because Nina never leaves those lights on."

"No. I don't."

"Anyway, I went back into The Stink Shoppe for something I'd forgotten, and when I got back to the car, the light had gone off."

"Curiouser and curiouser."

"So, you might want to check it out."

"I do want to check it out. Thanks for calling, Patty."

"No problem. Good night."

"Good night to you."

And she flipped the cell phone closed.

"Carol?"

"Yep?"

Carol was curled in a corner of the living room, reading.

"Somebody saw a light on down at Elementals."

"That's funny."

"It's a little funny, because I locked up at four thirty today, and I'm pretty sure I turned them all off."

"You want to go check on things?"

"Yeah, I probably do."

"Shall I come with you?"

Nina shook her head, and walked to the closet to get a windbreaker.

"Don't worry about it; it's probably nothing."

And, so saying, she walked outside.

She paused at the foot of the stairway and looked up at Bay St. Lucy's sky.

It hung, slate and sullen, over the city like a shroud.

She unlocked the Vespa, donned her helmet, got on, started the engine, and pulled out of her driveway.

She turned onto Breakers Boulevard, listening, as somewhere in the distance, a siren wailed in mournful harmony with the outgoing tide, which was going about its business some fifty yards to her right.

A light on?

What was that all about?

Should she call someone?

The police?

No.

It wasn't that important.

She'd probably just forgotten, and left the thing on.

But then, when Patty had looked a second time, Elementals was dark.

Maybe the light had burned out.

At any rate, it almost certainly was not worth bothering Moon Rivard.

She tried to think of other things, and succeeded.

Her paintings, which were still selling.

Her travel plans with Carol.

How much money did she have now? Well, last week, the statement had read…

…but no more of that for now, since the outline of Elementals was looming in front of her, and she was dealing with the risky job of slowing her vehicle from a dozen miles an hour to six miles an hour to three miles an hour to nothing.

She cut off the engine and dismounted.

All of the lights were off.

Nothing seemed wrong.

She walked up the stairs, peered into the cylindrical Bannister Canister and saw neither mail nor messages nor flyers nor small animals, reached into her purse, withdrew her key, and inserted it into the gleaming silver lock.

The door swung open easily as she pushed upon the key.

The shop was unlocked.

"Huh."

A strange thing. Nina was nothing if not a creature of routine, and she *always* locked up upon leaving. Which she had done a little more than five hours ago.

Oh well.

She stepped inside the darkened shop, reached to her right, and flipped the light switch.

Everything was as she'd left it. The hanging ferns over to the right, the row of paintings on the street-side wall—none of hers were hanging now, but a spot stood ready for *Owl*, which she would finish probably day after tomorrow—the cash register directly in front of her, the displays of silverware on tables in the middle of the room, several clay pots standing like dusky-brown fat soldiers behind them…

…no, nothing had been changed.

So she crossed the room and walked up and down the various aisles and crannies and semi-nooks and hallowed spaces that made up the store.

An urn by Amy Phillips. A display of books about backpacking in Mississippi. An embossed punchbowl.

She looked up at the ceiling light; a large, doped-up fly was buzzing around it.

Have to kill it tomorrow.

But, other than that, everything seemed to be in place.

So she turned, walked to the door, opened it, and walked outside.

No sound from anywhere in winter-sleeping Bay St. Lucy.

She got on the Vespa, started it, and pulled away.

Ten seconds later, she'd gone about fifteen yards down the street.

And the bomb went off.

Carol Walker heard two things almost simultaneously: the first was what seemed like a sonic boom that came from the direction of downtown Bay St. Lucy; the second was a knock at the door.

She opened it and saw standing before her, a beaming Tom Broussard, dressed in dungarees and a battered black sports jacket.

"Did you hear a noise?" she asked.

He nodded.

"Yeah. Sounded like a jet broke the sound barrier."

"Are there any military air stations around?"

"Not that I know of."

"Huh. Well, anyway, hi Tom!"

"Hi yourself. Nina around?"

"No, she had to go into town. We got a phone call, and— well, it doesn't matter. How's Penelope?"

"She's great. And that's what I'm here about."

"Ok, how can I help you?"

"I want to buy one of Nina's paintings for her. I think it would make a great pre-pre-shower gift. I went over to Elementals today, though, and she told me she'd sold the last one, but there were a couple here that she'd finished."

"That's true. Nina and I just finished *Owl* today. I was going to leave it out on the deck, but the air is so cold and wet I put it in the bedroom."

"Could I see it? I don't have my truck with me—I've just walked over here from my place—but if it isn't too big, I could give you a check for it and just carry it down to the wharf."

"Sure, come on it."

He did so, then made his way through the living room and into the bedroom.

The painting rested on the floor, leaning against Nina's bed.

"It's an owl all right. I like the way it's kind of hidden in that green leafy background."

"Yes," answered Carol. "Nina worked hard getting the colors right. It's a small painting, too, so you shouldn't have too much trouble carrying it."

"How much is she asking?"

"She always sells her paintings for the same price: three hundred and fifty dollars."

"The way the things are selling, she's going to have to start asking more."

"Yeah, I know. Well, if…"

There was another knock at the door.

"We seem to be popular these days. Look, Tom, there's some wrapping paper over in the corner, if you want to make the painting look like a present."

"Good idea. You get the door; I'll wrap the thing up."

"Right."

She turned; left the bedroom, crossed the living room, and opened the door again.

A very well dressed—charcoal gray business suit, red tie superlatively tied—tall blond man with ice blue eyes, was standing in front of her.

She'd seen only a few people dressed so well in all her life, and they were all doing the same thing.

He was, she could remember thinking later, selling bibles for Jehovah's Witnesses.

"Carol Walker?"

"Yes?"

"May I come in?"

She almost automatically took a step back into the living room.

Then a second.

Soon they were both standing in the middle of the room.

"How may I..." she began.

But he interrupted her, saying simply:

"Lorca Reklaw."

Then, very carefully, and with all circumspection, as though he were retrieving his sunglasses from the inside pocket of his Armani jacket, he took out a gun.

It was a small gun, hardly bigger than his hand, which was not a small hand.

It shone, oily and black, the light overhead reflecting upon its cylinder.

She remembered thinking it might have been a toy gun.

She also remembered thinking that she was not at all frightened. That she was watching a film. That she was watching an action scene in a made-for-TV movie starring actors very few people recognized, except that one of them was herself, Carol Walker.

The man stepped forward so that he was hardly a good stride away from her. Then, crossing his chest with his right arm, he removed the gun from its shoulder holster, and began to cock it.

She sensed movement behind her.

At this moment, Tom Broussard hurtled like a missile across the room, almost knocking her down and barreling into the gunman. The two bodies shattered against the wall just beside the door, cracking the plaster and then falling to the floor in what immediately became a writhing tangle of thick limbs, clutching hands, bellowed obscenities, and shoes—black shiny ones on the assailant, combat boots on Tom—scuffing the floor boards.

A part of her wanted to turn and escape onto the deck, but another part prevented movement at all, and so she merely stood, fixed as a statue while the gun slid across the floor and came to rest at her feet.

She stared at it while the two men fought.

Its hammer, she noted, was cocked and ready.

The fight could not have lasted more than fifteen seconds, and it was soon over, for, although Tom was big and brawling, and had obviously been in bar room scuffles for most of his life, his opponent was trained.

And had a knife.

She did not even see where it had come from, nor out of what secretive pocket it had been slipped.

She only heard the click, saw the blade flash open, and saw the hand holding it, free for an instant from the grasp that had held it, crawl upward toward Tom's throat, which pulsated red and vein-laced beneath it.

Six inches from the throat.

Now on the throat.

She could see Tom's eyes bulging wide.

The gun was cold in her palm.

She took a step forward, bent down—as though to pick up off the floor a coin she had inadvertently dropped—then pressed the barrel against a sweaty lock of straw blond hair hanging from the man's forehead, and squeezed the trigger.

Everything was going around and around.

Going around and around were: the Vespa's tires, which hung awkwardly a foot or so above the grass lawn fronting Clay Creatures; her running sneakers, but how could they be going around and around because they were securely tied to her feet, which extended a few feet away from the rest of her, and were lying quietly on the ground? The street lamp, glowing and buzzing golden on the other side of the street, and just going around and around in its merry way and orbiting like a planet the post on which it was supposed to be attached.

There were other lights though, of course, and they were going around and around too, especially the red ones, the ones that came attached to the sirens, and which were not only orbiting but approaching, as she lay there in the grass watching them.

She watched them and the fire.

It was spewing out of Elementals now, Elementals whose front wall could not be seen for the billowing black smoke.

It roared as it spewed, chewing up everything that had been part of the entryway, having eaten, she thought absurdly, The Bannister Canister, her little message tube, of which she and Margot were so proud.

The Bannister Canister.

It was gone now.

"Ms. Bannister!"

What was that?

People.

People were going around and around, and they were shouting, and they were all dressed in bizarre black and golden uniforms, and they getting closer to her.

Now they were all around her.

"Ms. Bannister! Ms. Bannister, are you all right?"

She watched herself try to answer the question and fail, laughed inwardly at herself for failing, enjoyed the show, all the round abouts, everything circling the way it was…

"Ms. Bannister, can you talk?"

"I…"

There it was, a word.

"I don't…"

Two words

The fire continued to roar like a freight train.

"Can you move your arms and legs, Ms. Bannister?"

"Can I…"

What a question.

Of course, she could move her arms and legs.

She tried.

One leg moved and one arm.

She knew they moved because she saw them.

Well, that was pretty good, wasn't it?

"Ma'am, can you understand us? We've got to get you into an ambulance, if you can stand up."

"I—I don't know. I just..."

"Are you in pain, Ms. Bannister?"

"I don't—I don't think so."

"Can you take deep breaths?"

Could she?

She tried.

"Good! Good! Just slow, deep breaths. That's the girl!"

How many of them were standing there in a circle around her? Three? Four!"

They were firemen.

No, firemen were down the street, and now a silver-glistening horizontal waterfall was attacking the beast that was the fire, attacking that roaring and smoking and bellowing and horribly angry animal, flooding right into it.

"Ma'am, can you tell us if you're in pain?"

Now she was shaking her head.

And now she was back into her own head, and could talk, not just watch herself try to talk.

How strange it all was?

"I'm—I think I'm all right."

"Can you sit up?"

She tried; she succeeded.

Now she was upright at least and not lying on the grass.

"Good job, Ms. Bannister! Can you tell us where you're hurting?"

"I don't hurt."

"You sure?"

"Yes. I think I'm all right."

"We need to get you into the ambulance, ma'am. We're going to put you on this stretcher."

"I don't think I need..."

"Just be real calm now. We're going to lift you, and put you on the stretcher."

And now she was floating, and more faces hovered over her—and now she was descending, slender cloth belts wrapping themselves around her wrists, faces bending down close over her chest, metal circular things cold against her skin.

"Just hold on—we're going to put you in the back of this ambulance..."

"I'm all right. Really, I am."

"Yes, you are, dear. Yes you are."

A woman's voice.

"I'm Judy. I'm a paramedic."

"Hi, Judy."

Laughter from the faces circled above her.

That was good sign.

"Hi, Nina! You probably don't know me. My daughter is a high school junior. She loved having you as principal last year."

"What's her name?"

"Tricia Sherwood."

"Oh, Tricia. She made the honor roll every six weeks I was there."

"Yes, she did."

"I talked to her a few times in the hallway, between classes. She told me she wants to go to med school."

"And you remember that?"

"Of course, I do!"

"Of course, you do. You do, dear, because that's just the way you are. Now, hold on: we're going to lift this stretcher into the back of the ambulance now. Just lay your head back on the pillow. You might even close your eyes if you can..."

They did, and she did.

And the world became a warm dark place where she could think about Tricia going to medical school.

CHAPTER THIRTEEN: THE BELLS, THE BELLS...

At midnight in Bay St. Lucy, all of the bells in the city went off simultaneously.

Bells of the Lutheran Church, bells of the two Methodist Churches, bells of the three Baptist Churches, Bells of the Evangelical Church, and, of course, the truly big and sonorous bells of the Catholic Cathedral, which was located in the dead center of downtown.

There had been some talk of quieting the din, of letting the proper people—pastors, music directors, etc.—know that the sound of church bells in an evening was edifying, of course, but...

...but midnight?

...and *every* evening?

Still, nothing was done about the matter, because to have done so would have seemed distinctly sacrilegious, and because it was better to be awakened in the middle of the night than to be labeled Ebenezer Scrooge by one's fellow citizens.

And so, the bells continued to chime, not *The Bells of St. Mary's* but *The Bells of St. Lucy's*, and that is what they were doing this particular night, and that is why Nina Bannister could hear them as she sat shivering and no longer quite shocked, on the end of a gray table in Observation Room 204 of Bay St. Lucy General Hospital.

People had been coming and going for what seemed to have been hours, but what had in reality been forty-seven minutes.

For that was the precise time—eleven-thirteen PM—that a bomb had detonated in Elementals: Treasures from the Earth and Sea.

"Can't I at least get my clothes on?"

The young doctor nearest to her looked at the older doctor farthest from her, who was standing in the way of the middle aged nurse who was trying to get out of the room with a chart she was writing on, and thus had almost run into a very old but still spry looking nurse who was shaking a thermometer.

"We just want to be sure you're all right."

"I'm all right. I keep telling you: I'm all right."

"You had quite a shock."

"Yes, I did. But I'm all right. I fell off my Vespa. But I'm not even scratched."

"You're not having any problems breathing?"

"No. I'm just breathing right along, in out, in out, just like I learned to breathe a long time ago."

"No dizziness?"

"No dizziness."

"The room doesn't seem to be going around?"

"The people in the room seem to be going around. But the room itself is just good old rock solid."

This seemed to be the very statement that was necessary to make all of the doctors and nurses leave the room together, saying that they'd be back immediately, and for Nina simply to rest calmly.

So she was left by herself.

Wearing a hospital gown which opened, impossibly, in the back.

And which was cold.

The whole room was cold; the bed was cold, the ceiling was cold, the ventilator screen *on* the ceiling was cold.

She remembered a line from an Austrian play she'd read; during these last weeks when she'd been throwing herself into the literature of the country she and Carol were perhaps preparing to visit. The line had been delivered from a hypochondriac who was also fiercely afraid of being buried alive, and who explained his fears by saying:

"The doctors, even when they have succeeded in killing a man, are never quite certain that he is actually dead."

She was fine.

She'd told them that.

She had been at least fifteen yards from the door of Elementals when the blast had gone off.

Then, true, it had been strange, as though someone had pushed the Vespa over.

This, she now realized, was a shock wave.

And, true, she'd certainly been dazed for a time, when the paramedics arrived and examined her initially.

But now she was fine.

Except for the possibility of getting pneumonia in this observation room.

She was considering making a break for it, when the door opened again and the man who had to be, she decided, the chief night physician of the emergency squad—she had recognized none of the people taking care of her, strange, she knowing every denizen of Bay St. Lucy, but indicative of the transient nature of midnight emergency crews, she decided—this man entered, nodded his head and said:

"Well, Ms. Bannister, the staff seems to be in agreement that the best advice might be for you to stay here tonight. Just for observation."

"No."

He shook his head:

"I understand that you want to go home, but…"

"I want to get dressed. I want to have my real clothes on. I want to wear garments that button in the front and don't tie in the back. I want to put on those garments, stop shivering, and go home."

"Well, we can't keep you here against your will."

"You are keeping me here against my will."

He smiled.

"We hope you'll forgive us for that, Ms. Bannister."

"Only if you let me go right now. Otherwise, I'll hate you forever."

"We would regret that. But, since we can't find anything wrong with you…"

"You're letting me go?"

He shook his head.

Darn, she thought.

Too good to be true.

"It's not quite that simple."

"Somehow I knew it wouldn't be."

"There are a number of people who are waiting to see you outside. We've pretty much held them at bay. And we can do so all night. If you'd like for us to give you a sedative, something to make you sleep, then you can get a good night's rest. You can have breakfast here tomorrow morning; we'll arrange a place for you to meet with all these folks, and the whole thing might be easier."

She shook her head.

"No. Let's get this over with. Who's out there?"

"Most of the town."

"Well. That's nice of them."

"The word got out quickly."

"It's Bay St. Lucy."

"Yes, it is, Ms. Bannister. And you're—well, you're Nina Bannister. Everyone wants to know you're ok."

She was suddenly aware of a tightness in her throat.

The doctor continued:

"As it is, we could get you out a back entrance. But, if you really think you're up to it, the police seem to feel talking to you is urgent."

"I'm up to it."

"All right. Then why don't you get yourself dressed— your clothes are there on the chair—and we'll set up a room where you can talk to people."

With that he left.

She dressed.

Then she waited.

All she could do was look at the charts and pictures on the wall.

THE HUMAN HEART AND INDICATIONS OF ARTERIAL SCLEROSIS.

TIPS FOR AVOIDING MENINGITIS

FIVE INDICATIONS OF INCIPIENT BONE DISEASE

"They need," she found herself saying, *Old Red Lighthouse #2.*

There was a knock on the door.

"Come in."

The door opened and was filled with the form of Jackson Bennett, who flooded over her like an African-American tidal wave, hugged her for a few minutes, picked her up, looked carefully at her in what was not quite good enough light, broke a few of her ribs, and finally set her down, in the way that a tornado sets down a cow it has carried a few miles.

"Nina…"

She found herself crying.

Probably, she thought, because her chest had been crushed.

But for whatever reason, she just sat there blubbering.

"Nina, how are you?"

Blubber blubber.

She wanted to say *fine*, because she was.

But, seeing Jackson sitting there, and realizing half of the town had probably come to the hospital to pray for her…

…as well as the fact that she had, in fact, missed being killed by a matter of seconds…

…she decided a few tears were not such bad things, anyway.

So she shed them, and then finally said:

"I'm all right, Jackson."

"Are you sure?"

She nodded:

"After all this time, with all these doctors prodding and measuring and listening and recording—I'm probably the healthiest I've ever been. They've listened to my heart, looked into my ears, taken several big bottles of my blood, and examined my urine. I've never urinated this much in my life when I didn't feel the urge to go. But I think now we can all say with some certainty that my urine is among the best urine in Bay St. Lucy."

He smiled and shook his head:

"There are a lot of people out there waiting to see you."

"I know. The doctor told me. He also said the police want to talk to me."

Jackson pursed his lips:

"Do you feel up to that?"

"Yes. I'm not sure what I can tell them."

"You want me to be there when you talk to them?"

"If you would."

"Of course."

"Is Moon Rivard out there?"

For some reason, Jackson hesitated, then said, quietly:

"Moon isn't here."

"Really?"

"There's—been another crime."

"What kind of a crime?"

He shook his head.

"Let's not worry about that right now. Maybe we can just get this interview with the police done, and then…"

"Then I can go home."

He rose.

"We'll see."

"Is Carol…"

"Come on."

He held the door for her.

She followed him and two doctors down a corridor, then down another corridor, and then into what seemed like a consulting room of sorts.

There was a large oaken table, comfortable green leather chairs, and paintings of what seemed either the various stages of the life of Warren G. Harding or the people who'd founded the hospital.

Two police officers stood as she entered.

Again, she knew neither of them.

A young man and a young woman.

The man spoke, deferentially:

"Ms. Bannister?"

"Yes?"

"I'm Officer Peterson; this is my colleague Office McReynolds."

"I'm happy to meet you."

"Yes, ma'am. We're—well, we need to ask you some questions. That is if you feel all right."

"Yes. I'm all right."

"Then," said Jackson, "maybe we should all sit down."

They all sat down.

There was silence for a time, and Nina, much to her own surprise, asked the first question:

"I have a question."

The young male officer leaned forward, his hands folded upon the table:

"Yes, ma'am?"

"What the hell happened?"

Some smiles.

Jackson answered:

"Nina, as far as the fire department and the police department can now tell, it looks like someone put a bomb in Elementals."

She tried to speak, but there was that tightness in the throat again.

That was going to come and go for a long time now, wasn't it?

Yes, yes, it was.

"Why," she was finally able to ask, "would anyone do that?"

"We don't know, ma'am," said the young woman.

"I thought, sitting there being examined, that it might have been something like a gas leak."

Jackson:

"That was what everyone thought, at first. It's an old building. But they got the fire out quickly. Good that the Fire House is only four blocks away. Anyway, the fire was out within ten minutes of the explosion. They found what was left of the...device."

"What was it?"

"A plastic explosive of some kind. They're analyzing it now."

"And Elementals?"

Jackson smiled:

"It's not that bad, Nina."

"Oh, Jackson—I saw the flames pouring out..."

"No, no, the town got lucky. We still have our Elementals. The blast was all outwards, into the street. The front wall of Elementals is gone, but the rest of the store was untouched."

"The garden?"

"Garden's fine. All the displays are just the way they were."

"Oh, thank God. Margot! Margot's got to be told!"

Jackson smiled.

"I've taken care of that. I called her half an hour ago, at The Candles."

"You woke her up?"

"Nina, it was eleven thirty."

"Oh, that's right. I'd forgotten that we're talking about Margot Gavin."

"She'd barely gotten up for the day and was only on her third gin."

"And tonic?"

"No, just gin. Anyway, the only thing she was really worried about was you."

"Not Elementals?"

"I told her ninety-five percent of the place was untouched. She just said 'Damn, with the insurance I've got, we could have rebuilt it in its entirety if it had been destroyed.' She said, in fact, that she herself had thought about dynamiting it a hundred times, but didn't have the courage."

"Yes, that sounds like Margot."

"Anyway, I assured her that you were fine. She's coming down anyway. Probably be here tomorrow. But Nina…"

Jackson looked at the other officers in the room:

"About the bomb…"

"Yes, Jackson?"

"Well, there's something that we've got to tell you…"

"Yes?"

"It's something we'd all rather not talk about, but…"

"Go ahead."

The male officer took a deep breath, then asked:

"Do you know of anyone who might have wanted to blow up Elementals?"

She shook her head:

"It's a curio shop, for God's sakes! Who'd want to blow up a curio shop? We sell clay pots! Who hates clay pots?"

Silence in the room.

Then, the same officer:

"Then...and I hate to ask this, but—then, do you know anyone who might have wanted to hurt you, specifically? You or Miss Walker?"

"No! Carol is new in town, hardly known, and the nicest person anyone might want to meet. And as for me...."

Jackson:

"Nina, no one in Bay St. Lucy is more admired than you are. But—during your time as principal, is there someone you might have angered?"

"I—I got thrown out of a basketball game once."

Jackson could not help smiling.

"I remember that."

"You think the referee..."

"No."

Silence again.

The wisps of inappropriate humor dissolved into the air.

And the young officer continued:

"The problem is this, ma'am. It appears that the bomb had been connected to a timing device they'd attached to the front door of the shop. It was set to go off a certain number of minutes after the front door opened."

"The front door," she said quietly, "was unlocked when I got there."

Nods.

"They probably picked the lock to get in; then they set the bomb up and left; but they couldn't relock the door."

"Why," asked Jackson, "did you go down there so late?"

"Patty Brewster called and said she'd seen a light on."

"You didn't call the police?"

"I didn't think it was worth calling the police. I thought I'd probably just forgotten to turn off the light."

The young officer continued:

"This is the hard part, Ms. Bannister: the bomb was planted under the front desk. Probably, the plan was, at a specific time tomorrow morning, one of the people responsible for this would call Elementals at precisely that time…"

"…and I'd answer the phone."

"You or Ms. Walker."

"And then the bomb would go off."

"Yes, ma'am."

"So the bomb wasn't meant to destroy Elementals."

"No, Ms. Bannister."

"It was meant specifically to kill one of us."

Jackson leaned forward and said, quietly:

"You, Nina. It was meant to kill you."

She stared at him:

"How can you be sure it was meant to kill me and not Carol?"

"Because Carol was already supposed to be…I mean, a short time ago, at your place…"

"What?"

Silence in the room.

What were they not telling her?

"Where's Carol?"

Then Jackson rose and said:

"Come on, Nina. There are some things you have to know."

CHAPTER FOURTEEN: THE BIG UGLY GOON

Nina spent the night at Jackson Bennett's house.

It was there, sitting on Jackson's couch, flames crackling in the fireplace—all right, it was only forty three degrees, but certainly that was cold enough for a fire, especially if one had a fireplace—it was there, a little after two AM, that she learned of the events that had taken place only a little over an hour earlier, in her house.

There she learned that a man of unknown identity or motive, apparently a well-dressed man by all accounts, had knocked on the door, been let inside by Carol, uttered two incomprehensible (at least to Tom Broussard, who, except for Carol, was the only one there to hear them) words, taken a 38 caliber pistol out of its shoulder holster, and pointed it directly at Carol.

There she had learned that Tom Broussard, good Tom, Tom who would never be able to acquire a table at Sergio's or be considered one of the better people of Bay St. Lucy, or even really one of the *people* of Bay St. Lucy, had, by his own words, "done what I could."

She could imagine the scene.

She remembered Tom, at what must have been the exact same location just inside her door (Why were fights always breaking out in her shack? But then, why were murders always breaking out in Bay St. Lucy?)—remembered Tom almost throwing out of her window one of Eve Ivory's 'security men.'

But this man had, apparently, been tougher.

Better trained.

For he'd placed Tom in what must have been a kind of judo hold ('I couldn't move! He had me!'), and held a switchblade knife against his throat ("I could feel it beginning to cut me—I knew I was dead").

At which time, Carol Walker—shy, meek, short, soft-spoken, from a farm in Georgia, just north and east of Athens—had picked up the gun and blown the man's head open.

These things Nina had learned.

Then Jackson had given her a strong sleeping pill—two actually—and she had lain on the couch, watching the fire, trying not to imagine what happened when a man's head was blown open—until the world went away.

Now it was nine AM the following morning.

She was sitting in one of the interview rooms of police headquarters, Moon Rivard at the desk across from her, a secretary of some sort seated beneath one of the windows, taking advantage of white morning light filtering through the blinds to set up her computer—and she was sipping a cup of coffee that tasted better than it had any right to, given that this was not Carol's Cup or Morning Wake Up!, but jail.

Or at least one of the rooms adjacent to jail.

Pre-jail as it was.

Jackson Bennett, who'd driven her here, was also seated a foot or so beside her.

He was her Atticus Finch.

He had been there all night, sitting beside her.

And he would be here this morning.

"Where is Tom now?" he was asking.

Moon rose and took two steps toward the door, then peered down the corridor.

"He should be here anytime now."

"Did he spend the night at home?"

"Yeah. He insisted on it."

"Is he," asked Nina, "all right?"

Moon nodded:

"As far as anybody can tell. It must have been a close thing though."

Silence for a time.

Then Nina asked one of the questions that was going to be asked inevitably, anyway.

"Moon. Who was this guy?"

A shake of the head.

"We don't know anything."

"But he must have had…"

"He had nothing on him at all. No ID of any kind. No credit card. No driver's license. He was just a blank slate of a human being. Even the vehicle he used has no identifying marks, at least none that we've been able to trace."

Jackson:

"Fingerprints? He must have had fingerprints. Please don't tell me he somehow burned them off."

"No, he didn't. His fingerprints are just as clear as you'd want. They just aren't any good for anything."

Jackson persisted:

"Why not?"

"We've sent those prints everywhere we know. The FBI. Interpol. All state and local agencies. All national data banks. The man clearly has no record."

"At least not in this country."

"And not anywhere else in the world, as far as we can tell."

Nina's turn.

Another of the inevitable questions.

Did she really want to ask it?

No, but…

"Moon, this attempt on Carol's life and the bombing. Do you think they're related?"

"Yes, Ms. Bannister, I do. We all do. It's a scary thing, but you need to be aware of it."

"Go on."

He nodded, slowly:

"This man's job was to assassinate both you and Carol Walker. He probably had just left the bomb in Elementals when you arrived."

"He saw me?"

"That's our thinking now. But if he did see you, he also saw the explosion, and knew that you were all right."

"My God."

She could feel herself beginning to shake.

The thought that this man had seen her go into the store; could have done anything to her while she was there…

"Why," she found herself asking, "didn't he just kill me while I was lying there on the sidewalk?"

Another shake of Moon's shaggy head:

"Too many people arriving."

"All right. So when I couldn't get me…"

"He knew that Ms. Walker was staying at your place. He decided that, if he couldn't get both of you…"

"He would at least get one."

"Yes. That's the way it looks now."

"If his plan had worked right…"

"You would have been dead the next morning, a few minutes after you'd opened the door—and the moment you answered the phone call, which would have been placed at the exact time the bomb had been set to go off. Then he'd have driven over, and…"

"…and Tom wouldn't have been there."

"No, ma'am. He wouldn't have."

Moon took another step forward into the doorway and said, quietly:

"He's here now though."

And he was.

Nina sprang up almost instantaneously when he appeared in the doorway, which seemed small given his frame. She buried her face in some part of his stomach, and for a time was unable to ascertain whether the shaking in her head came from her heart or his bowels.

Finally he moved her some inches away and peered down:

"Hey, teacher."

"Tom…"

He shrugged:

"I'm in trouble again."

"Tom..."

Was that all she could say?

Apparently.

He continued to smile through his great, black, tangled, shaggy mane:

"Another fight."

She could only laugh, foolishly.

"You ought to be ashamed of yourself."

He nodded.

"Just can't seem to straighten up. You're going to suspend me, I guess."

She shook her head, trying not to cry any harder than she already was.

"I don't know what we're going to do with you."

Then, impulsively:

"Tom, you saved her."

He shook his head:

"I don't know."

"You may have saved both of us. If you hadn't been there, then when I got home…"

"I don't know exactly what I did."

Moon interrupted.

"That's what we need to find out, Tom. We need to get your statement. A man's dead. This may be a difficult time for you, but…"

"No, I understand. I'll tell you the whole thing as well as I remember it."

"Ok, let's all sit down."

They did so.

The stenographer beneath the window was working, typing now.

"I'd walked over to Nina's place from my own. The truck was down at Penn's on the wharf."

"Why did you go to Nina's in the first place?"

Tom smiled:

"I wanted to buy a painting. Kind of as an early shower present for Penn. I still do want to buy a painting, Nina."

She shook her head:

"You'll never buy another painting from me, Tom Broussard."

"No?"

"Of course not. They're all on the house from this moment on."

"Even the visceral ones?"

"Especially the visceral ones."

"Go on, Tom," Moon said, quietly.

"All right. Well, Carol answered the door."

"Did she seem upset or nervous?"

He shook his head:

"No, she was fine. She asked me to come in and said Nina had gone down to Elementals. Something about a light being on."

"Yeah, we know all about that. Now, that is."

"So I told her I wanted to buy a painting but none were hanging in the store. I'd been over there that morning."

"Right. Keep going."

"She said there was a painting in the bedroom, and maybe I could buy it. I went in to look. The painting was propped against the bed. I'd just bent down to pick it up, when I heard a knock on the door. That seemed a little strange to me, I don't know why. Anyway, I put the painting on the bed, turned around, and walked out into the living room; all the time listening to the door open and this deep voice say something."

"Say what?"

"Sounded like two words."

"What two words, Tom?"

He shook his head:

"Damned if I know. Looking back, it must have been another language."

"And you have no idea what language?"

"No idea at all."

"Did Ms. Walker answer?"

"No, she didn't have time. By the time I'd reached the doorway, they were both standing in the middle of the room, and this guy was pulling back his suit jacket. I've seen my share of guns before, and I knew this one was a .38 automatic. I saw him take it out and point it, but then..."

"...then you weren't really observing anymore."

"No. I just did what I did."

"Thank God," said Nina, quietly

"Yes, Tom," Jackson Bennett chimed in. "Thank God."

"Yeah. Well. Sometimes you need a big stupid goon. And I happened to be available."

"You can," said Nina, "put it in your next novel."

Tom shook his head:

"I don't want to think that much about it. I'm trying to forget it as hard as I can, but I'm not succeeding. Damn the guy was tough. He was hell for strong, but he knew moves I've never seen. I thought I was at least holding my own with him for a few seconds; then he flipped me and I couldn't move anything, arms, legs, anything. I saw him slip the knife out of his pants' pocket, heard the 'click,' and thought: 'uh oh.' Then I felt it against my throat."

"Take your time," said Moon.

"Yeah. Well. Not too much more of it. I could see Carol out of the corner of my eye. She didn't seem panicked at all. She'd gotten hold of the .38 somehow. I guess it came loose from him during the struggle. Anyway, for a second I thought she was just going to shoot, kind of blindly. Looking back on it now, that would have been disastrous, because we were just wrestling there in one big knot. But she didn't. She bent down as calmly as you please, pressed the end of the barrel against the guy's temple, and pulled the trigger."

Silence in the room.

Tom went on, quietly:

"I don't know if you've ever seen what a .38 can do, point blank like that. I know I hadn't. I'd seen people shot. In the army. On the street."

More silence.

"But not like that, not right up against the temple."

And more silence still.

The explosion going through the minds of everyone in the room was sound enough.

"How," asked Moon, "did Ms. Walker react? What did she do?"

Tom shook his head.

"I don't know."

"You don't know?"

Another shake of the head.

"No. I'm not sure what either of us did. For that couple of minutes right after…well, right after it happened, my mind doesn't have anything in it. All I know is, I must have come over and—and got her, somehow, got her on her feet. We must have gotten through the door, stepping over—what all was lying there. But somehow, the first clear thing I remember was the two of us, sitting there at the base of Nina's stairs, huddled together and crying. There were sirens. Flashing lights. Finally, we were in an ambulance."

And one last bit of silence.

Followed by Tom saying:

"I was sitting in the back of the ambulance with my arm tight around her. She looked up—I remember she'd lost her glasses, and she was crying—and she said: 'Thank you for saving my life.' I said: 'I think it's the other way around….'

…and that's all I remember."

CHAPTER FIFTEEN: THE SMUGGLER

The quietest rooms in Bay St. Lucy Hospital are located on the building's fourth (and top) floor. These rooms are not large, but each is meant only for one patient, and each has thick, well-insulated walls. People assigned to these rooms have often undergone some kind of mental trauma, and do not need a roommate to chat with, a television to watch, or a constant stream of doctors and nurses coming and going.

It was late morning, when a small stream of such people reluctantly entered room 407, where Carol Walker had been placed the night before, just after having been given a strong sedative. The people in the stream—a stream which had been formed a short time earlier three floors below—were the primary care physician, Nina Bannister, Moon Rivard, and Jackson Bennett.

It was the physician who pushed open the door.

"Ms. Walker? You awake now?"

The room was bathed in the light of late morning, a kind of hazy white glow with what seemed like millions of tiny dust particles floating in it, but which must upon more careful reflection have been super-inflated air atoms, dust of any kind being alien to so sterile an environment as the hospital possessed.

"I'm awake."

The window behind the bed on which Carol lay revealed the still slumbering—not because of the time of day but because of the time of year—village of Bay St Lucy, with its slate gray rooftops spread out beneath a slate gray sky, and the restless ocean beyond, with its equally slate gray waves churning restlessly in toward shore, all of them, one after another, reaching the beach and turning around to head back out again, disappointed to find no small children waiting to dive in the ocean.

The rest of the party filed in.

Jackson, last in line, closed the door carefully behind them.

The windows were thick. Ambulances going and coming made no sound, nor did anything else from the outside world.

Nina, as though knowing instinctively what to do, pulled a chair, which was as gray as the universe outside the window, up to the side of the bed, sat down in it, and took Carol's hand.

Carol smiled wanly at her, then, with the other hand, reached over to the night stand beside the bed, picked up her glasses, and put them on.

No one in the room spoke for a time.

The men had formed a small semi-circle around the bed.

Finally the doctor:

"Were you able to sleep, Ms. Walker?"

Carol kept her eyes fixed on Nina as she answered.

"Yes."

"Good. How are you feeling?"

She gave a small shrug, but did not answer.

Then she turned her head slightly, and her eyes became fixed on the opposite wall.

Moon Rivard took a step forward and asked:

"Ms. Walker, do you remember what happened last night?"

"Yes."

"Well, due to the nature of the events, it's important for us to get a statement from you. Understand, Tom has told us what happened. There's no question at all of charging you with a crime. You clearly acted in self-defense. And you almost certainly saved Tom's life and your own. I have to tell you, Ms. Walker, you're a brave girl."

Another shrug.

Moon continued:

"For the record, though, if you could just tell me in your own words what happened, as you remember it—then I'll be able to pass that statement along to the proper people. We'll start processing all the paperwork, and we'll be able to leave you alone here so you can rest."

Carol continued to stare at something that was clearly invisible to everyone else in the room.

Finally she took a deep breath.

Her shoulders seemed, thought Nina, very small and delicate beneath the pale blue hospital gown.

"I am," she said softly, "a smuggler."

Moon leaned over the bed:

"I'm sorry. I didn't get that."

"A smuggler. I smuggle stolen paintings. For a while, I took the paintings on airplanes. Michael would give them to me in Chicago. Different places. Then I would take them on the plane in my backpack. Everyone saw them. No one cared. I'd take them to Frankfurt. Then to Graz, in southern Austria. I would just leave them in the hotel. Someone would come and get them, I suppose. Every time I did this, I would find a check for twenty thousand dollars in a drawer in the desk in the room. I had to have the money for papa. He's very old, and sick."

"Ma'am, if you can't…"

But Carol interrupted:

"A man has a castle not too far from Graz. He's collecting the paintings. All kinds of paintings. *View of the Sea at Schweiningen*. I had the painting for a while. On Nina's deck. I touched it. I could feel the sand in it. The wind was blowing the day Van Gogh painted it. I could feel the grains of sand in the paint."

Then she turned her head slightly and cocked it, so that she was looking up at Moon:

"His head just blew up. I pulled the trigger, and there was this horrible…"

"I know, Ms. Walker. Maybe for now you just better…"

"It was all over me. His head was all over me."

"We probably should leave now. Whenever you…"

Her grip tightened on Nina's hand.

Her gaze did not waver, but her voice grew softer:

"We had to change, you understand? It was The Red Claw. He found out. He found out everything. He wants the paintings back. They belong to his people, don't you see? He's going to kill us all, so that he can get them back. First he found out about the airports. So Michael came and told me that we couldn't do any more airports. He said we had to do frame changes. And that would be safe. I did them. But it wasn't safe."

The physician:

"We're going to be letting you alone now, Ms. Walker."

But Carol simply pulled Nina closer to her and said:

"His head was all on me. All over me. And it wasn't on him anymore."

"I know, baby. You just lie still and get it out of your mind."

"I keep feeling it. It's all so cold. Everywhere on me."

"It's all right. You're my brave girl. I'm here with you now."

"Will you stay here?"

"Sure, I will."

"Don't let him come back, because he doesn't have a head. It's all on me. All over me."

"No one will come. It's all right, my baby."

Jackson, who was standing by the door:

"Maybe if we could all meet out in the hall, just for a second..."

Nina:

"I have to go into the hall for two seconds, Carol. Then I'll come back and sit with you. I won't leave you."

"So many beautiful paintings—but they weren't mine. I shouldn't have done it."

"I'll be right back."

A moment later they were standing in the hall.

Jackson said, almost whispering:

"She doesn't know what she's saying."

The physician:

"She's clearly in shock. I've seen this kind of thing before. Painting is so important to her. She can't really face what must have happened up there in your cottage, Nina. So she retreats into this fantasy world of smuggling paintings. It's all a delusion."

"What was she saying about red claws?"

Jackson shook his head:

"It's all just fantasy. Like the doctor said, she's in shock."

Nina, to the physician:

"How long will this last?"

"No way of knowing. Physically, she's fine. I think we should bring in a psychologist from Hattiesburg. I know a good man. My feeling is, these delusions will pass. They usually do. Shock trauma can go on for a day or so—but, like I said, it will pass."

"That's good to know."

"We just need to keep her quiet, and let her sleep as much as possible."

"All right. I'm going back in now, and sit with her."

"Do that."

And Nina did.

CHAPTER SIXTEEN: ALPINE IDYLL

By mid-morning, a light snow had begun falling on Graz.

This was not a normal thing. The city lay in a kind of basin, ringed about by the Fischbacher Alps, and so its winter months were generally cold, gray, somber, and snowless, the citizenry forced to travel twenty miles or so in order to enjoy the delights of downhill skiing.

But this morning was different.

Franz Beckmeier enjoyed watching the world whiten beneath him as he sat by a plate-glass window in the second floor of Café Europa and savored his 'Grosser Brauner' (big brown one), which had been served steaming hot to him seconds before in a coffee cup that seemed as large as half a bowling ball.

There it was, all spread out, the Christkindle Markt, which was Graz' name for its winter market, held during the month of December on the Main Square.

Good to be back in Graz.

He preferred the summer months, of course. He preferred sitting outside on the café's balcony, looking almost straight down on freshly-washed streets and watching the vegetable stands do their business, watching the dirndl-clad Hausfrauen laugh and chatter as they threw baskets around and carefully fingered fruit.

But the winter had its charm, too.

The small light brown wooden shacks that hawked Christmas wares, dolls and aprons and clocks and every manner of non-necessities thinkable.

There, beyond the River Mur, the ruins of Castle Gosting. Beyond that, the dark green mountains, topped by a band of snow.

And beyond that, the taller mountains, cloud-shrouded now, but sure to be there shining and glittering in the afternoon when the snow clouds had dissipated by early afternoon.

Yes, he liked Graz.

And here he would stay.

The years of travel were behind.

The last of the corporations were sold. Let others take care of running them.

Of course, he'd never needed to be a businessman in the first place. His family's lands and fortunes had been secure by the early nineteenth century, and his fiefdom would never have been imperiled, even had he chosen to live his entire life as a recluse.

But what would have been the fun of that?

He's always been a man who took pleasure in the chase. The hunt.

Competition.

And so he'd competed all these years in the cutthroat world of business.

Where he'd cut his share of throats.

But that was over now.

Now it was time to live. While he still had a modicum of health. While he could still ski. And shoot. And do other things that a healthy man might be expected to do.

And which he was going to do tonight.

"Mein Herr?"

The waiter, tuxedoed, silver haired.

A fixture of Café Europa.

Standing before him now, holding a silver tray.

With a card on it

"Für mein Herr, bitte schon."

"Danke."

He lifted the card off the platter, turned it over, and read:

"Landeszeughaus. Dritten Stock."

Armory. Third floor.

"Ja. Danke sehr."

He put the card in his shirt pocket, and said:

"Ich muß momentan weg. Komm gleich."

Have to leave for a moment. Will come right back."

"Jawohl, mein Herr."

So saying, the waiter bowed and left.

No point in paying, Beckmeier told himself as he rose, taking a last sip of coffee. He'd be right back. Whatever he was to be told in the armory, he'd hear quickly.

Then he could come back.

For he had another meeting in fifteen minutes.

A meeting which promised to be much more enjoyable.

The armory was no more than a hundred yards away, just up Sackstrasse, whose cobblestones were being lightly covered by a film of snow. He looked up the street in front of him. 'Up' was the correct word, since the narrow passageway climbed the castle mountain at an impossible angle, twisting its way around and through the hedges and wall remnants of the old fortress, and segmented by windows just washed an hour ago.

There, just up the hill, Herzl Backerei: people leaned out the door, wicker baskets hung from crooked elbows.

He should stop there on the way back from the armory.

Seven-thirty was a bit late in the morning for the freshest baked goods; but he'd find something.

Of course, he had his own cooks, who would be serving croissants for him and his—friend—tomorrow morning.

But it was an old habit, going to the bakery, and he would not give it up.

He trudged on.

Now he was by the Solingen Steel store, with bigger knives on the obscured shelves toward the back, and swords gleaming on racks beside the green-baized counters.

He thought back to his university days.

His dueling scar.

Inflicted with a sword just like that one, that one third from the end of the row.

He himself had used a sword slightly different from any sold now.

Older.

In subtle ways, more effective.

Crueler.

And he'd inflicted his own number of scars.

He pulled his overcoat tightly around him as he walked, wincing a bit as the wind bit into his face.

He peered into the mélange of statue work and concrete stairways, that, had the great green metal door not been opened, would have remained unseen by him as he passed.

How many other secrets, treasures, palaces, chambers, dungeons, courtyards, and mysteries, were hiding beside him?

For Graz, essentially a medieval city, would always hide its secrets, even from a native.

Here: the signboard hanging above the street, announcing in Frakture Script:

Landeszeughaus.

Armory.

He pivoted, his boots scraping on gravel which could have been poured from horse-drawn trailers by knights in the service of Ferdinand II, and stepped into the dark forechamber, through a narrow, gothic-vaulted passageway, and through another turning—where a short staircase beckoned him.

He made a quick turn, climbed five steps, ducked beneath a worn oaken archway that seemed to have been built for beings six inches shorter than he, and then straightened, a vast hall looming before him.

"Mein Gott," he whispered.

As he always did, no matter how many times he entered this place.

He received no answer, for the chamber before him was inhabited by people made of metal.

It yawned before him, the vast and almost untouched, for centuries, arsenal of Graz.

Row upon row, row upon row, they stood gleaming silver in light filtered through beaded-glass windows: suits of armor.

There were hundreds of them, all lined along the wall so close that he could touch them, just to his right. And then, farther down, toward the end of the great hall, there were more suits of armor, just as brightly polished—but made for horses.

Metal horses, eight feet high, their heads encased in visors and every inch of flank, thigh, shoulder, upper leg, haunch—tightly covered by its own metal-segmented plate, screwed marvelously and flexibly to its overlapping plate, the whole impregnable horse-ship creating a vision unseen outside of these fine dust-infiltered walls for more centuries than could have been conceived by creatures, such as he, from the still slightly parvenu lands stumbled upon by Columbus.

"Mein Gott."

What else could one say?

It never grew old to him, even though he'd been coming here since childhood.

He began moving along the row of breast-plated and iron-expressioned soldiers, all at rigid attention, all held upright by the straight metal rods to which they'd been bolted.

He walked on; wooden boards creaking almost imperceptibly with each of his heavy-booted steps.

He made his way along the rows, fighting the urge to reach over the green-baize rope cordoning soldier after soldier who stood, never wavering, attention eternally perfect, swords at the ready, awaiting his approval.

Fighting the urge to touch one of the suits of armor.

Just touch it.

Of course, this was forbidden.

Later on in the morning, there would be guards, sternly watching each of the visitors making their way down the aisles, admonishing them that even a slight touch could begin the process of rusting.

There were no guards here now, of course.

Too early.

His agent had taken care of having the armory opened.

So that they would be alone.

One could not be too careful.

Hopefully, the agent would have satisfactory news. Then all this secrecy could be ended.

Then he would not be at war any more.

Muskets.

There, behind Sergeant King Arthur and General Sir Galahad…were rifles like blunderbusses—and there beside them, pistols.

And so, for a time, he simply wandered, his gaze drawn away for a second or so by the huge windows through which he could see more courtyards, some serving as parking lots—and briefcased bureaucrats walking to work in municipal buildings—but then drawn back constantly to these quiet ornaments reminiscent of unthinkably brutal wars and battles.

Stairs at the far end of the chamber.

He climbed them: second floor.

Third floor.

He'd begun to inspect the collection of gunnery wagons and powder holders, when he noticed, on the wall to his left, a solitary chair in which sat a wax-like gnome of a figure seated and surveying the weaponry. He would almost have taken this image to be a part of the collection itself, had it not spoken to him.

"Herr Beckmeier."

"Jawohl."

"Bitte. Setzen Sie sich."

And there was a chair, usually occupied by one of the guards.

He sat down opposite, who looked like nothing other than a human version of Rumpelstilzken, and was doubly useful because of this.

No one feared him.

That was a mistake.

But this was one of his most trusted men. And had been for some time.

"You are back. Im Lande."

"Ja. Im Lande."

They sat for a time.

Then the question:

"News?"

A shrug from the fairy tale figure:

"Yes, there is news."

"And?"

"I received word from one of Red Claw's people this morning."

"How?"

"Doesn't matter."

"Also. So what is this 'word' you have received?"

"He and his men will be coming."

"To Eggenburg?"

"Yes."

"When?"

"Soon. The next few days."

"You told him I have men, too."

"He knows that. Red Claw seems to know everything."

"Well. Then we shall do what these armor-covered fellows around us spent their lives doing. We shall have a little war. And that, I think, will be the last of the inscrutable Lorca Reklaw."

"Do you want me to…"

"I don't want you to do anything. I myself shall know what to do when the time comes. I shall know how to protect my paintings."

He rose, then said:

"And tonight I shall entertain a guest."

"An art lover?"

"A lover."

"I see."

"Thank you for your services. You may disappear now, as is convenient for you. I shall know how to contact you, if I need you again."

"Jawohl."

Beckmeier turned and left.

When he returned to the Café Europe, fresh coffee had been poured.

Both for him and the dark-haired woman sitting at his table.

She rose, smiled, extended her hand:

"Herr von Beckmeier."

He took the hand and kissed it, bowing as he did so.

"We do not use the 'von' for some decades now."

"I apologize."

"No need."

They sat.

She was, he thought, ravishingly beautiful.

Even more so offstage than on.

"I took the liberty," she said, "of ordering more coffee."

"Excellent. I had to leave for a short time to do an errand."

"I'm sure you're a very busy man."

"Not so much now. These are the first days of my…well, my 'retirement.'"

"Oh! You are not so old as all that!"

"I am a mere relic."

"Do not say such things. I would never consent to spend the next two evenings with a relic."

"All right. I shall, from now on, simply view myself as an experienced man of the world."

"Much better. A man of the world, who collects paintings."

"I do have a modest collection."

"So I have been told."

"But I should apologize."

"And why?"

"I was not able to attend the performance last night. The flight arrived late."

"Oh. A pity."

"A great pity, since all of Graz is talking this morning about the great Anya Celline, who is the greatest Violetta in the world, in the greatest performance ever of *La Traviata*."

"I hope it went well. You will come…"

"For Tuesday's performance, of course."

"Wonderful."

"But between now and then, I will have you as my guest."

"As we have arranged?"

"As we have arranged."

And so, for a time, Franz Beckmeier sipped his coffee.

And stared wonderingly into the eyes of one of the most beautiful and talented women in the world.

And forgot about Lorca Reklaw.

CHAPTER SEVENTEEN: AN INVITATION

At eleven AM, the door to Carol Walker's hospital room burst open and three nurses, in single file, entered carrying flowers and baskets.

"Good morning, lazy bones!"

She raised herself on an elbow and smiled back at them, but said nothing.

"How do you feel?"

"All right."

"Your vital signs are fine."

"That's good."

"Everybody in town has sent you flowers or written you cards. These are only part of the whole shebang."

"I didn't know that many people in Bay St. Lucy even knew me."

"Well, they do, honey."

She knew nothing to reply to that.

"The doctor's going to want to see you again in an hour or so. After that, it's a little unclear. We don't know where would be best for you to stay tonight. The main thing is, you're all right now. Nothing will happen to you."

"Thank you."

"You just went through a bad trauma. It's going to take a while, but everybody in Bay St. Lucy is looking out for you. For you and Nina."

"Am I," she asked, "going to need to go to the police station?"

A shake of the first nurse's head:

"I don't know, honey. Maybe later on, but only when you feel like it. I wouldn't worry about it. You have some very fine folks looking after you."

"I know. And I appreciate it."

"Now," said the nurse, placing the letter basket on a chair next to the bed, "we're going to get out of here and let you enjoy the flowers, and read some of these cards."

The nurses left, the door closing quietly behind them.

Carol began to feel her way through the cards:

"We're all pulling for you!"

Alanna Delafosse.

"All Bay St. Lucy is thinking about you."

Edie Towler

"Be brave, be strong, trust in the Lord."

Emily Johnson

"The Bennett family is with you!"

Jackson Bennett and Family.

And on and on.

Until, the next one in the pile, a letter and not a card.

She opened it.

It had been carefully typed, on an elegant, though unmarked, sheet of stationary.

It read:

IT IS TIME.

LORCA REKLAW WILL RETRIEVE THE PROPERTY OF HIS PEOPLE

ALL THE THIEVES WILL LEARN WHAT THE JEWISH PEOPLE HAVE HAD TO LEARN, AND ENDURE WHAT THEY HAVE BEEN FORCED TO ENDURE.

AS SOON AS YOU READ THIS, COME TO THE WHARF, SLIP 15.

YOU ARE BEING AWAITED.

IF YOU DO NOT DO THIS IMMEDIATELY, YOU AND MS. BANNISTER MAY WELL BE KILLED.

THIS WAY, SHE WILL REMAIN SAFE.

AGAIN; THE TIME HAS COME FOR LORCA REKLAW TO DO WHAT MUST BE DONE.

The letter was not signed, but there was a crude drawing of a claw where the signature would have been.

She lay in bed for a moment, staring at the ceiling.

Then she got up and walked to a closet, where her clothes were hanging.

She got dressed, folding the hospital garments neatly and putting them on the bed.

She took pen and paper out of her purse, sat down beside a small bedside table, and wrote a letter, sealed it in an envelope and placed it when finished on the table beside the hospital bed.

She walked out of the room, her purse slung over her shoulder.

The corridor was deserted.

She went down the stairs and out into the entry vestibule, where people—nurses, doctors, patients, visitors—were coming and going.

No one noticed her. She walked out the main door, blinking in the sunlight.

There were several ambulances and police cars scattered around, but, again, no one noticed her.

She made her way toward the ocean. In fifteen minutes, she had reached the wharf.

Slip 5.

Slip 10.

Slip 15.

She sat down.

Within five minutes, a boat arrived.

She made her way onto it.

And in that way, Carol Walker was taken by agents of The Red Claw.

Nina Bannister, having surveyed the damage done to Elementals and satisfied herself that the first reports had been accurate (the damage being surprisingly minor) returned to the hospital at noon carrying a bouquet of roses and a box of Kentucky Fried Chicken (breast, wing, mashed potatoes),which she knew Carol would love.

Damn all hospital food, anyway.

She waved to the woman at the desk, spoke cheerily to two nurses in the main corridor, pushed the button beside the elevator door, stepped inside, and pushed the button for the third floor.

She got out of the elevator and entered the quiet corridor. Room 302. Room 304. Room 306.

She pushed open the door, saying, as she did so:

"Chicken time."

The empty bed smiled back at her. She noticed an envelope with her name on the side of the bed. She slipped it into her pants pocket.

She walked into the room and put down the things she was carrying.

"Carol?"

The bathroom.

Empty.

Carol was clearly not there.

She walked back out into the hall, where a nurse was leaving one of the rooms at the far end.

"Hey!"

The nurse looked at her.

"Yes, ma'am?"

"Where's Carol?"

A shake of the head:

"I'm sorry?"

"Carol Walker. The patient in 306."

"Isn't she in there?"

"No, she isn't."

The nurse approached her, then passed her, then stuck a head in the room.

Then the nurse emerged, saying:

"Well, she's not in there."

"That's what I just told you. Where is she?"

"I don't know."

"Somebody has to know."

The nurse pulled a pager out of her pocket and said quietly into it:

"Assistance in 306."

Then she put the pager away, and re-entered the room.

She walked around it, brushing her hand against the flowers, peeked into the bathroom, and came back out into the corridor.

"She's definitely not in there."

"No. No, she isn't."

Two more nurses arrived, one a younger woman, the second clearly someone in charge.

This was the person who said, with an authoritarian ring to her voice:

"What's happening here?"

"The patient in 306 is gone."

"What do you mean, gone?"

"She's just not in there."

"Has she gone for testing? Maybe they took her down to the lab."

"Can you call down there?"

"Here. I'll do it."

Another pager produced.

"Hey. We're trying to locate a patient. Room 306. Walker. Carol. Dr. Stephenson. No. No, I'm not showing any testing on the schedule, but we're checking anyway. Is she down there?"

Pause.

Shake of the head.

Pager back in its holder.

"She's not in the lab."

Nina:

"Well where the hell is she then?"

"Ma'am, if you'll just…"

"I don't want to 'just' anything. I want to know where my friend Carol is!"

"I'm sure she'll turn up."

"'Turn up?' This is a hospital! People don't just 'turn up!'"

"She must be somewhere."

"Well, that's a profound statement!"

"Please, ma'am. If you'd lower your voice…"

"My voice is not the problem here! Do you realize someone tried to kill this woman last night?"

"Yes, ma'am, we do."

"There ought to have been a guard at her door!"

"Yes, ma'am, but the doctor thought an armed guard would disturb the rest of the patients. There are officers downstairs to be sure no one suspicious came in."

"Ok, so no one did. But are you sure no one suspicious went out? Like your patient?"

"She may simply have taken a walk down one of the corridors…"

"Oh, the hell with you!"

And, so saying, Nina turned and walked away.

She was running when she reached the stairway.

There was a welter of people coming and going in the entry vestibule. She looked around madly but could see no sign of Carol.

Outside, a young policeman was leaning against a corner of the building, smoking a cigarette.

"Hey!"

He turned and looked at her:

"Yes, ma'am?"

"Did Moon Rivard assign you to be here?"

"Yes, he did."

"What were your orders?"

"I'm not sure I'm supposed to…"

"What were your orders, dammit?"

"Well. I was just supposed to be sure nobody suspicious came into the hospital."

"And has anybody suspicious come into the hospital?"

"No, ma'am. Not during my shift here."

"How long has that been?"

"Four hours."

"You've been here at the door all that time?"

"Yes."

"And you haven't seen Carol go out of the building?"

"I don't think so."

"You don't *think* so?"

"No, ma'am."

"Do you know what Carol Walker looks like?"

A pause.

"Do you know what Carol Walker looks like?"

"Well. Not really."

Another pause.
Nina looked around.
No Carol Walker.
She flipped open her cell phone and dialed a number.
Buzz.
Buzz.
"Sheriff's office."
"Give me Moon Rivard. And quick."

CHAPTER EIGHTEEN: THE JOYS OF CROSS COUNTRY SKIING

Swissssh.

Swissssh.

Snow had continued to fall through the day, and the trails were perfect. Loose but dry. It was quite cold—Beckmeier had no idea exactly how cold—but he knew that if he did not keep moving, keep working quite hard, he would begin to lose feeling in his extremities, despite the extra warm woolen socks over his ski boots, despite the thick gloves, despite the added layers of sweaters and scarves and whatever else he'd been able to wrap up in.

Swisssh.

Swisssh.

Left pole, right pole, alternate stride, alternate stride—the darkened forest slid by.

His darkened forest.

God he loved it here.

And he was not in bad shape.

Tomorrow, he'd have some of his men re-open the ski lift—a private lift he'd constructed for intimate parties of those close friends who did not care for the crowds that thronged each winter to Innsbruck and Salzburg—and he'd see how much rust his downhill abilities had accumulated over his period of absence.

He did not think there would be much rust.

He was still as active a man as ever.

Swissssh.

Swissssh.

Yes, by God, he was active.

He'd proven that last night with the opera singer.

She'd been impressed, both by the paintings—she had especially loved the three Correggios—and by his own performance.

Of course, this was the kind of life that international beauties deserved. They deserved to be supported by royalty. That was the way great European art had come into existence in the first place. The patronage system. Great books, great paintings—these were done at the behest of The Duke of Something or Other, or the Baron of Buxtehude, or...

...or the Graf von Beckmeier.

Damn the modern world.

Damn the bourgeoisie.

There, just to the right, twenty feet away, almost hidden in the dark pine boughs—a deer, probably a buck, its horns magnificent, its eyes shining like little points of starlight. The animal stood perfectly still, looked at him for an instant...

...just long enough to get a shot away, if that was his intent on this snowy evening...

....but it wasn't.

Perhaps tomorrow.

God, there was so much to do.

So many pleasures to resume.

And, as he thought these things, the buck disappeared, simply dissolving in a haze of snow and pine brush.

And he began his homeward trek again.

Swisssh.

Swisssh.

Yes, it certainly was quite cold.

He could see the faint haze of what would have been the full moon straight above him, would have been, had the clouds dissipated, would have been and almost certainly would be tomorrow night, for snow storms seldom lasted long in the southern Fischbachers in December.

January was another matter.

By January, the entire castle would be snowed in.

Narrow mountain roads almost impassable.

Trips to Graz or even Moorbach on the lake difficult at best.

So for the next week they would carry in stores of supplies and become a fortress.

As in the old days, when they were a fortress permanently.

He glimpsed an opening in the woods before him and knew that the trek was done. Good. He was tired. Not exhausted but tired. Tired enough so that he was perfectly prepared for the dinner that awaited him. First a glass of champagne in the library, with its massive windows letting him watch snow fall on the front lawn, letting him enjoy the statuary—the Diana and Achteon done in bronze by Klaus of Innsbruck.

Then the table itself, his dinner table, graced last night by one of the great Violettas of the modern stage, but quite empty tonight, save for himself and bottle of St. Emilion and a pheasant, shot this morning.

Swisssh.

Swissssh.

He swept out of the forest and glided effortlessly across the opening, drawn as if by a second source of gravity to the black RV that sat waiting, patiently as a hunting dog, as he skied up to it.

"Whew! Mein Gott!" he whispered to himself as he reached the vehicle. "Mein Gott ist es kalt!"

He stopped, put a hand against the fender of the vehicle, propped his ski poles securely, and caught his breath.

Even as he did so, he could feel his fingers begin to grow numb.

He needed to get inside the RV, get the engine going, get some warmth circulating.

He'd almost finished the job of taking off the skis and securing both them and the poles to the rack on the vehicle's roof when he heard the sound.

Rrrrrrrrr.

An engine.

There, in the distance, between him and the lake.

He opened the door, climbed inside, turned the key, and enjoyed the comfortable soft roaring of his own motor.

Then he turned on the heater, took off his gloves, and waited.

The sound grew louder.

Now he could see the vehicle's lights, hazed beneath a floating cloud of snow, moving slowing toward him.

It was another Landover, a vehicle from Eggenburg.

One of his own men.

He sat and watched it approach, sat and warmed himself as it stopped, sat and savored the meal to come and the champagne and the wine and the music he would play afterward on the sound system in the music room and Amontillado he would have on his night stand while drifting off to sleep even as this snow was drifting over his forest...

The door of the second vehicle opened and one of his men got out.

A hatchet-faced man, eyes barely visible behind the black toboggan that covered most of his face and neck.

The figure approached.

He pushed a button; the window opened.

"Mein Herr."

"Ja?"

"Es ist wohl Zeit."

It is time.

He felt his heartbeat quicken.

"Wie meinst du?"

What do you mean?

Although, deep within, he knew quite well what the man meant.

"Red Claw. His people are close by."

"Schon gut."

There was nothing else to say.

Eight o'clock at night in Austria meant one o'clock in the afternoon in Bay St. Lucy, where chaos reigned.

Sirens were going off everywhere as police cars raced toward and away from the city hospital as though they were taking part in a re-filming of The Keystone Cops.

Everyone was yelling at everyone else.

The primary care physician of Carol Walker was yelling at the nurse at the reception desk, who was yelling at the nurse in charge of the third floor, who was yelling at an orderly, who was also being yelled at—for some reason—by two other nurses, who were listening while Jackson Bennett, having just arrived, was yelling at Moon Rivard, who did not have time to respond, because he was yelling at the young officer he'd assigned to guard the hospital, who was simply repeating the words:

"Yes, sir."

And:

"No, sir."

And:

"I don't know, sir."

...over and over and over, so that he did not have time to yell at any body at all.

Nina was simply running in circles, her hands alternatively covering her face and balling themselves into fists that went up and down beside her like little pistons while she yelled at anybody who'd come close to her:

"What were you *thinking* about? Is this a hospital or a lunatic asylum? You can't simply *lose* people here, can you? What is this, a supermarket? Do you think somebody shoplifted her out of here like she was can of asparagus?"

"Ms. Bannister..."

A good many people—Moon, the doctor, the head nurse, the assistant head nurse, Jackson—were calling her this, trying to calm her down, but it did no good, of course.

She was near tears.

This could not be happening.

And it all swept over her: the explosion, the tale of what had happened to Carol, the vision of what had almost happened to Carol...

After a while, she found herself simply sitting on a chair in the main hospital waiting room, a copy of *People* magazine sitting opened on the gray chair beside her.

She cried like a baby, tears falling on the bare abdomen of Celine Dionne.

This went on for a time.

Finally, through a window that opened out onto the hospital parking lot, she spied Jackson Bennett and Moon Rivard standing beside a squad car shouting at each other.

The only way she had to stop crying, she realized, was to start shouting herself, and so she rose, tore the picture of Celine Dionne out of the magazine, crumpled it up, hurled it viciously into a wastebasket, and left the building.

Moon, when she reached his squad car, had stopped yelling at Jackson Bennett for a moment, and was yelling into the two-way radio:

"I don't care. No, I don't care; I want you to find that girl! No, put everybody on it. Get hold of Hattiesburg! Yes it's a Code Four; that's what I'm trying to tell you! No. No! We don't know anything, don't you understand that? Of course, she could be in a car! She could be in a damned pick-up truck for all we know! The only thing we *do* know is that she's not in the damned hospital."

Jackson, spying Nina, hugged her—it seemed like she was being hugged frequently by Jackson these days—and whispered:

"I'm so sorry! I'm so sorry!"

She shook her head:

"How could this have happened?"

"I don't know. Nobody knows."

"It's not like she was getting her tonsils out, Jackson!"

"I know."

"Somebody's trying to kill her! We put her in the hospital so she could be *observed*. *Observed*. Doesn't anybody know what that means?"

"Nina, I can't tell you how…"

"It means *watched*! *Watched!* And so what does Moon do? He puts Dobie Gillis at the door of the hospital and then goes fishing!"

"He wasn't fishing, Nina."

"Well, he just as well could have been fishing!"

"I know. I know. I'm as furious as you are…"

"No, you're not! If you were, somebody would be dead! *Damn!* Why do I have to be so little? I can't break anybody's head; I can't beat anybody up—I can't even break anything!

But look at you! You're huge, you're tough! Why aren't you *hitting* somebody!"

"Nina, if I…"

"What did football *teach* you, anyway, if not how to *hit* people!"

"All I know is, Moon and his people are doing everything they…"

"I want to go home."

Jackson stared at her for a moment, then said:

"I don't know if you should do that."

"Well, I'm going to damn well do it! Try and stop me!"

"Your home is a crime scene, Nina. The people from the lab are there, and it can't be cleaned until they finish their job."

"Then get them the hell away. It's my home! I live there, and I want to go home!"

Moon Rivard had gotten off the intercom. He stepped forward and asked:

"What did you say, Ms. Bannister?"

"I said I want to go home!"

"I'm not sure we can let you do that."

"So who are you, dad?"

"No, ma'am, but…"

Jackson intervened:

"Moon, are the lab people still there?"

He shook his head.

"No. They finished up about six this morning. But we don't know if it's safe for…"

Nina, furious now, shouted:

"Safe! Safe! Yeah, that's right isn't it! The Moon Rivard safety team! If anybody knows about safety, it's you guys!"

He blushed.

She calmed down a bit.

When she was able, she said, quietly:

"I'm sorry I said that."

Both men had their heads hung.

"I had no right to say that. It's just…well, listen:"

She took a deep breath.

"I've been thinking about this. We all heard Carol last night. She was confused, delusional."

"Yes, Ms. Bannister. That's why…"

"Just give me a minute, Moon."

Silence

She continued:

"She was saying all this insane 'international smuggler' nonsense. As though Carol could ever be an international smuggler. She's a farm girl from Georgia, for God's sakes. She was completely off her head. Now it's just possible that after Dobie—who was probably trying to find Maynard—let her walk out under his very nose, she went, I don't know, down to the beach or something. She could just be wandering around."

"We'll keep looking for her," said Moon, "but in the meantime, Alanna has offered you a room at the Auberge until your place is cleaned up."

Nina thought for a moment. "What about Furl?"

"I'll instruct my officers to keep an eye out for him. If they find him, we'll bring him to you at the Auberge."

And with that assurance, Nina agreed to be a temporary guest at the Auberge des Arts guest residence.

While at precisely the same time, two Land rovers were making their way slowly, single file, over the narrow snow-covered road that led to Eggenburg Palace.

The great pale yellow building, floodlit and shimmering through a haze of slow-falling snow, seemed to encircle them as they made their way around the gravel driveway.

The main façade was two-hundred feet long.

At intervals of every twenty feet, stood an armed guard.

These men all seemed the same height.

They seemed, in fact, identical in every way.

They were Franz Beckmeier's private army.

Just as there were urban gangs in cities such as Chicago and New York, so were there private armies in parts of Europe.

This, its members outfitted in black uniforms and carrying automatic machine guns, was such an army.

Beckmeier surveyed it as he stood down from his vehicle.

The hawk-nosed man from the second vehicle walked to his side.

Beckmeier turned and looked at him, then asked:

"So, where is this army of the Red Claw now, at this moment?"

No answer.

The snow could be heard hissing through pine boughs in the surrounding forests.

Beckmeier reached into the vehicle, picked up a bullhorn that lay on the floor in front of the passenger seat, turned it on, put it to his lips, and spoke into it:

"Na, Manner…"

All right, men.

"Jetzt ist so weit."

Untranslatable.

The closest thing?

The time is at hand.

"Kommt denn nah."

Come close.

"Ich will euch ganz klar sagen, welcher Kamp vor uns liegt."

I want to tell you as clearly as possible, about the battle that lies before us.

As though he knew.

But he did know.

He knew his men were well trained.

And he knew they were experienced fighters.

They would prevail.

"So," he repeated, "kommt euch her!"

Come here.

He watched them.

They remained precisely where they were.

His heart began to pound erratically.

Then he looked at the hawk-nosed man next to him.

The man was holding a machine gun trained upon him.

And suddenly, he knew where the Red Claw's army was.

CHAPTER NINETEEN: SEE THE REAL PAINTING

Nina was relieved to leave the hospital, and sank thankfully into an overstuffed armchair in the Auberge study. She heard a crinkle and remembered about the note she'd crammed into her pocket.

She took it out, glanced at it, and read:

"Dear Nina…"

My God.

This was from Carol.

She read:

"I'm so sorry for what has happened. It's all my fault. I just want you to know that I love you very much, and I love Bay St. Lucy, and I'm sorry for the violence I've brought to your little town."

"It's over now, though. I've gone somewhere else. Please don't try to find me for a while. I'm sorry, but that's all I can say now. The police may want to ask me more questions. I'll try to help as much as possible."

"The main thing is, and I want you to believe this: you are all safe."

"There will be no more bombs."

"There will be no more guns."

"Again, I love you all,"

"Carol"

She was crying by the time she finished the letter.

She was still crying as she walked out of the study and into the garden.

She thought about the letter. None of this made any sense.

That Carol had been able to leave the hospital unseen was insane enough—but this letter?

How was any of this conceivably the fault of Carol Walker?

Carol was a college teacher and a museum docent.

How had Carol been responsible for that?

And where was Carol now?

She could not have gone far.

Georgia. Clearly she was going home.

So, what was she—Nina—to do?

Take the letter to Moon Rivard, and to Jackson Bennett.

There must be a way to find Carol's parents. East of Atlanta, north of Athens. In a small town. A farm family named Walker.

There had to be some record.

So thinking, she walked back into the study, resolving to call either Moon or Jackson—she was not entirely sure whom.

She glanced out beyond the sliding glass door.

There, sitting on a bench in the garden, where she'd just walked, was a man.

She caught her breath.

For a time, he simply stared at her.

She was frozen, her hand paralyzed on the phone.

He rose, took a step toward the closed glass door....

...and smiled.

Then she recognized who he was.

Five minutes later, the two of them were sitting at the table in the Auberge parlor.

"I hope you don't mind the intrusion. You were easy to find; I just asked at the hospital."

"This is not making any sense to me," she was saying.

He was the same man who'd come to Elementals a few weeks earlier.

Michael.

The man who'd been close once to Carol.

Who'd even wanted to marry her.

Who had come to Bay St. Lucy in order to attempt to persuade her to go back with him to Chicago.

"I'm genuinely sorry," he was saying. "I've caused you both a great deal of pain."

"That's just what Carol said in her letter."

"What letter?"

Nina took it out of her pocket and handed it to him.

He read it and smiled.

"Yes. This sounds like her."

"Michael, has she gone back home?"

"I think I should say 'yes' to that. Then you will not worry."

"What you should do is tell me the damned truth. I think we've all earned that. We may be small town rubes..."

"You're not rubes. Not any of you."

"Ok, we're not. But whatever we are, we deserve the truth."

He nodded his head, slowly:

"All right. But you may find some of this hard to believe."

"As opposed to last night and this morning? Which are easy to believe?"

There was just the smallest hint of a smile. Then he continued:

"What do you know about international art smuggling?"

Nina stared at him for a time, then said:

"Last night. Carol had just been forced to—well, to do that awful thing. We went to see her in the hospital room. She seemed out of her head. She kept talking nonsense about being a smuggler..."

"It wasn't nonsense."

"What?"

"It wasn't nonsense. It was the truth."

"Are you insane?"

A shake of the head:

"No, I'm a criminal. And so is Carol."

"That's impossible!"

"Smuggling, my dear Ms. Bannister, is not impossible."

"Smuggling drugs, yes, but..."

"Drugs are cheap, compared to paintings."

"But, but—what paintings?"

"In the last month? Van Gogh's *Poppy Flowers*. Said to be worth fifty million dollars. *View of the Sea at Schweiningen*. Also a Van Gogh. Priceless. *The View of*

Auverse sur Oise, Paul Cezanne, not signed by the artist, who felt it unfinished. Seventy million dollars. *Nativity with St. Francis and St. Lawrence*. Caravaggio. Priceless, as are all Caraveggios."

"But how—why…"

"When I first hired Carol, in the early fall, I merely wanted her to take paintings from Chicago through the Frankfurt Airport and into Austria. She was to leave them in a hotel in Graz. There the representatives of a—let's call him a 'private collector'—would pick them up. For each painting she delivered, she was to be paid twenty thousand dollars."

"My God. But the story about your relationship beforehand…"

"Was a complete lie. A complete and utter lie. When I first saw her, she was doing her presentations at The Chicago Art Museum. I felt that she would be perfect for my purposes. She knew her way around paintings, and around Europe. She was plain. Unassuming. And, I instinctively felt, completely honest. I found out all I could about her. No alcohol use to speak of. No boyfriends. No drug habit that had to be supported. She was perfect."

"So the trips she made in the early fall, after she came to live here…"

"Were made for me."

"But how did that lead to…"

"How did it lead to yesterday? It led there because things are simply never perfect. All of the paintings we were delivering to the collector I spoke of were at an earlier point in time stolen by the Nazis."

"From whom?"

"From a group of wealthy Jewish families named 'Reklaw' who lived in the Caucasian Mountains of Russia. One of the descendants of these families, a character called 'Lorca Reklaw,' has apparently gone on a mad binge to get the paintings back. He heads an organization—we are not certain how large it is—that calls itself the Red Claw."

"After the family name 'Reklaw.'"

"Precisely. At any rate, as this organization somehow became richer and more sophisticated, it began to be, almost impossibly, aware of every move I made. My operatives were taken at various airports around the world."

"Taken?"

"Yes."

"Were they murdered?"

"We don't know that. It's still an open question. All I—and my employer—knew was that they simply disappeared. We thought they were to be sold back, for a huge ransom. We simply didn't know."

"You know now?"

"Let me continue: at any rate, once it became too dangerous to go through airports, we needed a new—well, a new method."

"Which was?"

"We used you, Ms. Bannister."

You used…

And finally, Nina began to see.

"The paintings I sold…"

"Covered the masterpieces I told you about."

"Oh, my God."

"I'm sorry. It was cruel to use you in this way. But neither I nor Carol ever thought Reklaw would find out what was happening."

"And the people who paid $350 each for Old Red Mill and Old Red Barn…"

"…were actually taking away from Bay St. Lucy some of the most valuable masterpieces in the world."

She could only sit for a time.

Finally she said, quietly:

"My viscous luminosity…"

Again, the figure across the table from her shook his head.

"As I say, I'm sorry."

Silence.

The screeching of peacocks on the grounds interrupted the silence…

"And so, Carol, now…"

Michael pursed his lips, then said:

"This is going to be very difficult for you, Ms. Bannister."

She looked at him:

"What? Is Carol…"

He shook his head:

"I received a phone call a short time ago."

"Is she dead?"

"No. But the caller claimed to be a representative of Lorca Reklaw. He said that Carol was now en route to Austria."

"Oh no…"

"He said that I would very soon be in the same situation. That, within days, all of the thieves would be brought together at the castle. That the castle would be burned, just as the Jewish ghettos were burned during the war. The thieves would be made to watch the burning, just as the Jews were forced to watch the destruction of their homes and property. That after watching this, the thieves would be loaded into trucks, taken away, and…dealt with."

"This is unthinkable. Inhuman."

A shrug.

"I suppose those adjectives could be made to apply to a great deal that was done in the twentieth century."

"So…what are you going to do now?"

Another shrug.

"I could go into hiding."

"Do you think that would work?"

"No. If Reklaw's people could find Carol in Bay St. Lucy, then they could find me."

"So what will you do?"

He stood up, walked to the railing of the deck, and looked out over the water. Then he said, as much to the gray incoming tide as to Nina:

"I'm going after her."

She stood, too, and joined him at the deck.

"You're what?"

Again, the hint of a smile.

"I'm going after her."

"What does that mean?"

"It means I'm still in possession of several priceless paintings. They are well hidden. Even Red Claw does not know their location, of that I'm certain. So, I intend simply to go to Eggenburg…"

"To what?"

"Schloss Eggenburg, the estate of Franz Beckmeier, the 'collector' I've been telling you about. I believe that by tomorrow, the palace will have been overrun by Red Claw's men. I'm going to go there. And I'm simply going to beg for her life."

"You think he will listen to you?"

"No. But she's not like me, nor my other operatives. They were people of the world. Callous people, who, as myself, felt above the law. Carol is a simple girl. She has an elderly father waiting for her on a farm in rural Georgia. Maybe, by offering to give up the paintings, tell where they are—maybe that and…well 'turning myself in' as it were…maybe I can persuade the man to show some mercy."

"How are you going?"

"I have flights arranged. This is an easy thing to do for someone in my business. I'll leave this evening from New Orleans and be in Austria tomorrow. Perhaps it will be in time."

"I see."

Nina turned, went back to the table, and sat down.

"I'm going with you," she said, quietly.

He stared at her.

"That's stupid."

It was her turn to shrug:

"Thinking that I had 'viscous luminosity' is stupid. Going to get Carol is not."

He continued to stare, incredulously.

Finally, he took a step toward her and said:

"And when the horrible Red Claw, the Jewish Revenge, the man who's supposed to be seven feet tall and have a true claw instead of a hand—when this man looks at you and says: 'Why should I let you go?' What are you going to say?"

"I'm going to say that I don't much care if he lets me go. I've had a good life, and it's coming to an end anyway—and that maybe it's time now to be with Frank."

Michael sat down.

Then he asked, quietly:

"And when this creature asks, 'Why should I let the young girl Carol Walker go, what are you going to say then?'"

Nina merely looked at him:

"I'm going to say: 'because I'm begging you to—and I'm her mother.'"

An hour later, Nina found herself in front of Jackson Bennett's law office, listening to the buzz on the door lock that told her that her approach had been noted.

Jackson, she knew, had been sitting by the window, watching for her.

She pushed the door open and stepped into the narrow stairwell.

He appeared at the top of the steps, gesturing for to come up:

His voice rattled the walls.

"We still don't know anything! I'm in contact with Moon all the time—he's gotten permission to use some extra people from the force in Hattiesburg. Cops are all over the county, trying to get some leads."

She walked on up, saying nothing.

"Nina, everybody in town is stunned that this thing could have happened. The hospital especially. They were all so worried that some killer might get in, they didn't think to worry about Carol getting out."

They entered the office.

It did what it always did: gave her a sense of melancholy, because she could visualize Frank sitting behind the desk.

But it also reassured her.

It was a kind of legal womb.

When she'd been here, with Frank, she'd always known things would be ok.

But now?

Despite Jackson's massive, comforting presence, were things going to be ok?

What kind of insane thing was she planning to do?

"I'm going to put another call in to Moon now. Maybe we can…"

"Jackson, wait."

She took the letter out of her purse and handed it to him.

"What's this?"

"A letter from Carol."

"From Carol? How the hell is that possible?"

"I don't know. It was on the table by the bed in the hospital. You need to read it."

He did, quickly.

Then he looked up:

"This is crazy."

"I know."

"You believe she really wrote this?"

"Yes. I recognize her handwriting. She's written several things to me over the last weeks—notes, memos, things that she's done at Elementals while I wasn't there, or errands that needed to be done. No, she wrote this all right."

"But—where is she?"

"I don't know."

This was a lie, of course.

But in another way, it was the truth, too. She did not know where Carol was at the moment.

She only knew where Carol was going.

And where she herself was going.

"Nina, what is this woman thinking?"

"I don't know that, either."

Jackson leaned forward on the desk:

"She just shot someone! It was clearly in self-defense, but still…she can't just walk out of town and disappear."

"That's just what she's done."

"How? She has no car!"

"Maybe she took a bus. Maybe she's hitchhiking. I just don't know."

"And you have no idea where she's headed?"

Nina shrugged.

"She could be going home."

"And where is that?"

"Georgia. She grew up on a farm north of Athens. Maybe she's gone back there."

"Where exactly is this farm? What town is it near, exactly?"

"I don't know, Jackson. I just don't know."

"Great. So all we have to do is find all the people in Georgia named 'Walker,' and ask them if their daughter is home, because she has to testify in a shooting."

"Yes, that's all we have to do. That and search Chicago, because for all we know she may have headed there."

"Oh, for God's sake…"

Now it was Nina's turn to learn forward, saying as she did so:

"Jackson, I know you have to go on looking for Carol."

"Of course, we have to go on looking for her! Somebody tried to kill her! Whoever it was, may try again. For that matter, somebody tried to kill you, tried to blow up Elementals! I still don't like it one bit that you even went back to your place! For all we know…"

"All you know, Jackson, is not very much."

And for a time, the room was silent.

Jackson sat back in his chair.

Finally he said softly, his voice rumbling like a throaty volcano:

"And you know more?"

She shook her head:

"I know little Carol is a woman of the world. She doesn't say a lot. And she's not too impressive to look at, not too formidable. But she's not dumb."

Jackson placed his palms down on the desk and stared at them for a time.

Then he looked up and said:

"That description could fit another woman I know."

Nina merely nodded.

"Yes. Maybe."

Another pause, then:

"Nina, what the hell is going on?"

To which Nina replied:

"Jackson, I may have to go away for a few days."

His eyes narrowed:

"Go away?"

"Yes."

"To where?"

"I'd rather not say."

"Why not?"

She stood up, walked to the window, and looked out over downtown Bay St. Lucy. She whispered into the window glass:

"You have to trust me on this."

"You know where Carol is, don't you?"

"Not at this time."

"Listen, Nina, for God's sakes…"

Then she returned to her chair, sat, and looked at Jackson.

"I think I'll be back in a few days."

"You think we're going to let you go flying off…"

"You don't," she interrupted, "have any choice."

"The hell we don't! I don't know what you've gotten yourself caught up in, but…"

"You don't have any choice. Now. If you want to arrest me, do it."

"If we have to arrest you, then…"

"Then I'll get out of jail immediately. Because I haven't done anything. And you know it."

"All right. Then I'll have Moon arrest you as a material witness."

"To what?"

"To…to…"

She smiled.

"You forget. I'm a lawyer's wife. I'm no more a 'material witness' to anything than Furl is. Besides, that whole phrase only has meaning on Perry Mason shows."

He could not help smiling.

"But that reminds me, Jackson. I don't know, exactly, how long I'll be gone. If you would take care of Furl…"

He nodded.

"You know I will."

"During the Aquatica mess you even took him over to your place for a while."

"Sure. The girls love him."

"And if—well, I don't get back soon…"

"Nina, what the hell are you talking about? Where are you going?"

She forced herself to smile.

"I'm going on a trip, Jackson. Frank and I never had the time to take one. And Carol and I have been planning one for the entire fall. Ever since she came here to stay with me. Well, now I'm going."

He looked at her for a time, then said:

"You're going to try to do something dangerous. And you're going to try to do it alone."

She shook her head, as she stood up:

"I'll never be alone, Jackson. Whatever happens to me— and I'll be honest with you, I'm not sure what that will be— I'm a part of Bay St. Lucy, and Bay St. Lucy is a part of me. Just—just take good care of Furl, and say good bye to everybody for a while. Tell them I'll write."

"Nina, don't…"

"And by the way, be sure to tell Moon's deputy I'm sorry for calling the young man Dobie Gillis."

Jackson stood up:

"I wouldn't worry about that."

"Why not?"

"I overheard him talking to Moon just after you'd left."

"Was he upset?"

"No. He didn't know who Dobie Gillis was."

"Good bye, Jackson. And thanks for everything. Always."

And so saying, she turned and went down the stairs.

END OF PART THREE

CHAPTER TWENTY: GOING TRAVELLING!

The Hotel Erzherzog Johann—or Archduke John—is the oldest in Graz. Named for the city's favorite Habsburg (because he was born in, and loved the Styrian state in which the city was located), it sits just on the eastern side of Hauptplatz, or main square. During summer months, the windows of its café open out onto the sidewalk, so that one can reach out, tap passers by on the arm, and sing out a morning's greeting.

Winters are more somber, of course, but the hotel is still not without its charm.

There's an inner atrium, the table and sofas flower-bedecked, around which, a wrought-iron grillwork bannister corkscrews its way up seven stories, at the top of which, a guests finds it possible to lean over and peer down sixty feet upon the bald heads or cleavages of card players or conversationalists in the lobby below.

It was in this lobby that Michael Gellert was seated, a 'kleiner Swarzen' (little black one) swirling and steaming in its demitasse before him, when the dwarf arrived.

There was nothing else to call him. He was no more than four feet tall, walked in a crooked way, and smiled upward with eyes that twinkled black like coal particles.

"Not the best place," said Gellert, "to meet."

The figure pulled out a chair and sat down, gesturing for the waitress to come.

"It does not matter now," he said. "There are no secrets anymore."

The waitress appeared.

"I shall have what my friend here is having."

"Kleiner Scwarzen?"

"Ja."

She disappeared.

The two sat in silence for a time, as people came and went around them, and an occasional maid appeared going in or coming out of the rooms above.

It was one in the afternoon.

The hotel was only half full.

The rooms needed to be ready by two, though, and this caused a bit of last minute bustle.

"So. What is the situation?"

A shrug:

"The situation is lost."

"How can that be? Beckmeier had at least twenty good men. Paramilitary. Well trained. How many more could Red Claw have had?"

"He had no more. He had precisely twenty. The same twenty Beckmeier thought that he himself had."

Gellert thought for a time, then nodded, and said, quietly:

"Red Claw bought them off."

"Jawohl, mein Herr. That he did."

"How much did he…"

"Twenty thousand dollars apiece. With more, probably to come. My sources tell me much more."

"How is this man, this 'claw,' getting his financing?"

"Keine Ahnung."

No idea.

The second cup of coffee came.

"Danke."

"Bitte schon."

The small man, who was dressed in a Styrian gray-green hunting suit that seemed to have been tailored for a child, sipped, winced at the burn, then sipped again.

"Where," asked Gellert, "are my smuggling operatives?"

"Again, I have only a few sources still reporting to me. Many have left Styria. Or Austria."

"I understand."

"But one of them I do trust. The man tells me that these people you employed have been kept, let us say 'under wraps' in various estates, all of whose owners are loyal to Red Claw. They are now being brought to Eggenburg, even as we speak."

"And when they arrive, Red Claw will burn the palace down. For them all to see. And for Beckmeier to see."

"You are well informed."

"I have my sources, too. Before the great conflagration, I assume all of the paintings in Eggenburg will be loaded in trucks and taken away."

"Almost certainly."

"How many paintings?"

"Fifty three."

"My God. Beckmeier was quite a collector."

"Or quite a thief."

"Many would say they are one in the same," said Gellert, quietly.

"Possibly."

"So, all right. Red Claw wants his paintings back. What does he plan to do with my people?"

"No one knows. But the story seems to be that he's recreating what the Holocaust must have been like. The Jews were forced by the Nazis to watch their ghettos burn—then they were herded like animals into trains or vans, and then…"

"Yes. I know what 'then' means. Beckmeier was no Nazi, though. Nor were my people."

The small man shook his head:

"Beckmeier was no Nazi. But his father was."

"Beckmeier's father fought with the Nazis?"

"Beckmeier's father owned factories that supplied weapons to the Nazis. No Hapbsburg actually goes to war in this century, or the last. Once the cavalry was eliminated, so was all military honor and glory, at least in the eyes of old aristocrats. Crawling around in the mud, machine gun fire—no, better simply to get rich and let the poor people die."

"And Beckmeier's father did get rich?"

"The family fortune quadrupled."

"And now is payback time. But this still does not explain why this monster wants to send my operatives to gas ovens."

"I did not say he did. I have no idea what he plans to do with them. But I do know that *your* plans, if I have understood them correctly, are completely insane."

Gellert merely shrugged and said:

"That is my business. The question remains: can you get me to Eggenburg tonight?"

"If you go to Eggenburg, you will be taken like all of the others. Whatever happens to them will happen to you."

"Perhaps."

"Not 'perhaps.' Certainly."

"Then it will be a kind of adventure."

"Your last adventure, Gellert. Certainly your last one. How can you possibly think of surviving, of getting out of there, even if you do get in?"

"Paintings."

"Which paintings?"

"I have several still in my possession. I'm certain that Red Claw wants them. Perhaps we can bargain."

"Or perhaps Red Claw will prove to be a man of medieval spirit. And he will simply put you on the rack. Then you will divulge the location of these masterpieces. And that will be the end of you."

"That might also happen."

"But Gellert—all right, you have the paintings! Disappear, for God's sakes!"

Michael Gellert shook his head:

"The man is too smart. I don't know how he derives his intelligence—but derive it, he does. I'd never feel safe. He'd find me somehow. And the paintings. No. I want there to be an end of it, one way or another. And besides, there's someone who should not be at Eggenburg now, someone…"

He paused, then shook his head:

"Does not matter. The bottom line is, I shall go there tonight and beg. Now. Can you get me out there?"

"It's a difficult thing. Besides the twenty armed men, there are others to deal with. You must know that Eggenburg Palace lies some kilometers to the south of Lake Moorbach, above which sits the small village of Altdorf."

"All right. Go on."

"For tonight, all ways into Eggenburg are closed off. Red Claw wants no chance witnesses to what he's going to do. There are several places along the lake where boats can land.

But they're all being watched. Watched carefully. If you're found attempting to cross Moorbach, by any of the villagers who've been paid off by Red Claw—why, then you will not be escorted into Eggenburg to plead with Reklaw. You'll be shot, and your body will be thrown into the lake. Punkt. Schluss. Fertig."

"So how can I…"

"As I say, I'm not without a few contacts. One of them— one of the paramilitary—still remains loyal to me. At least, I believe he does. Now. You have money?"

"Yes."

"Let me see it."

Gellert opened a portfolio which sat on the floor beside him.

He shoved it across the table.

The man sitting opposite him opened it, examined the contents, then said quietly:

"That is satisfactory. All right. Here's how it will work. If it will work at all."

"Go on."

"There's only one village tavern in Altdorf. Drive down into the village; you'll see it. Go there. Try to arrive in the early evening."

"All right."

"Wait for a call. If no call comes, then go home, the thing has failed."

"But if it does come…"

"Then you go up the hill to the cathedral which overlooks both Altdorf and Lake Moorbach. The cathedral houses an ossuary, a charnel house."

"A boneyard."

"If one wishes to be crass about the thing."

"Bones are bones."

"At any rate, the cathedral is never locked. Most village sanctuaries such as this remain open, for villagers who want to go in at midnight or later to pray. If one is old, and one is in Altdorf, there's nothing more to be done."

"I understand."

"From the cathedral, you can enter the charnel house. In the charnel house, you enter a tunnel. This tunnel leads down to the lake."

"Why in God's name would anyone have built such a tunnel?"

"It goes back hundreds of years, as does the cathedral itself. It was meant as an escape tunnel, to be used by the villagers when the place was besieged by whatever local warlord thought he'd achieved enough power to thumb his nose at the Hapsburgs."

"We take the tunnel down…"

"It leads to a landing which cannot be seen. It was built that way. You will at least be able to get on the boat. Maybe snow clouds will cover the moon. The boat will be small. You may remain unseen."

"And one on the other side?"

"My man will pick you up and drive you the three kilometers to Eggenburg. Where you will almost certainly be killed."

"That is my problem."

"It most certainly is. At any rate, you should stay here in the hotel for the afternoon. You have a room?"

"Yes."

"Stay in it until five. There will be a rental car waiting for you, parked on the sidewalk outside on the Sackstrasse. You know the way to Altdorf?"

"I'll find out. I can read a map."

"Then do so. The car will be locked, but the key will have been left at the front desk."

So saying, the man sitting across from Gellert rose, turned, turned back, said:

"You are insane."

And then left.

Gellert stayed where he was for another half hour.

Then he climbed the spiral staircase which led to his room on the fifth floor.

He slipped the key into the lock and opened the door.

The room had been freshly made up, the down comforter lying two feet thick on the bed beneath as if it were a hibernating polar bear.

He threw himself on it, made his mind be blank, set a mental alarm clock for five o'clock, and immediately went to sleep.

The mental alarm clock did not go off.
It did not have time.
He was awakened, instead, by a knocking.
He was groggy for a time.
Then he rose, crossed the room, and opened the door.
Nina Bannister stood before him.
"I'm insane," she said, "but I'm here."
"Well, there's a lot of insanity going around."
"What do we do now?"
He shrugged.
"We go see the Red Claw."
And they left the room together.

Michael negotiated the narrow banks of the parking lot concrete with more ease than she'd expected, and within minutes, Nina found herself watching the Mur River and its traffic of coal barges more closely than the traffic lights and turn signals that she'd expected to worry about.

They passed the city administrative buildings, then paralleled the Number Eight streetcar tracks which skirted the train station.

The traffic began to lessen. Villas began to dot the lush hills mounding around them, and wisps of fog hovered over the forest as the sun began to set.

"All right. This is how I read the map. We turn in two miles. Turn left, to the west. The road is 465. We follow the arrows. We go to Althofen. In the town is an ossuary. Just beside it is a tavern. Go there. Sit outside and wait."

The world was darkening, as the sun had dropped below the range of mountains to their left.

No snow was falling now, but limbs in the surrounding forests were white,

At approximately quarter mile intervals, there were street lamps along the side of the country road. These lamps were beginning to turn themselves on, and could be seen shimmering a translucent blue.

"How was your flight?" Michael asked.

"Ten hours in first class, direct from New Orleans to Graz. Thanks for the ticket."

"My pleasure."

"What airline was it? The plane wasn't marked."

"Not all planes," he said, "belong to airlines. How was the food and drink?"

"I'm sure it was wonderful. They served lobster and champagne."

"It was good?"

She shook her head.

"I'm a little off my feed right now."

"I'm sorry. A little…"

"Off my feed. It's how your digestion gets to be when you're about to be murdered."

"I see. I did warn you not to come."

"I know."

"How did you explain Carol's disappearance to the authorities in Bay St. Lucy?"

"I told them to forget it, and that it wasn't any of their business. Which is what I told them about my trip."

"And they accepted this?"

"I'm a school teacher. They do what I tell them."

"I see. But, Ms. Bannister, I still must insist that you…"

"Nina. I want to be on a first name basis with people I get killed with."

"All right. Nina. I still must insist that you…"

They drove on, as the world darkened around them.

What a strange thing, Nina found herself thinking. *The great trip she'd never taken with Frank, and that she had planned so eagerly with Carol.*

It was merely a dark, frightening and somber thing.

She was too exhausted to be frightened.

Why was she here?

This was not her business.

And yet, of course, it was her business.

Carol was her business.

She could not sit idly in Bay St. Lucy, and walk along the coast.

Which she had done with Carol.

And putter about in Elementals.

Which she had done with Carol.

And plan a wonderful trip to Austria.

Which she had done with Carol.

And so…

…and so, she was taking a terrible trip to Austria, a dark and horrifying trip to Austria.

But it was the only thing she could do.

At seven o'clock, they entered Althofen.

The village proved to be the postcard that does not quite exist in real life, except that it did exist, below a massive gray castle-fortress, and abutting a lake that was a black sheet of water set in snow white hills.

She could see Michael braking as the road leading down into the village became steeper.

Beside them on the right, just outside the village limits, were farmhouses. These were half-timbered structures, also half barn, in which the open haylofts gave out onto courtyards where chickens squawked and panicked their way between and around troughs of water, and massive mounds of decaying compost.

The village itself was perfectly white—partially this came from the fact that it was snow-covered, but it was white in any season, from the whitewashed walls of stucco cottages, to the white and gleaming needle-towered cathedral overlooking them as the Opel crawled over a cobblestoned main street.

The shops themselves were closed now, but the windows had, of course, just been washed, and whatever was inside looked as though it were sitting outside. She felt she could reach in and touch bicycles arranged as though they were beginning a race that would lead from the interior of the shop out into the main square itself; or ready-to-broil chickens hanging despondently, like victims of war, interspersed with hams and massive sausage cylinders, all reaching to within a foot or so of equally massive barrels of cheese.

They'd descended halfway down to the lake when they saw the tavern on the right side of the road.

Michael parked the car.

The building they walked into was tripartite.

Stretching before them was the garden, a few tables laid out beneath the carnival lights, their checkered tablecloths dotted with twigs and smaller leaves that had fallen from the massive oak overshadowing them.

Directly across from them was the interior of the tavern. They could see a bar, a few stool, two haggard women in black dresses and aprons, and ornate turn-of-the-century mirrors that invariably stood behind such bars, so that people could enjoy watching themselves get drunk.

Other than the two women and a bartender, no one was in the bar area.

Nor for that matter was anyone seated in the garden.

That was for summer.

Directly to their left though was another building, almost an addendum to the bar area itself. This was a plain structure, and might have been taken for a garage, had cars been parked inside it instead of people.

It was packed.

People squeezed themselves through the single entry, hung out of windows, pushed, prodded, and alternatively shouted and shut completely up, so that whatever event was happening in there provided alternatively the most intense moments of a tent show revival and a presidential funeral.

People had packed into this small house in order to die and go to heaven, or to reverse the process, except more often, and with more animation about them, than is generally the case.

"What are they doing over there?" asked Nina.

"Soccer. In a village like this, everybody comes to the tavern at night to watch soccer."

One of the women came out of the bar carrying, balanced on one palm, a brown plastic platter with six steins of beer on it.

She skirted the two of them, then walked into the TV building, then returned.

There were cheers from time to time.

Finally, she came over to the table where they were seated.

"Was darf es sein?"

What will it be?

"Zwei Pils."

"Jawohl."

She left.

"What did you order?"

"Two beers."

"I don't think I can…"

He shook his head.

"You don't have to drink it. Just let it sit there. We had to order something."

"Ok. So. What happens now?"

"We wait for a call. If everything works out all right, there will be a boat."

Silence for a time.

A few cheers.

The clink of beer steins from the adjoining room.

An hour later, the call came.

Michael Gellert clicked open his cell phone, listened for a few seconds, then shut it.

He looked across the table at Nina.

"Let us go," he said, "and meet our Mr. Red Claw."

The chandelier resembled a helicopter made of crystal and diamond. It must have been, thought Carol, ten feet high and at least as massive in diameter.

What was the rope doing…

"Oh my," she whispered, almost to herself.

She'd never seen such a thing.

For the rope, taut now, led to a pulley on the ceiling, the entire apparatus designed to haul the magnificent sparkling and flickering monstrosity upward, where it would reign over the great dining hall, the heat of a thousand candles wafting through huge open windows which looked out over the lawns and showcased the peacocks.

There was, in this room, obviously no electricity.

So that the innumerable white candles that fitted into the gold holders sprinkled like bits of icing around the birthday cake of a chandelier, had to be lit, one by one, by the young men and women who were now busily engaged in doing so, forming a kind of candle-bucket brigade, taking a candle out of the box lying on the floor, passing it, watching it be lighted, and then repeating the action until the room grew lighter, as the smoke from the smoldering wicks eddied and swirled more densely beneath a baroque hunting scene painted upon the ceiling, and the pulleys began to squeak and groan more threateningly as the chandelier prepared, like a hot air balloon, to rise.

"Also," said Franz Beckmeier, who had seated himself at the head of the table. "Beginnen wir."

Several leafs had been added to the table in order to make room for the prisoners who were now preparing to eat off it.

Carol could remember each one of them, as well as the paintings each had brought or taken away.

There, sitting beside Beckmeier: the woman in the zebra striped pants. She'd taken the St. Sebastian. And there, at the other end of the table, the innocuous man who'd climbed Nina Bannister's staircase with an equally innocuous thing wrapped in brown paper.

A van Gogh.

They were all seated here, looking at each other.

Frightened to death.

Beckmeier, either too old to be frightened or too angry, went on about his business of being the head of the estate.

All around them, men in paramilitary uniforms were carefully taking paintings off the dining room walls, then stacking them carefully in separate piles on the grounds, which could be seen from tall windows.

Beckmeier's ex-guards, bribed, and now in the service of

...

…the Red Claw.

What a name for an organization, she found herself thinking.

Food was being put before them.

A gourmet meal, fit for an Austrian king.

Which Beckmeier obviously thought he was.

A gourmet meal:

Dishes in highly polished silver platters, the subtle clicking of silverware mixing with a continual gurgle of white wine being poured, and the host's unending commentary describing the various dishes as they were placed around the table.

"As for the roast beef you see there before you, we grow the cattle here on the estate. And the venison is from our deer."

He seemed hardly to notice that his wondrous museum, the greatest illegal museum in all Europe, in all the world, probably, was being disassembled around him.

Strangely, Carol watched it all taking place with a complete lack of emotion.

She had felt no emotion at all, since earlier in the afternoon, when the armored car had delivered her like a sack of money to the front door of the estate.

And she'd been told of the situation.

Had been told by Baron Beckmeier that she, and at least a dozen of his other—operatives—had been kidnapped.

By Lorca Reklaw.

Now, as the paintings continued to be brought down the staircase, she could only think of the scene months earlier in the museum, when Rebecca Simpson had fired her.

Boxes. Boxes in wheelbarrows, coming from many rooms at once, clattering down the staircases.

Boxes.

"As for the Beilagen—I think the English would say, 'side dishes'—the one there in the center of the table is called, in Austria, Aubergine. The Germans have a different word for it. It is in English, 'eggplant,' I believe. Strange word. No egg connected to it. But you should all try it. With the rhubarb sauce. Quite a delicacy, the way we fix it here."

One of the soldiers—could one call these men 'soldiers'?—at any rate, one of them tripped slightly going out the door.

Beckmeier rose quickly, stared at him for an instant, then bellowed:

"Can't you be careful, you idiot? It's not enough that you betray my trust and sell yourself out like whores! Now you destroy my paintings!"

The man righted himself and kept to his job, seemingly not hearing.

Beckmeier continued to shout:

"So when does he come? When does he make himself known to us, seen by us—this 'Lorca Reklaw'? Is he frightened that I should see him? That we all should see him, finally, face to face?"

No reply.

But now it was time for one of the guests to speak.

The English woman, the one in the zebra-striped pants.

The St. Sebastian woman.

This woman rose, her face flushed, her hands knotted into fists on the table in front of her:

"And, for God's sakes, what's going to happen to us?"

No answer.

Just the clattering of boxes.

Of paintings.

And Carol continued to feel nothing at all.

For she knew exactly what was going to happen to them.

CHAPTER TWENTY ONE: THE RED CLAW

The church, as Nina could see when she came abreast of it and topped the hill on which it sat, overlooked the lake which she and Michael had glimpsed upon entering the village earlier. This lake had transformed itself in the last hour though, for the snow clouds had dissipated and a full moon was shining, so that Lake Moorbach was now black cloth crisscrossed with silver lines that were wavelets, eddies, currents, motions in the water, twinkling across the surface like slender, luminous threads.

"Damn."

"What is it, Michael?"

"The moon. It would have been better for us if it had not come out."

"You don't think the boat will come now?"

"I don't know. Come on."

The church stood beside her now, a sign of some kind, backlit and legible to anyone who cared to read it, and could.

She could not, save for a number that repeated itself, and seemed to be a part of each paragraph.

846.

Eight hundred and forty six.

Surprising, she thought, *that so many people would belong to a church in a village of this size, where hardly so many people could be thought to live anyway.*

Then she realized.

She was indeed a long way from Bay St. Lucy.

Eight hundred and forty-six was not the number of people on the roll.

It was the year of the church's founding.

Almost thirteen hundred years ago.

The thought preoccupied her for an instant or so.

Then she let it sift back into her mind, where it milled and jostled with other thoughts, sensations, sounds, tastes, smells, remembrances—all things, ultimately, that would bury the thoughts she did not want to deal with.

Somewhere behind her, down the hill that led past the tavern, a dog started barking.

Thirteen centuries.

The figure kept re-entering her mind.

Had the trees been different then? The lake? Had dogs barked, signaling to each other on a cold moonlit mid-December night?

Did people steal paintings then, and kidnap each other, and blow up buildings?

"All right. Here we are. Last chance to back out Ms.—sorry, Nina."

"No. I want to go see Carol."

"Well, then…"

He pulled the church door open.

It swung easily toward them.

The church revealed itself.

Like so many of the churches of Austria, it had begun as a primitive edifice of some sort, then, transformed itself into a sparse Romanesque one, then been rebuilt for the purpose of attacking heaven with spectacular flying buttresses and gothic arches, and finally modified by the middle class so that it served now more to inundate the senses of the citizenry here below than frighten the essences of angels somewhere above.

Colors, candles, circles, gold paint, fat celestial arms, children's faces robed in saffron and white—a baroque world painted over a gothic one. Nina sniffed. She perceived a never before smelled odor of ancient stonework, centuries of incense and timeless human suffering.

She stopped for a second, let her hand rest on the back pew, and prayed:

"Let Carol be all right," she found herself asking the darkly painted Christ just to her right, encased in gold frame and headed by the numeral *one*, "and take care of all of us."

The numeral *one*.

The first stage of the cross.

Perhaps their first stage.

"Help us through all of this."

They walked further into the church, toward the ambulatory.

They'd passed beneath the pulpit—it still seemed impossible that a minister should be up there, halfway to the roof, preaching down at people instead of looking out toward them—when she began to look more closely at the paintings on the walls of the church.

Some marked the stages of the cross, certainly.

But others…

…they were like the ossuary itself.

Full of bones.

Paintings full of bones.

Not separate bones, she realized as she moved closer to one and examined it. Death's Heads. Skeletons. All images of skulls and scythes, horrid, gaping mouths, ribcages blown open with organs spewing from them.

Here and there, human forms—either dead or dying, gaunt, meager, being carried toward graves by monsters.

The other face, she found herself remembering, of the Baroque world.

Swirls and angels plastered across light blue ceilings above.

But just beneath, remembrances of past plagues, floods, invasions, armies, and wagon loads of rotting corpses.

"In life," she found herself whispering, "we are in death."

And there, before her, written on the wall, was the word:

KARN.

"What does that mean, Michael?"

"Charnel House. Ossuary. Repository of bones."

They approached the altar.

A door stood closed before them.

Michael opened it.

Stairs descended.

"We go down here."

"All right. Lead the way."

"Close the door behind us."

For some reason, she dreaded doing so.

There was no reason, she told herself, for being afraid.

No.

Actually, there were plenty of reasons for being afraid.

But none of them lurked in this tunnel.

The stairs corkscrewed down before them, a black metal rod acting as banister, colorless concrete steps adding to the general feeling of thickness, of solidity, of immobility that enveloped her, as though she were descending through not a religious edifice but a Masonite glacier.

Yellow electric lights glowed in the stairwell.

Were they kept on at all times?

Apparently.

The church was open at all times.

The tunnel was open at all times.

Death was always near.

Escape from enemies was always to be possible.

She could see now that net wire enclosed them.

What was beyond the net wire? What were all those objects through which this downward leading tunnel was taking them?

"Oh God."

For the first time she realized, not merely intellectually but viscerally, what an ossuary really was.

"Oh God."

Everywhere around them there were bones. To the left, the right, immediately above them…

…just bones.

Not merely were there bones that had been thrown in indiscriminately, haphazardly, a shovel full at a time. No, these bones had been arranged by type—skulls in one section, clavicles in another, legs in another, arms in another—and carefully, artistically, jammed so tightly together that not one space remained unfossilized, not one millimeter of breathing room remained available for these no-more-breathing parts of human beings, who would never again care one way or another.

This. This was a charnel house.

And it seemed to go on forever.

She thought of Dante's lines:
"I had not thought, death had undone so many."
So many.
On down they went.
On and on and on...
Finally they took a turn.
And beyond it, a different kind of light.
Could that be moonlight?
Then sounds.
Water.
Water lapping on stone.
The opening appeared as though by magic. Within half a minute, they found themselves standing at the entrance to the escape tunnel.

And silently, a dark black shape approached like flotsam over the surface of the lake.

"All right," Michael said quietly, motioning to the oarsman, who merely grunted in response. "We go to Palace Eggenburg."

Nina stepped gingerly into the boat, which rocked beneath her as she thought of stages of her journey, and of the human bones that she and everyone else would ultimately become.

The room in which Carol was to spend the night—if that was, in fact, what remained in store for her—was like a salon in an elegant clothing store.

There were full-length mirrors everywhere. Armoires stood side by side, like burnished, twin-corpse coffins upended and standing mute, elegant wood carvings tracing their exterior while subtle keys protruded from their bellies.

There were small tables, small sofas, small ashtrays, small silver platters with nothing on them—and large windows, two of them, lace-curtained, overlooking a magnificent pond in the middle of which, at the precise moment Carol spied it, a fountain began to erupt in blue and neon red, its splashing barely audible through the window glass.

"How can they do this to us? What are they thinking?"

She did not respond to the woman opposite her, whose voice was shaking with anger and fear.

"They have no right! They have no right."

"But they do have," she found herself saying, quietly, "the power."

She opened one of the armoires. Then she stepped close to it, inhaling an aroma of dead money and enchanting perversity so strong as to be undeniably French.

She let her fingers slide across the inner collars of the gowns hanging before her.

The labels:

Elie Saab

Collette Dinnigan

Oscar de la Renta

Vera Wang

Miu Miu

She found herself reading descriptions of the gowns.

And sizes.

Red Plus Size Formal Dress Halter Rhinestone Beading Full-Length Long V Neck (Turquoise/Size 20).

Look at it.

Full-length it was, the hem brushing the bottom of the armoire. A magnificent red, a burgundy wine red, the red of a zodiac scar.

Rhinestone beads like stars about the décolleté…

She understood the reason for the dresses, the reason many of these upstairs castle rooms had been transformed into salons.

Beckmeier would bring women out here from the village, or perhaps from Graz.

Or for that matter, from Vienna. Or Paris.

The guest for the evening would be led here, offered champagne, and given the opportunity to dress for the evening meal. With the understanding, of course, that whatever gown was chosen, and whatever jewelry, was to be accepted as a gift.

A gift for services rendered.

Or to be rendered, sometime after the meal was finished.

A dessert, so to speak.

"It would have been better if they'd simply shot us!"

"No," she found herself whispering into the hem of a Vera Wang. "No, it wouldn't have."

She found herself becoming very sick of this woman, whoever she was.

"What we did was not that wrong! We carried paintings from one place to another!"

"For a lot of money."

"All right, so maybe we deserve to go to jail. But not to…to…"

"Die?"

"Don't say that!"

"All right. I won't."

"And where is this man, this Claw?"

"Lorca Reklaw."

"Yes, whatever the name is! Is he too ashamed even to show himself to us?"

"I doubt that."

"Then where is he? Where?"

"Probably," she said, "closer than we think."

"Then why does he not…and look! Look at that!"

The woman pointed to a corner of the room.

There on a small stool, undoubtedly designed for it, sat a magnum of champagne, its neck protruding from glistening ice crystals, two glasses sitting rim-down around it, as though they were champagne planets caught in mid orbit around the bottle that, being their sun, was to fill and replenish them.

"He expects us to drink champagne?"

"It would probably," said Carol, "not make things any worse."

Had Lorca Reklaw left this champagne? she wondered.

Or had Beckmeier left it earlier in the day, before his grounds were invaded by armed troops, many of whom he'd thought were in his own employ?

Was there to have been another special guest for the night?

Probably Carol would never know.

Certainly it did not matter.

She walked to the corner, grasped the bottle, took it into the small alcove that was the bathroom, and poured it out.

The woman behind her was continuing to rant:

"If they would only allow us to…"

But they were not going to, whatever it was that she was about to demand.

For the door opened behind her at that moment and a uniformed guard—or soldier, or Ranger, or paramilitary operative or whatever Red Claw had chosen to call his men—took a step into the room.

He gestured curtly at the woman and barked:

"Out!"

"But I only want to…"

"You do not need to be here! Go back to your own room! One thief, one room!"

"I want to talk to…"

His hand moved toward the firearm hanging from his thick black leather belt.

"Go."

And the woman did, pursing her lips, and disappearing silently into the corridor.

The armed figure stared at Carol for a time, then said, more quietly:

"You should sleep."

"All right."

Upon hearing these words, he disappeared.

Carol took off her clothes, turned off the overhead light in the room, got into bed, and thought.

She knew that she would never sleep.

She was wrong though.

She must have been exhausted by all of the events of the previous two days, for sleep she did—a sound, noiseless, dreamless sleep that lasted for two hours.

She awoke shortly before midnight, although she did not know precisely why.

She looked out the window. The snowfall had stopped, and the estate glowed silver in the cold light of a full moon.

There was a small, golden, jewel-encased clock, ticking and glowing eerily on the bed stand beside her.

Eleven fifty-five.

There was a knock on the door.

She got out of bed carefully, and made her way across the room. The tile floor felt cold to her feet.

She made her way to the door and opened it.

A hatchet-faced man dressed in fatigues, with a forty five automatic strapped at his side, confronted her.

"You must come."

"What is it?"

He simply shook his head and repeated, in a thick indeterminate accent:

"They are waiting for you downstairs."

So saying, he turned and left.

She returned to her room.

There, on a small writing desk beside the bed, was a candelabrum.

She hefted the metallic and porcelain thing before her, taking note of shepherds and minor goddesses waving playfully around and beneath the wicks, set it down again, and lit the three white candles that it held in trident shape, like Neptune's scepter quivering with smoky light.

Thus armed, she re-entered the corridor.

She found herself accompanied along it by the ghost of herself, huge, furtive, simultaneously jerking and floating on the wall to the left of her as her right hand quivered with the weight of the candle.

She turned to the left, remaining in the center of her small sphere of light, felt her slippers sliding noiselessly on the alternate marble squares of black and tan beneath her.

There, some steps farther on, the corridor turned sharply to the right.

Then she took two, three, four steps forward…

….placed her palm over the wall-corner…

…and leaned forward.

Spread out below her was a vast library. It was doubly partitioned, books below, windows above.

Innumerable books. Books which, she could tell by flashes that now came every five seconds or so, were earthy in color and massive in form, books transcribed and not published, illuminated and not printed, copied one at a time on parchment, and destined to dissolve if read.

Even from this distance, the titles smelled of Latin.

And surrounding this library, were men identical to the one who'd knocked on her door.

They stood at five-foot intervals.

Between them, huddled, holding their hands before their eyes were the guests of Lorca Reklaw.

Beckmeier's mules.

The people whom Red Claw had captured, and to whom he was now preparing...

What punishment?

One of guards looked up, saw her standing there, and gestured for her to come down.

Whatever was going to happen, it was about to begin.

Yellow lights showed themselves through the trees. Barns and stables appeared, dark and deserted.

The truck carrying them, the one that had met their boat at the lakeshore, turned sharply and Nina saw the main building of the castle itself, sitting back beneath a canopy of trees, folding its arms and waiting for them, smiling in the way that only a true seat of royalty can smile.

It was, of course, 'Schonbrunn Gelb,' that kind of off-yellow that must have been invented to harmonize perfectly with the deep blue or the deep red of cavalry officers' uniforms, as they danced within its salons, their horses feeding quietly in stables scattered about the grounds, the sound of canon fire rolling over the mountains in the distance.

And there were peacocks strolling in front of them.

She'd imagined peacocks—if she thought of them at all—as day creatures. But these, their huge fans of tail feathers wafting gently back and forth, might as well have been parading and courting at noon, so white-bright and radiant had the moon become in its niche between the central garret of the building and two chimney tops that seemed to have been sculpted just to hold it.

"Well," whispered Michael, "now you get your chance to meet the Red Claw."

"So do you."

The vehicle came to a stop.

The entire front of Eggenburg Palace was glowing, huge floodlights bathing everything within a mile's perimeter.

There were at least a dozen trucks, troop carriers more accurately, all black, with no insignia, all ringed around the driveway where carriages once would have disgorged Dukes and Duchesses.

They got out, took a few steps toward the entrance, and stopped in their tracks.

For there before them, came a line of people out of the front door, guards with machine guns and pistols, and between these guards, some of the people Nina recognized as customers who'd bought her paintings.

Her visceral, translucent paintings.

Her vivid, scintillating, paintings.

They were art smugglers.

And now they'd been caught.

They were, as she watched, being loaded like cattle into the backs of the troop carriers.

And there, at the very end of the line, came Carol.

Nina involuntarily took a step forward.

Carol's head turned to the left, her mouth opened wide…

…and then they were running across the storm-soaked lawn of the palace, their shoes drenched, their voices yelling uselessly, all sounds covered over by the drone of motors and the movement of huge cans of some kind of liquid.

Finally, just a few steps from the reflecting pool, they ran together, embraced, sobbed, continued to embrace, attempted to talk, succeeded only in stuttering, sobbed a bit more, and finally contented themselves by wiping tears out of each other's eyes.

They were, Nina ultimately realized, surrounded by a ring of guards.

She could hear Michael shouting behind her:

"Red Claw! I want to speak directly to Red Claw!"

His words had absolutely no effect on the guards, who continued to gaze dispassionately at the two women standing before them.

One of these women, Carol, looked at the guard closest to her, and said:

"You must let us talk. Please."

No change in expression.

Another guard arrived, this one the hatchet-faced man, who said:

"It is time. The trucks are leaving."

Carol merely shook her head:

"We must talk."

"Yes, but…"

"This is my mother."

Silence.

Then the ring of guards opened, and the three of them were led to a small stone bench, which faced two metal chairs.

They sat, now some distance from the parade of prisoners being loaded before them.

"What are you doing here, Nina? Michael? How did you get here?"

Nina found that she could not speak, and so Michael was the one who held forth.

"You have to know, Carol. Nina came here because she wanted to."

"But how…"

"I found out what was going on. I still have a few contacts. One of them told me that you'd been taken out of Bay St. Lucy. I went to Nina's place and explained everything we'd done. The way the paintings had been smuggled. Everything."

"But…"

"I told Nina I had a plan for getting you out of here."

"What plan?"

"I still have several paintings hidden away. I want to talk to Lorca Reklaw. If he'll let you go, I'll tell him where the paintings are."

"But don't you think he'll kill you after he gets them?"

"It doesn't really matter. I don't want to live my life in hiding."

"But…but Nina, what are you doing here?"

"Nina refused to stay in Bay St. Lucy, knowing that you were being held here."

"Oh, Nina. Nina, my second mother…"

"We'll get you out of this, Carol. We'll talk to this man Red Claw. We'll get you out, I promise."

"Nina, what makes you think he's going to let you leave Eggenburg?"

"He has to."

"Why? Why does he have to?"

"Because if he doesn't, he'll have Moon Rivard to deal with."

"Oh, Nina! Nina, I'm so sorry I got you into this!"

"It's all right."

"No. No, I'm an idiot! I thought it would all be all right. That I could do everything I planned to do

Carol was crying now.

Nina was crying, too.

No one could speak.

And as they watched, Beckmeier was led from the building.

He wore all white, as though he were on safari.

His hair was unkempt and wild, as were his eyes.

"Let me go, you swine! I'll have you shot!"

He was able, of course, to have no one shot, being a prisoner himself, in the center of a group of armed men, each of whom seemed a foot taller than he himself was.

"You thieves! You all should have been killed in the war! We should have burned all of you!"

And then, as she watched the scene unfold in front of her, Nina finally realized what the things that had appeared like oil drums being rolled into the building really were.

They were gasoline drums.

Beckmeier would be forced to look on, as his palace, Eggenburg, was burned to the ground.

And farther on, beyond the line of 'operatives,' or smugglers, this line of people who would have become instantly wealthy for doing no more than take part, comfortably, in a private and illegal re-distribution of the world's art treasures, continued to be herded into the dark, featureless trucks that were to transport them.

But transport them where?

Carol looked at the same scene and whispered, as much to herself as to Nina and Michael:

"That's what it must have been like."

Nina found that she could, in fact, speak, though hardly above a raspy whisper:

"What, Carol? What must have been like?"

Carol's gaze seemed to contain no fear at all, but only visualization of something that was not really there, that had happened half a century ago:

"The razing of the ghettos. Poland. France. Everywhere. All the buildings burned. Probably at midnight, just like now. The people who'd lived there, who'd been happy there, forced to look on. Then the flames. Women screaming while their possessions, their treasures, burned up in front of their eyes."

"Carol…"

"And then the thing that had to follow, of course. Follow as the night the day. The ultimate solution. All of the people, uncertain what was going to happen to them—herded into great trucks, like cattle, to be gassed to death. Gassed to death by the millions. By the tens of millions."

Then she was silent.

All of them continued to watch.

The last of the people had now disappeared into the last of the trucks.

"Nina. Michael."

"Oh, Carol, maybe you could…maybe if we could…"

And Carol smiled:

"You're the bravest two people in the world. The very bravest. I'll never forget you. Whatever happens, throughout all of time, all of eternity…I'll never forget you. Either of you."

"Carol…"

"And Michael, it's all forgiven. Just one thing. Just one thing, I can never forgive you for."

Michael stepped toward her; she embraced him.

He asked:

"What?"

"What you said about my breasts."

Insanely, they were laughing then. He asked:

"What breasts?"

And they continued to laugh.

The hatched-faced man stepped close to them and said:

"All right. But now is time."

Carol nodded:

"Good. Just, just one more thing: listen, the two of you. They will put you both in the same car, I know."

"But," said Nina, "can't you…"

Carol shook her head:

"No. That's not possible. I know that. It's not possible. We part now. But know this: it will be all right. *You* will be all right. Just remember, Nina, what I told you a long time ago. At least it seems a long time ago now, looking back. Just remember, it's the same thing in life as it is in paintings. Always look below what you see on the surface. Look at the painting underneath, at the *real* painting. Don't believe, ever, what seems to be true. Look at what is really true. Now good bye, and know how much I will always love both of you!"

And with that, she was gone.

Somehow, she simply disappeared into the crowd of soldiers.

Nina and Michael allowed themselves to be led toward the last of the trucks.

They walked carefully up a wooden ramp that led into the back of it, where two other of Nina's 'customers' were holding hands and sobbing.

Nina looked around.

She could see flames starting to pour out of the upper windows of the palace.

Then a tarp was thrown over the back of the transport, and the truck pulled away.

CHAPTER TWENTY TWO: DREAMING IN THE ERZHERZOG JOHANN

She was aware of several things simultaneously as she and Michael huddled together in the back corner of the truck. There was the warmth of his small hand in hers, and the somehow supportive sound of his breathing, which seemed to mask the sobs of the three groups of people also riding with them.

But there was also a memory of Carol's face, and the sound of her voice:

"Know this: it will be all right. *You* will be all right."

And:

"Always remember: look beneath the surface of the painting."

What was she talking about?

All right. She, Nina Bannister, had been made a complete fool of. Had been vain enough to believe that her own silly paintings could be worth money, and had been for weeks on end unaware that those same paintings had masked invaluable art treasures: Rembrandts, Van Goghs, Monets…

But there was something else.

There was another painting that was deceiving her.

Think, Nina.

Think.

What is the painting you're looking at, have been looking at, have been for all this time misperceiving…

…and what is the real painting underneath?

For had not Carol been trying to tell her only minutes ago what Jane Austen had been telling her for a lifetime?

'A mind lively and at ease can do with seeing nothing, and can see nothing that does not answer.'

Her mind had been lively for these past months.

But it had also been at ease.

It had been quite satisfied to see nothing at all.

And it had seen nothing that did not conform to her preconceived notions.

Where was the real painting, Nina?

And how could it be uncovered?

Thinking these things, listening to gentle sobbing, feeling the warmth of Michael's hand, being aware of a popping in her ears as the truck rolled upward into mountainous terrain, and feeling absolutely confident that Carol had been right, and that there was nothing to fear…

she drifted off to sleep.

She awoke some hours later.

All of the people in the back of the truck were asleep.

Sunlight was filtering through the cracks between the tarp and the truck's frame.

She looked at the watch: seven fifty-five.

They'd all slept through the night.

And, as she became aware of these things, the tarp was pulled back.

Light came flooding in, and they all awakened at the same time.

"What…"

Michael stirred, rubbed his eyes, leaned forward, and peered over her.

There were eight other people doing the same thing: rubbing eyes, stretching…

Two men were standing outside the truck, peering in at them, and smiling.

They were workmen, dressed in the dark blue uniform of city sanitation people.

"Heraus! Heraus mit euch!"

"Michael?"

He shook his head:

"They're telling us to get out of the truck."

"But…"

"It's ok. They're not soldiers. They've got brooms, not guns."

Nina rose, feeling as though her joints had rusted. She followed Michael over the floor of the truck, waited for the other people to disembark, and somehow got down onto the pavement, which was moist with patches of now-melting snow.

She looked around.

They were back in Graz.

The truck was parked squarely on what she remembered to be Hauptplatz.

The main square.

She looked at Michael.

He was peering around the same as she was.

Some of the other people who'd ridden with them—and who clearly had not been harmed and so were hugging each other and laughing—were asking questions of the workers, and were getting only shrugs and grins.

"These workers," Michael said, quietly, "don't know anything. They say they found the truck parked here. It was here at sunup, they think. They have no idea where it came from."

"So we…"

"Let's go into the hotel. We go to my room. Perhaps there, we make some sense of this whole thing."

They crossed the square.

The hotel looked just as it had yesterday, when the limousine which met her plane at The Graz Airport dropped her off there.

She looked at the city waking up around her, sparkling in the sun.

All that had happened since…it was like a dream.

She found herself repeating the lines:
If we shadows have offended
Think but this—and all is mended—
That you have but slumbered here,
While these visions did appear.
And this weak and idle theme
No more yielding, but a dream.

They walked into the hotel.

Michael went to the desk to get the room key.

"Hola! Ms. Bannister?"

This from a tall blond woman who'd apparently been seated in the hotel's coffee shop.

"Ms. Bannister?"

The woman approached, with a large manila envelope clutched in her hands.

"Are you Ms. Nina Bannister?"

"Yes."

"I'm Gertrude Henninger."

The woman reminded Nina, surprisingly, of Margot Gavin. True, she wore an impeccably tailored business suit and not a Kandinsky abstract, and, true, her hair was straw blonde and not silver, and, true, it was well combed and not wildly displaced.

But she was at least as tall as Margot.

That was something, in itself.

"I must tell you, our office in Vienna has received a phone call only a little over an hour ago."

Office in Vienna.

Interpol?

What actually *was* Interpol, anyway?

Whatever was going on, this woman had to represent the police in some way.

They were being arrested.

That was not so bad.

At least they were alive.

At least the Red Claw had let them live.

Or so it seemed.

The woman continued:

"Yes. The call came directly to our director, at her home. It was quite urgent."

"I'm sorry…I don't…"

"A great deal of money was involved…was transferred to us…but we were told you'd be arriving at this hotel shortly before eight o'clock. And that the trip should be planned by then. And the itinerary given to you."

"The itinerary?"

"Yes. And that's what I've brought here, to give to you."

The international smuggling police were giving her an itinerary?

How many prisons was she going to?

"I'm sorry. I still don't understand. Your office…"

"Yes. We are the largest in Austria. We have representatives in all major Austrian cities. I have the honor to be the president of our branch here in Graz. Here. Please accept my card. It's written in English."

She took the business card and read it:

Gertrude Henninger

Sales Representative

International Travel Bureau

"You're a travel agent?"

Gertrude Henninger beamed:

"Yes! And we hope the trip we have laid out for you will be satisfactory!"

"The trip?"

"We've booked you for four days in Vienna. Then three in Salzburg. Two more in Innsbruck. And finally you come back here to Graz. The hotels are the best available. There are also opera performances. We had little time to prepare of course, but…"

"I can't afford all of this."

"Oh, it has all been prepaid!"

"By.."

A shake of the head.

"I'm sorry. I don't know that. My director merely said that I was to tell you, it was a gift."

"A gift."

"Yes. You have a great admirer. But…I see that your young man friend is waiting for you."

And Michael Gellert was, in fact, standing at the base of the stairway, room key in hand.

"Our office is on the Sackstrasse. After you have breakfasted, you might perhaps come by? We can talk more of the details!"

"Yes. Yes, of course."

And the woman turned and left.

Michael was waiting for her.

"Who was that?"

"A travel agent."

"A what?"

"A travel agent."

"That doesn't make any sense."

"None of this makes sense. It's more and more like we dreamed it. I don't know what else to think. The castle last night, all those flames coming out of it, those terrified people being led out and herded into cattle carriers; Beckmeier, shouting and railing, the guards, the machine guns—and before that the tavern, and the charnel house, and the tunnel leading down to the lake…"

"…all of these things happened, Nina."

"They couldn't have. Look around us. Look at the people coming and going, doing business as usual. It's as though it was all just a part of our imagination. No more yielding, but a dream."

But the guns, she thought, as they climbed the stairs, *had been no dream.*

Nor had the paintings.

Where were the paintings now?

And where was Carol?

She walked up the stairs, a step behind Michael, looking down into the vine-enshrouded atrium below, as she did so, letting her palm—which was already becoming sweaty—run along the grillwork stair rail, and seeing her own door grow larger as she approached it.

He put the massive iron key with its equally massive key ring into the lock and turned it. There was a 'clicking' sound. He mashed down on the lever that functioned as a doorknob, and pushed open the door.

White light flooding through the wall-length windows bathed the unslept in bed, the giant armoire, the heavy, oaken desk.

And there, lying propped against the desk, was a painting.

"What is that?" she whispered, entering the room and stepping toward it.

Michael did not move from his place in the doorway.

"It's a Monet," he said, quietly. "An original, not a reproduction. One of the 'Flower' pictures, from his garden at Giverney."

Nina approached it, then bent down and touched it, gently.

"One of the paintings that Carol made come alive in her presentation."

"Yes. The same presentation I saw her give at the museum."

Then something else caught Nina's eye.

Two things, actually.

One was a letter lying on the desk itself, its corner barely touching the large mirror that sat atop the desk.

The other was a map of the world, which had been taped to the wall beside the mirror.

Several lines, and several circles, had been drawn with dark black marker on the map.

"What is it?" came the voice from behind her.

She looked for a time at the map, at the regions circled there, and the lines connecting them.

"Oh my God," she found herself whispering. "Oh my God."

"What?"

She shook her head, knowing even as she began, carefully, to open the envelope.

Knowing.

Seeing.

The real picture.

The picture beneath false picture.

She took out the letter, lay it gently on the desk, and, as Michael approached behind her, read aloud:

"Dear Nina,

I'm sorry to have been forced to deceive you. Both you and Michael, actually. You must believe I never thought anything last night would happen. But Michael was too smart. He found out that I had been 'taken' from Bay St. Lucy. He decided to come and rescue me. And you decided to come with him.

How brave. Of you both.

You deserve a reward.

You deserve many rewards.

Hopefully, you've been given a travel itinerary. It is not much, admittedly. But it is the closest I can come to the grand trip we planned together. I do hope you enjoy it, and that you think of me as you see the places you have only dreamed of before.

Michael can come with you, if he pleases. But I suspect he'll wish to get on with his other affairs of business.

Michael.

How amusing he was.

As for myself, my business is done.

It took four years, and such careful planning...

...such careful planning.

It began when I arrived in Chicago from Georgia.

I had to take a teaching job first, but then I was hired at the museum by the wonderful Margot Gavin.

Then I met you, Michael... Although I must tell you that I'd been told of you, and of your business, sometime before.

And, yes, I seduced you. In Pilsen.

For that, I hope you will forgive me.

But I knew that you dealt in stolen paintings.

That you would come to have access to the very paintings I so desperately wanted, needed—that this would happen someday I could only hope.

And it did.

I needed to know where all of the paintings that I needed were going to wind up.

You found out these things for me.

You began working for Beckmeier.

And Beckmeier was collecting—re-stealing, actually—all of works that had been taken from my family. And the families that lived near us.

I began carrying paintings for you. And then we began the operation in Bay St. Lucy.

You paid me very well, Michael.

Twenty thousand dollars a painting. Twenty paintings, total.

And with that money, I could hire to work for me the very guards Beckmeier thought, stupidly—such people are always stupid—were working for, and loyal to him.

Last night it all came together.

Four years work.

And during all of that time, I would have hurt no one.

All of Michael's operatives have been released by now. They needed to experience what it must have been like, the burning of the ghettos. The things my people must have seen.

Just not the ovens.

No one deserves that, even thieves.

Even Beckmeier has not been harmed.

He can sit and look at the smoldering ruins of his palace.

But he has not been harmed.

The man I did shoot…well, I had no choice.

He was not working for the Red Claw, but for Beckmeier, who'd found out about the operation.

He would have blown you up the following morning after you had opened Elementals. And he would gladly have killed me the night before.

How Beckmeier found out where I was, I don't know.

But I have my family's paintings now.

Except for one.

The Monet.

That one is for you, Nina.

Dearest Nina, who took me in, and showed me Bay St. Lucy, and introduced me to Tom and Penelope—I wish I could be there for her shower, please give her all my best wishes—and the Bagattelli's and Sergio's Not By The Sea and, of course, magnificent Margot and her husband and Alanna and the Auberge—

—no, that painting, that Monet, is for you.

The papers proving ownership are in this envelope.

Please hang it in Elementals.

No one will steal it. I have placed a spell on it.

It will be safe. And it will keep Elementals safe.

And it will keep Bay St. Lucy safe.

And it will keep you safe.

Forever.

Now I must close. You have, of course, by now, looked at the map, and at the lines, and at the circles.

You have seen that there are at least two Georgias.

Who knows, there may be more.

There is one in the United States, near, I believe, Florida.

And there is another.

My Georgia. A part of Russia.

My Jewish family's Georgia.

Nestled in the Caucasian Mountains.

A little ways east, and somewhat north, of Athens.

Athens, Greece, that is.

My Georgia, where I grew up, and helped raise sheep, and wandered in the mountains.

Where I will now go back and live.

But you will live with me, dear Nina.

My second mother.

And I will never forget you, not ever, not ever...

Your dearest...

(By the way, now it is time for you to hold the letter up to the mirror, and read my name, my real name...

...and see the real picture...)

Your dearest...

Carol Walker."

And Nina did hold the letter up to the mirror.

So that the signature read:

Lorca Reklaw.

CHAPTER TWENTY THREE: GEORGIA ON MY MIND

In the late afternoon, almost thirty hours after she'd left Austria, Lorca Reklaw arrived at the Manor.

She'd chosen to go by train not because of any fear of being discovered. There were no such fears now.

The proper people at various borders had been paid off; the paintings had gone before her, and were back where they belonged.

No, she'd gone home by train simply because it was something she had savored doing for the four years she'd been away. Papa would still be there, still recognize her; she knew that. But the old Orient Express, subdivided as it now was into fours...the train itself, its routes, its magical city names...held the same fascination for her as it always did, and she wanted to reward herself with the moments that only it could offer.

Going over the Fischbacher Alps just before darkness, the villages in twilight far below...and the bells of the wine carts rattling by...

And the sleeper. The sound of the whistle at midnight, the clacking of the wheels...

...morning, looking out over the Hungarian plains...

Thirty hours. Nothing at all, a blissful time...

...and now here she was at home. A car met her at the small station. The driver, newly hired, had never seen her before. No matter.

The forests remained well tended; two sections, she could see, were ready for cutting.

Sheep surrounded the car as it made the final turn to the house itself.

And Mitja, her aunt, stood at the door as the car pulled up.

Mitja, beaming, beautiful and radiant as always, tall and stately and muscular as a drover's horse...Mitja would not have run the few yards to the car, for running did not befit the manor's mistress now...but she covered the distance quickly and was able to lift Lorca in her arms as effortlessly as she always had done. Looking up...for Lorca's face was well above hers now, suspended in air as it was...looking up, the magnificent Mitja said simply:

"Achai Hym."

Welcome home.

"Acai Hym, Mitja."

She was set gently on the ground again, and the two women entered the manor house.

It was as she remembered it. The men, hardly noticing her arrival, sat smoking in the corner of the Great Room, which, of course, was not cluttered with the superfluous chairs that had been placed in it by the Chicago museum's miniaturist. There was always activity, servants running here and there, carrying dishes, finishing the last day's cleaning.

They sat together in the parlor, golden sun pouring through the latticed windows.

"Did the paintings arrive, Mitja?"

A nod.

"Yesterday. Twenty large wooden cases. Forty-eight paintings. You did it."

"Yes."

"All of Mossad could not...all of the people we hired...none of them could find these paintings, and get them back for us."

"And they were all taken to the right places?"

"Yes. All of the men helped. Even on wagons, some of the pictures were carried. But every family has its treasures back. Seven paintings of ours. Look. I hung Monet's flowers over the mantelpiece. Like I was told it used to be before the Nazis came."

"I saw it when I came in. It's beautiful. Look at the way the light makes it shimmer and radiate."

"Yes."

"There is one special painting though that I did not send with the others."

"The one you have with you there? In the brown wrapping paper?"

"Yes. This one. Special to Papa."

"It isn't large."

"No. Fourteen inches square."

"Shall we take it up to him now?"

"Is he awake?"

"I think so. We told him last night that you would be arriving this morning."

"All right."

"He held on. There were times we did not think, Lorca, that he would survive the sickness. But he would not die. Not until he saw you again."

"Let us go up to him."

And, with the painting between them, they ascended the staircase.

The old man lay in bed, seemingly sleeping. A few rays of light filtered through the small window beside the bed.

He was not sleeping, though, and when Lorca entered the room, his face blossomed. She could hear the cracked voice, as he tried to raise himself.

"Lorca?"

"Yes, Papa; I'm home."

"Oh, Lorca...mein Haserlchen!"

My little rabbit.

"Yes, Papa," said Lorca, bending over him and lifting him, so that his back was against the bedstead:

She unwrapped the painting, Dürer's Hase, and held it before him.

He beamed, nodding, then crying, unable to speak.

Finally she said:

"Both of your little rabbits are home."

And she simply sat for a time, until the old man went to sleep.

EPILOGUE

Margot Gavin could remember the day perfectly.

She would never forget it.

She could, in fact, remember everything about the conversation. Down to the last word, the last gesture.

How strange!

It was almost nightfall, late December, and the light in Bay St. Lucy had changed. It was a pure winter illumination now, spread over the whole town.

She could remember walking into Elementals, hoping to see her best friend Nina Bannister at the cash register and, instead, spying her deeper in the store, staring up at a painting.

"Nina! You're back!"

And Nina was back, of course.

Back from what was certainly the trip of her life, it being practically the only trip of her life.

Margot had half-lived it herself; getting Facebook pictures every day (and even a few post cards, Nina remaining one of the few beings of the twenty-first century who still sent such things).

Pictures, in whatever form they'd arrived, of the great castle on the mountain overlooking Salzburg; of St. Stephen's Cathedral in Vienna; of the basement of The Franziskaner Church, the dark green leaden coffins—at least fifty of them—holding the remains of Hapsburg emperors; of the Prater, the great amusement park…

…and yet more pictures still, not of Vienna, but of the magical—at least it had seemed so as described in Nina's letters and cards—city of Graz.

City of another time, another world.

City of slate roofs and suits of armor and marketplaces and coffee shops and smiling people; of heurige, outdoor wine taverns spread across the meadow on hills overlooking the town; of palaces with no electricity, where great dining salons were still illuminated by massive twinkling chandeliers containing a hundred candle holders, each filled by hand with a small candle, each candle carefully lighted, the entire immense construct then hoisted over the main table by ropes and pulleys...

...of the opera Nina had attended...

The Merry Widow.

"Dann geh ich zu Maxims
Dort bin ich sehr intime
Ich dutze alle Damen
Ruf sie bei cosinamen...

And...

Villa, oh, villa

And the "Merry Widow Waltz"...

Dancing, and marvelous gowns and uniforms, and the beloved emperor Franz Josef.

About all of these things, her friend Nina had written, about the golden last days of the empire when the situation was hopeless but not serious, and a thousand years of history seemed to waver in the golden twilight, about to be erased by machine guns, and the horrible machines of war and the twentieth century, and visions of troops marching over the cobblestone streets.

"Nina! Nina; it's Margot!"

She could remember her friend turning, smiling the warm smile that always illuminated Elementals better than a thousand lamps could do.

And she could remember Nina pointing up.

At a place on the wall where the best painting in the shop, at the time, usually hung.

She could remember her astonishment.

"That—that's not a reproduction!"

"No, Margot."

"But...but..."

"It's my painting."

"Nina, it's a true Monet! It's one of the most famous paintings in the world. One of the series of flower pictures, from the gardens of Giverney!"

"I know."

"But how..."

"I don't know how, exactly. And if I did, no one would believe me. I just finished living a dream. And out of the dream, came this painting."

"Nina it's a priceless thing! You can't hang it here! We have no security!"

And she could remember Nina looking up at her, with a mixture of firmness and complete implacability:

"It's my painting, Margot. I have the papers to prove it. And we will hang it here; and no one will bother it. No one will bother Elementals while it's here. Because it's got a spell on it."

"But how long..."

"For four months. We'll hang it here for four months. Then we'll wrap it up. In plain brown paper, the way it was given to me. And we'll give it to Penelope and Tom's daughter, on the evening of the baby shower."

"Their daughter?"

"Yes. They're expecting a son, but I know it will be a daughter. And I'll beg them to name her 'Carol.'"

She could remember looking at her friend and saying, quietly:

"They admire you more than anybody in the world, Nina. If you suggest Carol, then that's what it will be."

"Yes. I know. And they'll protect the painting for Carol, until she grows up. And when she goes away from home, she will take it with her and prize it, always. Because it's the most beautiful thing in the world. And it's from us."

Then she could remember sitting down beside her friend, and simply looking, as the sun sank lower and lower in the winter sky, at the marvelous painting that hung there before them.

Halfway around the world, the same sun that was setting on Bay St. Lucy rose over the Caucasian Mountains.

Over an isolated farmhouse.

Carol Walker, having risen shortly before dawn, sat in the great room of the manor, a cup of coffee before her on a small table.

...where the magic that was the light in the air and the magic that was the wonder and mystery of their minds and the magic that still lived in colors of Monet...

...all gathered simultaneously...

...and the flowers began to dance!

THE END

ABOUT THE AUTHORS

Pam Britton (T'Gracie) Reese is an Assistant Professor in the Communication Science and Disorders Department at Indiana/Purdue University at Fort Wayne. Previously, she worked as a speech pathologist in schools in private practice. She was also a supervisor in communication disorders at Ohio University. She likes nothing better, professionally, than helping small, silent two-year-old boys start talking. She has also published books about autism with LinguiSystems for the last 15 years. *The Circle of Autism* was previously published online at *ken*again e-magazine.*

Joe Reese is a novelist, playwright, storyteller, and college teacher. He has published four novels, several plays, and a number of stories and articles. When he's not teaching (English and German), he enjoys visiting elementary schools, where he tells stories from his Katie Dee novels and talks to students about writing. He and his wife Pam have three children: Kate, Matthew, and Sam.